SEEKERS

SMOKE MOUNTAIN

Explore the World of ERIN HUNTER

SEEKERS

WARRIORS

WARRIORS: THE NEW PROPHECY

WARRIORS: POWER OF THREE

SEEKERS

SMOKE MOUNTAIN

ERIN
HUNTER

HARPERCOLLINS*PUBLISHERS*

Smoke Mountain

Copyright © 2009 by Working Partners Limited

Series created by Working Partners Limited

Library of Congress Cataloging-in-Publication Data

Hunter, Erin.

Smoke Mountain / Erin Hunter. — 1st ed.

p.   cm. — (Seekers ; [#3])

Summary: When the bears learn of the legendary Last Great Wilderness, a fabled bear paradise, they believe that this must be their
ultimate destination.

ISBN 978-0-06-087128-4 (trade bdg.)

ISBN 978-0-06-087129-1 (lib. bdg.)

[1. Bears—Fiction.   2. Fantasy.]   I. Title.

PZ7.H916625Sm 2009   2009001405

[Fic]—dc22   CIP

                                                                      AC

Typography by Hilary Zarycky

09 10 11 12 13 LP/RRDB 10 9 8 7 6 5 4

❖

First Edition

With special thanks to Tui Sutherland

The Bears' Journey: Bear View

Lusa   — — —
Kallik   — · — · —
Toklo   ··········

The Melting Sea

BURN-SKY
GATHERING
PLACE

BlackPath

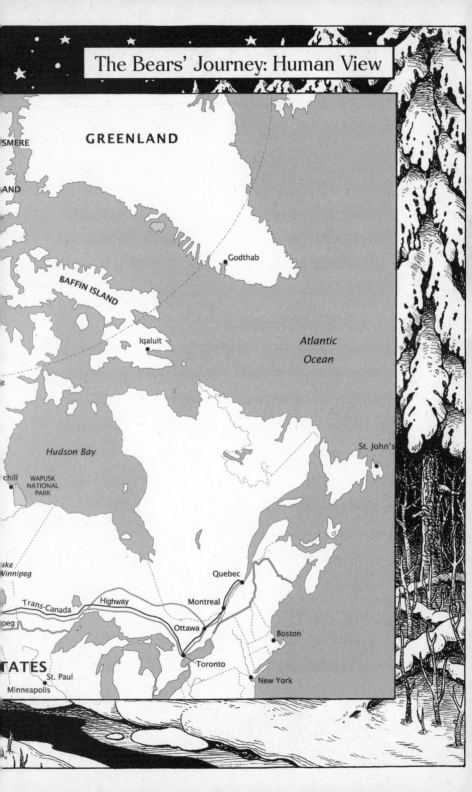

The Bears' Journey: Human View

CHAPTER ONE

Kallik

A soft breeze ruffled Kallik's fur, bringing with it the scents of fresh water and strange bears, as she climbed the rocky slope behind Toklo and Ujurak. Scrubby tufts of grass poked through cracks in the boulders, and tiny pebbles rolled under her paws. A faint orange glow lit up the edge of the sky; the night was already ending, although it felt as if they'd been walking for only a short time.

Kallik turned to look for her brother, Taqqiq. He was shambling along several steps behind her, batting small rocks down the hill with a ferocious paw swipe every few paces. He didn't look thrilled to be on this journey with the brown bears. Kallik wondered what he was thinking. Once, long ago, she used to be able to tell just by looking at him. Now, after so many moons apart, he felt like a stranger.

Beyond him, far below the ridge they were climbing, Kallik could see the vast blue shimmer of Great Bear Lake reflecting the rising sun. She spotted several shapes moving on the lakeshore. Bears were steadily leaving the Longest Day Gathering,

1

heading back to their homes in forests, on mountains, and on the vast stretches of ice that would return now that the sun had given up its hold over the sky. There were so many bears that Kallik's keen nose could smell them all the way up here— the mingled scents of damp fur and muddy cubs. All the white bears she'd met were going back to the Melting Sea, where Kallik and Taqqiq had been born . . . where their mother, Nisa, had died. From her high position she could see how most of the bears were staying away from one another, deliberately picking out separate paths so they could travel alone.

Not Kallik. She wasn't alone anymore.

A cold black nose nudged her left side, and Kallik swiveled her head around to look down at the tiny black bear cub beside her.

"It's strange to be leaving them all behind, isn't it?" Lusa said in a hushed voice, matching her tone to the quiet predawn stillness around them. Her eyes were huge in the pale light. "I hope they all make it back to their homes." There was a wistful note to her voice as the cub watched every other black bear set off in the opposite direction. She shook herself. "But I'm glad you're here, Kallik. It feels right having you with us."

"Me and Taqqiq," Kallik prompted.

Lusa glanced back at the other big white bear. Kallik followed her gaze and saw that her brother had a tendril of moss hooked around one claw. He was twitching his paw angrily, trying to get rid of it. His teeth were bared, and he muttered something under his breath.

"Yeah, you and Taqqiq," Lusa said, but Kallik could hear the drop in enthusiasm in her new friend's voice. She decided to change the subject. Hopefully Taqqiq would start acting like her brother again soon, like the cheerful, playful cub he had been when they lived on the ice with Nisa, and then the others would feel friendlier toward him.

"I can't believe the sun is coming up already," Kallik said, tilting her head toward the horizon at their flanks. She and Lusa had started walking again, padding over the cold gray stone to catch up to Toklo and Ujurak. "I thought that after the Longest Day the nights would be longer. We've barely had any time to follow the Pathway Star."

"We'll still be able to see it for a while," Lusa said, raising her nose to the sky where the bright star glittered. "And we have Ujurak. He knows where we're going."

Kallik blinked, remembering the endless scorching days she had spent traveling to Great Bear Lake, never knowing where she would end up. "It's nice to have someone to follow for once," she commented quietly. "I've been lost for so long." She looked up and saw that the two brown bears up ahead had stopped to drink from a small stream that trickled between the rocks. The rising sun tinged their fur a golden color.

"But you did what you were trying to do," Lusa reminded her as they quickened their pace, both of them thirsty after the night's walking. "You found your brother."

"Yes, I did," Kallik said. *Although that didn't go quite the way I expected it to.*

Toklo swung his shaggy head around to watch them

scramble across the rocks toward him. His brown eyes were expressionless, as if he didn't care if they made it or not. Kallik wished she knew how she could make him like her. Maybe if she proved that she could be useful . . . or if Toklo realized that Taqqiq was not as bad as he thought.

The stream bubbled icy and cold against Kallik's paws. She wished it were deeper so she could lie down in it and cool off.

"Brrrrr!" Lusa huffed as she dabbed her paw in the water. She lapped up a few drops, her long pink tongue flicking in and out. "It's freezing!"

"It's perfect," Kallik said. She buried her nose in the water and then shook her head as Taqqiq caught up to her, spraying him with icy droplets. "Taqqiq, it feels like snow, doesn't it?"

"Not really," Taqqiq growled. "You told me we were going to find real snow. How do we even know there will be any in this direction? At least back at the Melting Sea we know there *was* snow, once."

"It'll snow again here sometime," Ujurak said. He looked up at the cloudless pink-and-gray sky. "I mean, maybe not soon. But I know it will, once fishleap is over."

"Fishleap?" Taqqiq curled his lip. "What is that?"

"Black bears call it leaftime," Lusa jumped in. "When the days are long and hot."

"Oh—they mean burn-sky," Kallik said to Taqqiq. "We just have to wait for snow-sky to return."

"*If* it returns," Taqqiq muttered. He raked his claws across the bare rocks with a harsh grating sound. Kallik winced.

"Why don't we just keep going?" Toklo suggested, and

Kallik could hear the forced patience in his voice. "Lusa, there's a tree up ahead. Maybe you could climb it and tell us what's in front of us." He jerked his head at a tall, scraggly tree that stood on its own among the rocks. The rocky slope of the hill kept going up beyond it, covered in patches of yellow grass and a few leafy green bushes.

"Sure!" Lusa agreed. She bounded across the stream and trotted over to the tree. Her paws flashed as she leaped onto the trunk. In a few moments, she was racing up through the branches.

"Wow," Kallik said. "She climbs fast!"

"Doesn't she?" Toklo said, giving Taqqiq a faintly smug look.

Taqqiq snorted. "I guess black bears have to be good at something—they're useless otherwise."

Kallik could see the fur rising on Toklo's shoulders. "Taqqiq," she said quickly, "do you smell any prey? It would be great to eat before we move on."

Her brother sniffed the air. His eyes narrowed. "Maybe . . ." He began pacing up the stream toward a clump of bushes.

"Toklo," Ujurak said in a low voice, "I could have changed into a bird and scouted ahead for us."

"I know," Toklo said, glancing at Kallik. "But I figured Lusa would like to be useful." Kallik saw his eyes go to Taqqiq, and she realized that the real reason was that Toklo didn't want her brother to know that Ujurak could change shape . . . at least, not yet. She sighed. There wasn't anything she could say; Taqqiq hadn't exactly given them a reason to trust him, not after he and his friends had stolen a black bear cub at the Longest Day Gathering. It would take time, that was all—that and for Taqqiq to stop being so difficult.

Toklo splashed across the stream and headed for Lusa's tree, with Ujurak a few pawsteps behind him. Kallik let the water bubble around her paws for a few more moments before she waded out onto the rocks. She took a deep breath and noticed a faint scent on the air. *Prey!*

Dropping into a crouch, she crept forward on silent paws, her nose twitching. There was a dip in the rocks downstream surrounded by tall, dry grass. Something could be hiding in that grass . . . something edible.

If I could catch some prey for us, wouldn't Toklo be pleased! Kallik held her breath, trying to edge forward without scraping her claws against the rocks. Her stomach growled, and scratchy thistles tickled her belly fur. For a moment it seemed like the world went still, just as out on the ice when Nisa had waited for seals to pop out of their breathing holes.

Kallik inhaled again, and this time she recognized the scent: It was a bird, the kind that built their nests on the ground. Now she could see the flutter of brown feathers behind the tall grass. It hadn't noticed her yet. She crept forward another pawstep.

Suddenly she felt vibrations in the rocks under her paws. With a bellow, Taqqiq shot past her and threw himself at the patch of grass. His mouth was open and his claws outstretched. There was an explosion of squawks, and the bird burst out of the grass, scattering feathers in all directions.

With an outraged shriek, it shot away into the sky. In despair, Kallik watched the bird flapping away into the distance. It was plump and young looking, and would have made the best meal she'd had in a while. Now she was even hungrier.

"Stupid birds," Taqqiq said. He shook himself and backed out of the tall grass. "Salik was really good at catching those."

Good at catching birds and harmless black bears, you mean, Kallik thought bitterly. She blamed Taqqiq's friend Salik for turning her brother into this unfriendly, arrogant monster. Salik had acted like he was the leader of a group of young white bears who had insulted every bear at the gathering and tried to provoke war against the black bears. They had been nothing but trouble, and Kallik had been horrified when she realized one of them was her brother, whom she had been looking for ever since their mother was killed by orcas, out on the ice.

Taqqiq sat down in the grass and began scratching an itch behind his ears. Kallik turned away and saw Toklo watching them from under the tree. He must have seen the bird escape. She padded up to him. "Sorry," she whispered.

Toklo pawed at the tree roots. "It's all right," he said gruffly.

Lusa scrambled down from the upper branches and dropped to the ground beside them. "It looks like this hill keeps going up to a ridge pretty far ahead of us. I think I saw trees off to the left. And I saw lots of bears leaving the lake behind us. There's a white bear several bearlengths to our right, going kind of in the same direction as us, but heading that way." She pointed with her nose to where the stream came from, between two large boulders higher up the hill to their right.

"A white bear?" Kallik said uneasily. Had one of Taqqiq's friends decided to follow them?

"Not one I recognized," Lusa told her, and Kallik knew she was thinking of Salik, too. "I think it was a female. There was a cub with her."

"Well, we don't want to run into them," Toklo said. "We can't afford to share any prey in this area. We should stay away from other bears if we can."

It's going to be hard enough to feed five of us traveling together, Kallik thought. *Especially if Taqqiq and I are such useless hunters.* She was grateful that Toklo didn't say so out loud, but she was afraid he was thinking the same thing.

"We keep going up," Ujurak said, pacing around the tree. Taqqiq gave him a suspicious look, his massive shoulders hunched. But as the small brown bear scrambled over the rocks, Taqqiq followed him. Ujurak glanced back when he heard the white bear's claws clicking against the boulders. His gaze was questioning, as if he wasn't sure why Taqqiq was there.

Kallik dropped back to walk beside Lusa again. It was strange how she felt so much more comfortable with this little black bear than with her own brother.

"I'm sure Taqqiq just needs time to get used to us," Kallik blurted out after they'd walked for a moment in silence. A bird trilled from somewhere nearby, as if mocking them for losing their prey earlier.

Lusa looked surprised. "Well, sure," she said. "I mean, he's been traveling with those . . . other bears for so long. He probably misses them."

Kallik stepped over a tuft of sharp-looking grass. "How could he miss those awful bears?" she said. "You all are much nicer."

"I bet Toklo would be surprised to hear you call him nice," Lusa barked with amusement. "But he really is, deep down."

"So is Taqqiq," Kallik insisted. Lusa dipped her head, not arguing. But as they kept going up the slope, feeling the sun warm the cold rocks under their paws, Kallik wondered. Was it too late for Taqqiq? Had it been a good idea to make him come with them? Or had he changed too much to ever again be the brother she had known on the ice?

CHAPTER TWO

Toklo

Toklo was glad to be traveling once more, away from Great Bear Lake and the gathering of bears. He had felt trapped on the lakeshore, with too many bears telling him how to act and what he had to believe in. The only time he had felt free and strong was when he had swum to Paw Print Island, to prove to the Great Bear in the sky that brown bears deserved to have fish in the rivers and territories of their own. He had fought Shoteka there, and won. He was equal to any brown bear; he had nothing more to prove.

The sun rose higher in the sky as they climbed the rocky ridge. They hadn't passed a tree since the one Lusa had climbed; nor had they seen any more streams. There was no shade up here, and the plants were dry and withered. But it felt good to be with his companions again. It even felt good to be following the strange brown cub Ujurak.

"I don't think he knows where he's going," Taqqiq muttered.

Toklo shot a sideways glance at Taqqiq. The white bear's

shoulders rolled as he paced forward, his eyes narrowed against the bright sun.

"Yes, he does," Toklo corrected him. This was one *companion* he could happily have left behind at the lake, he thought.

Lusa let out a little sigh, and Kallik looked anxiously at Toklo.

At least Kallik wasn't so bad. She had walked all night without a single complaint, though her paws had turned brown with dirt and her fur was matted and dusty. Toklo figured his pelt was equally stained, but it didn't show as much against his russet-brown coat.

Lusa padded beside Kallik as if they'd known each other since their BirthDens. They'd been chattering nonstop since leaving Great Bear Lake, as far as Toklo could tell. There had been a lot more peace and quiet when it was just Toklo and Ujurak traveling together.

"You really flew?" Lusa was saying. "In the sky?"

"Well, I wasn't flying," Kallik explained. "I was being carried by a giant metal bird."

Lusa's eyes were enormous. "That must have been the biggest bird in the world!"

"It was like a flying firebeast," Kallik said. "It had the same kind of smell, of burning and no-claws."

"I've seen lots of no-claws—I mean flat-faces," Lusa said. "Flat-faces were the ones who brought us food and let us live in the Bear Bowl."

"And they never hurt you?"

"No, never," Lusa said, shaking her head. Then she paused,

and something darkened in her gaze. She looked at Toklo, and he knew she was thinking about his mother, Oka, who was taken away by the flat-faces after she attacked one of them. "They . . . they fed us and gave us somewhere to live," she repeated.

Toklo's muscles ached from all his swimming the day before in Great Bear Lake. Oka had come to him in a vision during the swim, Oka and his little brother, Tobi, who had died before they reached the Great Salmon River. They had saved Toklo from drowning in the waves and given him the courage to make it all the way to the island. After moons of believing that if he went out of his depth in water, his mother and brother would drown him so that his spirit could join theirs, they had shown that they loved him and wanted him to stay alive. He missed them even more now.

As he climbed, listening to the chatter of the she-bears, he let his head hang and stared down at his paws. He felt tired, though he would never let the others know that, especially Taqqiq.

"Oomph!" He walked right into the white bear, who had stopped on a wide, flat boulder.

"Hey," Taqqiq snarled, flexing his claws. "Watch where you're going. Are brown bears blind as well as stupid?"

Toklo took a step back, swallowing a snarl. The rocks here leveled off into a shallow ridge cresting the top of the hill before it began to slope down again. Ujurak was standing on one of the tall gray boulders, staring down at the landscape spread out before them. Toklo scrambled up to join him.

A rocky plain rolled out below them, shifting from gray stone to rippling green grass farther out to the edge of the sky. Narrowing his eyes against the wind, Toklo spotted a few small lakes and darker green patches, which were probably trees, in the distance.

Ujurak lifted his black nose and sniffed the wind. A hawk soared overhead, far up in the thin trail of clouds that stretched across the bright blue sky. Toklo saw Ujurak watching it and felt a stab of alarm. What if the bear cub suddenly transformed and flew away? *Please don't do that,* Toklo prayed. Then Ujurak lowered his muzzle, and Toklo let out a sigh of relief.

The other bears clambered up beside them. Toklo glanced at each one—a brown bear who wasn't always a brown bear, black and white she-bears who couldn't stop talking, and a white bear with wasps for brains. He watched Taqqiq out of the corner of his eye. What would *he* make of Ujurak turning into a bird, or a frog, or a mouse? Who knew? It was probably best Taqqiq didn't find out.

Toklo shook his head to clear his thoughts and stared down at the landscape below. Ujurak was no doubt trying to read the "signs" he kept talking about. One direction seemed more obvious to Toklo, since it led to a small lake surrounded by trees at the bottom of the hill, but in his experience that usually meant Ujurak would choose to go the opposite way.

"That way," Ujurak announced at last. Sure enough, he pointed with his nose at the craggy rocks that led down to the open plain, which stretched far into the distance before reaching any water.

"What?" Taqqiq objected as Ujurak took a step forward. "Are you as dumb as a seal? There's nothing in that direction for *skylengths*!"

"Taqqiq!" Kallik said, hunching her shoulders. "Don't be rude."

"What's a seal? Is it like a flat-face?" Lusa asked curiously. "What's a skylength?"

"It's the distance from here to the edge of the sky," Kallik said, nodding at the horizon ahead of them. "And a seal is . . . um . . . like a big, blubbery squirrel. Only better tasting. And without any fur."

Taqqiq was looking scornfully at his sister. "Look down there." He jerked his head at the woods below. "There's a lake and trees. We could probably find prey. I'm *starving*."

"No," Toklo said, although his belly was rumbling, too. He was irritated that Taqqiq had the same instinct he'd had himself. He was nothing like this white bear! "Ujurak says we go this way."

"Who made him chief bear?" Taqqiq snarled. "Why should I listen to a scrawny pile of brown fur like him?"

Toklo's claws sank into the hard earth as he pictured slashing at this white bear's tiny ears. "If you want to go your own way, that's fine with me."

Taqqiq's eyes were like burning black stones as he glared back at Toklo. Toklo tried not to look at Taqqiq's giant paws or think about how the cub was already bigger than him. He needed to teach this fish-smelling cub a lesson.

"I told you they wouldn't want me!" Taqqiq snapped at Kallik.

"Well, stop being so disagreeable!" she said. "They've been traveling together for moons—we should listen to them."

"I *have* been!" Taqqiq growled. "But it's past sunhigh, and we haven't had anything to eat since we left the lake!"

"I guess the legends about the strength of white bears aren't true, then," Toklo muttered.

"Do you want to find out exactly how strong I am?" Taqqiq snarled.

Toklo bunched his muscles and rooted his hind paws more firmly on the rock. A fight was just what he needed to show Taqqiq who was really in charge. "I'm not scared of you, fish-breath," Toklo growled.

"You should be, tiny paws!"

"I'll claw your face off!"

"Stop it!" Ujurak barked.

Toklo shuffled his paws on the ground, a growl rumbling in his throat. Taqqiq's fur bristled on his neck.

"He's a stupid badger-face," Toklo huffed.

"Listen," Ujurak said before Taqqiq could snarl a retort, "it does make sense to rest before we go on. Let's go down to the lake." He turned and began padding away down the rocks. "And after we've rested we can keep following the signs," he called.

Toklo couldn't believe what he'd just heard. Ujurak never agreed to leave the path when *he* suggested it. Not even if they'd been traveling for a whole day without stopping.

Taqqiq lifted his head and looked smugly at Toklo. Then he swung around and took off down the hill toward the lake. He was moving a lot faster now that he was getting his own way, Toklo noticed grumpily.

"Come on, Kallik!" Taqqiq called over his shoulder. "Race you there!"

"Not fair!" she cried. "You got a head start!" She took a step forward, then turned and lowered her head at Ujurak. "Thanks," she murmured. With a swish of her stubby tail, she began running down the hill with Lusa close on her heels.

"It won't take long," Ujurak said to Toklo. "It does make sense to eat something while we can. I always forget to look for that practical stuff when I'm figuring out where to go."

"Oh, that's reassuring." Toklo snorted. He followed the other bears down into the shade of the small woods. He could see Lusa with her head stretched up toward the branches, flexing her claws in a little dance. He guessed she was happy to be among trees again. The leaves whispered softly overhead, casting rippling puddles of shade and sunlight on the ground and across their backs.

It was much cooler once they were under the trees. Toklo made sure to check the bark of the trees for signs of any other grizzlies, but there were no clawmarks that he could see. No other bears lived here. He wasn't surprised: The woods were too small to feed a full-grown brown bear for more than a half moon, and there was nothing else around.

Twigs and fallen leaves crunched gently under his paws.

The soft sound of water lapping called to him from the lake ahead, so he pushed his way through the undergrowth and padded down to the shore. Compared with Great Bear Lake, it was hardly more than a puddle: He could easily see to the far side, and the surface of the water was flat and shiny, not whipped into waves. Taqqiq and Kallik were already up to their bellies, splashing and rolling in the water. Kallik cuffed a sparkling wave at her brother and he pounced on her.

"Look out, I'm going to get you!" he yelped.

He knocked her backward into the water and she wrapped her paws around him, rolling until she was on top and could pin him down.

"I win!" she cried.

"Never!" he spluttered, surging up out of the water and throwing her off. She landed with a splash, her mouth wide open with amusement.

Toklo watched them playing. He wished his brother, Tobi, had been strong and that they could have played like this. Then his mother would have loved them both the same, and they would all still be together. For a moment he could see why Kallik had traveled so far and for so long, looking for her brother. If he thought Tobi was still alive, he'd have kept on searching for him, too.

Then Taqqiq noticed Toklo watching them and he abruptly stood up, shaking his fur so that droplets rained down on the water around him. He pawed at his nose and waded back to shore. Kallik floundered in the lake for a moment, waiting for him to jump on her again. Finally she sat up and noticed he was gone. Blinking as water streamed off her muzzle, she stared after her brother with a confused look.

Lusa barreled up to the lake and leaped in with all paws. "Whee!" she yelped, disappearing in a glittering wave of water. "It's amazing! It's perfect! It's *really cold*! Brrr! I'm getting out!" She charged back onto the shore and shook herself vigorously. Drops of water spattered Ujurak and Toklo.

"Hey," Toklo growled.

Lusa bounced around him like a jackrabbit. "Try it, Toklo! Your paws will feel so much better! And then so much colder! Brrr!"

"Are there fish in there?" Toklo called to Kallik. "Or did you great lumbering beasts scare them all off?"

"Oops." Kallik looked worried. "I didn't even think of that. Sorry!" She lifted her front paws one at a time as if there might be a fish hiding under one of them.

"Fish," Taqqiq scoffed. He lay down on a patch of grass under a tree, gazing at them all with narrow eyes. "They're barely a mouthful for a real bear. What we need is a fat seal."

"Why don't you go get one, then?" Toklo snapped. "If you're such a great hunter, surely you can find one."

Taqqiq bared his teeth at Toklo, but Lusa nudged in between them, trying to draw Toklo's attention back to the lake and Kallik.

"Tell me more about seals," Lusa said to Kallik, who was wading back to the shore. "Do they taste like squirrels?"

"Not really. A seal is like a great big fish, only much better." Kallik padded onto the stones and let the water stream from her fur, which was noticeably whiter. "They're crunchy and chewy and delicious, and I could eat nothing but seals for the rest of my life and be perfectly happy. I wish I could catch one for you! I bet you'd love the taste even more than blueberries."

"More than blueberries!" Lusa echoed. "Wow, they must be really tasty. Do you think there will be seals at the Place of Everlasting Ice?"

"Of course," Kallik said. "That's why it'll be the perfect home for us."

Trying to block out the nattering, Toklo took a long drink. He stared at the pebbles wavering below the surface, wishing he could see a flash of silver. Catching a fish right now would make Taqqiq look like a dopey squirrel for chasing away that bird. And maybe it would make everyone shut up about stupid seals.

But all he could see were tiny darting shapes no bigger than a claw, and the swirls of sand the other bears had kicked up as they jumped around in the lake. He'd have to sniff around the trees to see if he could find prey there instead.

His sharp ears caught a new sound—something nearly lost under the growling and babbling of his noisy companions. He lifted his head and froze.

"What is it, Toklo?" Kallik asked.

Lusa had been dabbling one of her paws in the water, but she stopped moving. Her ears, the biggest of any of the bears', went up. Beside her, Ujurak glanced around, searching the bushes.

"Shh," Toklo hissed.

"Why?" Taqqiq grunted. "I don't hear anything."

"Anything but yourself," Toklo muttered. There it was again—a low moan, deep and guttural. This time Lusa heard it, too. She gave Toklo a wide-eyed look. He nodded at a large clump of prickly bushes not far from the edge of the lake. He was sure that was where the sound had come from.

Lusa took a step back, her fur bristling along her back. "Should we run?" she whispered.

It could be anything, Toklo thought. It could be a wolf like the ones that had chased them on the Sky Ridge. Or another enormous grizzly like Shoteka, waiting to attack them.

Then again, it could also be prey.

Taqqiq leaped to his paws. "Well, *I'm* not a frightened mouse, like the rest of you." He stomped over to the thicket and swatted aside the branches in his way.

"Wait!" Toklo barked, but it was too late. With his broad shoulders and sharp claws, Taqqiq cleared a path straight to the middle of the thicket.

And there, lying in a tangle of brambles, was an enormous white bear.

CHAPTER THREE

Lusa

Lusa gasped and dug her front paws into the pebbles to stop herself from fleeing up the nearest tree. The full-grown white bears at Great Bear Lake had been huge, but this one seemed even bigger. Or perhaps she was just used to Taqqiq's and Kallik's size—which was still too big for a cub, in Lusa's opinion. For a heartbeat she wondered if this was the bear she'd seen from the top of the tree, but that one had been a female with a cub, while this one was a giant male. A giant, scary male.

But the strange white bear didn't leap up and attack them. He didn't open his jaws and snarl at them with his enormous teeth. He whimpered with pain as he slowly scooted his head around to look at them. His dark eyes looked fuzzy and unfocused, as if he could barely see the cubs, and his fur was filthy and matted. He looked worn out . . . old and tired. His eyes drooped, and his long blue-black tongue flopped out between his teeth as he panted and groaned. Streaks of mud had turned his white muzzle brownish gray.

Lusa felt a stab of pity for the old bear. She remembered

the same dull, defeated look in the eyes of another bear: Oka, Toklo's mother. This white bear didn't have any fight left in him. Lusa hadn't been able to do anything for Oka. She had lain beside her on the other side of the fence the night before the flat-faces took her away, but she hadn't been able to touch her, or fetch food for her, or do anything to fill the gaping hole left by the loss of both her cubs. Maybe there was something she could do to help this bear.

She padded closer, nosing past Taqqiq. The white cub was staring in shock at what he had uncovered.

"Lusa, be careful," Toklo growled behind her.

"It's all right," she whispered. She crouched beside the strange bear's head and sniffed him. He smelled horrible, like rotting fish and hot, grimy fur. Lusa tried not to wrinkle her nose. She didn't want to make him feel worse than he already did.

"Hello," she said. "I'm Lusa. Who are you?"

The older bear blinked at her. "I . . . I'm Qopuk," he wheezed. His eyes rolled sideways to stare at Taqqiq. The white cub shuffled his paws and backed away. Behind him, the other three bear cubs were peering into the thicket. Kallik edged forward first, but she stayed away from the big bear's enormous paws. Each paw was nearly the size of Lusa's head. If this bear had had any strength left, he could have knocked her out with a single blow, and he wouldn't even have to try very hard. But he had no strength left. She could tell that from the scent of him, from his sunken frame and dull eyes.

"What happened to you?" she whispered.

Qopuk drew a long, raspy, clattery breath, like claws scraping across bark. "Death," he grunted. "Death . . . so far from the ice."

Lusa felt as though freezing water were running under her skin. "Death? What do you mean?"

"I'm dying," Qopuk rasped. "All my life I wanted to get there, but now it's too late."

"No," Lusa protested. "Don't say that! We'll help you. Ujurak knows all about herbs that will make you feel better, and I can fetch food for you. And some nice soft grass to lie on." She sniffed the crushed undergrowth beneath the old bear. It smelled like he'd been lying there for a moon.

"It won't help." The old bear's eyes closed and he sighed.

"But we can try," Lusa insisted. "What do you want?"

Qopuk tried to twist his head toward the lake, but his fur snagged in the brambles and he winced, then lay still. He opened his mouth a little and his tongue pushed forward again.

"Water?" Lusa guessed. "Ujurak, can you get him some water?"

Ujurak's eyes were full of pain as he gazed at the wounded bear. Without a word, he turned and padded down to the lakeshore.

"We should just let him die," Taqqiq growled. "He'd let us die if he had a choice."

"We don't know that," Lusa pointed out. "And if there's anything we can do to help him, we must do it."

Taqqiq scratched the ground, leaving deep furrows in the

dirt. "It's not our problem," he snarled.

"Toklo doesn't mind if I help Qopuk," Lusa said challenging-ingly. "Right, Toklo?"

The brown bear cub glowered at Taqqiq. "Do what you like," he growled. "I'm going hunting." He turned around and stomped off into the trees.

Ujurak came back from the lake, carrying a bundle of soaked moss between his jaws. He dropped it into Lusa's out-stretched paws.

"Here," Lusa said, dribbling some of the water into Qopuk's mouth. His jaws twitched open as she pressed the moss to his dry snout. He licked it gratefully, his tongue nearly brush-ing her paws. Lusa forced herself not to think about the giant teeth that were only a clawslength from her fur. *Not thinking about it. Not thinking about it. Not thinking about big . . . giant . . .* enor-mous *teeth . . .*

Qopuk stopped licking up the moisture, and Lusa gave the moss back to Ujurak. The old white bear stared up at the tan-gled branches above his head, outlined against the sharp blue sky. "The Longest Day," he murmured. "Am I almost there?"

"Oh—you were traveling to the lake?" Lusa guessed. "That's where we just came from."

"No, no." Qopuk shook his head. "I'm on a journey . . . but I thought I would try to go to the gathering. Only I got lost. . . . "

"The ceremony was yesterday," said Kallik. "I'm sorry. You missed it."

"So what?" Taqqiq grunted. "You didn't miss anything.

Blah, blah, fat old bears muttering about spirits and how much they miss the ice. Blah, bl—"

Lusa shot Taqqiq a stern glance and the white bear shut up.

"It would have been my last gathering," the old bear rasped. "I wanted so much . . . to tell them . . . what I learned."

"Right, I bet that would be *fascinating*," Taqqiq said. "Lots of old stories about *fishing* and how much better everything was when you were a cub. Don't worry; every other old bear in the world can fill us in."

"Taqqiq, stop," Kallik whispered. "He's one of us."

"You can tell us," Lusa said, lightly pressing the bear's fur with her nose. "We'll listen." She lay down with her paws tucked under her muzzle and her ears swiveled toward Qopuk. More than food, more than rest, this bear wanted an audience. Well, that was something she could give him quite easily.

"Huh! *You* might be happy to listen to some old fool rambling about the good old days!" Taqqiq snorted. "I'm going to show that oaf Toklo how a *real* bear hunts!" He turned and charged into the woods, crashing through any bushes that dared to get in his way. Lusa was sure Toklo would be ever so pleased about sharing his hunt with Taqqiq, but at least it meant Qopuk could speak in peace.

Qopuk blinked at the three bear cubs who were still gathered around him. One black, one brown, one white. Lusa realized how odd they must look together. But Qopuk didn't seem to care.

"It's so far," the old bear whispered. "Too far . . . How could a group of little cubs ever get there alone? No, it's too dangerous . . . if only I could take you there . . . take us all there . . ." His voice trailed off. Lusa reached for the moss and dribbled some more water onto his tongue.

Ujurak's ears twitched forward. "Where?" he prompted. "What's too far?"

"The Last . . . Great . . . Wilderness," Qopuk murmured.

Lusa shot Kallik a hopeful look. The Last Great Wilderness? She'd never heard of it before, not even from Ujurak. "What is that?" she asked.

"I only know the stories," Qopuk admitted. "It is a place where the forests are full of prey and the no-claws stay far away. There's enough space for bears of all kinds, white, brown, and black. And there is sea-ice all year round." He sighed.

Ujurak's eyes shone. "That's where we're going!" he barked. "That must be it—that's the place we've been looking for!"

"Do you know how to get there?" Lusa asked Qopuk. She wanted to leap around with excitement, but she made herself stay still so Qopuk would keep talking.

Kallik had crept close enough to press her nose into the white bear's fur as well. She leaned gently against him, and Lusa wondered if this was how Kallik had rested against her mother to hear stories about the everlasting sea-ice and the dancing bear spirits.

"I do know how to get there," Qopuk croaked, gazing up at the bramble branches as if he weren't really seeing them. "But it's very dangerous. Few bears survive the journey over Smoke Mountain."

"Smoke Mountain?" Lusa echoed. She looked up and saw

that Ujurak's fur was bristling and his eyes were so wide she could see white circles around them.

Kallik pressed closer to Qopuk. "What a horrible name," she whispered.

"Why is it dangerous?" Lusa pressed. "Qopuk, what's there? What's on Smoke Mountain?"

Qopuk's eyelids were drooping. "Smoke Mountain," he murmured. "The fire giant . . ." His head lolled to one side and his paws went limp. His eyes closed.

"Qopuk!" Lusa cried. "Wait, tell us more!"

"Shhh," Kallik told her. "Lusa, he's sleeping. Let him rest."

"Oh," Lusa said softly. "Sorry, Qopuk." She took a step backward, trying to move quietly.

"He's so tired," Ujurak said. They watched the bear's grimy fur rise and fall as he breathed.

"Can we stay here tonight?" Kallik asked Ujurak. "To be with him?"

"Oh, yes," Lusa said. "And tomorrow, after he's rested, he can come with us! He can show us the way to the Last Great Wilderness!"

Ujurak shifted his weight, twigs crackling under his paws. "I think it's a good idea to stay," he said. "Maybe if Toklo catches something we can share it with him."

"Or Taqqiq," Kallik reminded him.

"I'll get him some more water," Lusa said. She closed her jaws around the damp moss and backed out of the brambles. As she trotted down to the lake, the leaves of the trees around her rustled and whispered. She thought the bear spirits in them approved of her taking care of Qopuk, even though he wasn't a black bear.

She dipped the moss in the clear, cold water, soaking it through. The sun was sliding down toward the horizon, and the shadows were getting longer across the rippling lake. Lusa twitched her ears, listening for sounds of prey. She could hear thumping paws and branches cracking and some bear muttering nearby, which sounded like Taqqiq trying to hunt.

A twig snapped behind her, and she turned to see Toklo emerging from the trees with a hare in his jaws.

"Good job!" Lusa exclaimed. "I knew you would catch something!"

Toklo rolled his eyes. "No thanks to certain noisy bears," he mumbled around the newkill.

"We're going to stay here tonight," Lusa went on, lifting the soaked moss out of the lake. "Qopuk knows the way to the Last Great Wilderness, and Ujurak says that's where we're going. Isn't that great? He can take us there!"

"Terrific," Toklo said. "Just what we need, another bear to slow us down."

"But he'll be useful," Lusa pointed out. "And it's his dream to get there—we can help him." She was cross that Toklo was being so selfish. Qopuk deserved to reach the end of his journey as much as they did.

She picked up the wet moss and trotted back into the brambles with Toklo close behind her. Kallik was curled up beside Qopuk, her fur lifting and falling in rhythm with his. Her eyes were closed.

"Shhh," Ujurak warned, nodding at the two white bears. Lusa set the moss down next to Qopuk's nose.

Toklo scratched a pile of leaves together under a tree a few bearlengths from Qopuk and settled down to eat. "We'll save some for them," he said.

Lusa had just taken a mouthful when Taqqiq came crashing back through the trees. "There's nothing to eat in these woods!" he grumbled. "Forests are a stupid place to hunt."

Lusa couldn't help but think, *So why were you trying to steal forest territory from the black bears at the lake? Dumb fur lump.*

"Sure, Taqqiq," Toklo said. "Nothing but squirrels, birds, foxes . . . hares." He nudged the newkill in front of them.

Taqqiq glared at the brown bear as if he were thinking about eating *him*. He tore off a strip of meat and glanced around as he chewed. His gaze fell on Kallik sleeping next to the old white bear.

"What is she doing?" he snarled. "He's not family! Is she going to act like a seal-brained cub with every big lump of fur that comes along?"

"Leave her be," Ujurak growled, sounding fiercer than Lusa had heard before. His eyes looked like little black berries, glaring at Taqqiq.

Taqqiq twitched his ears but said nothing. He bent his head, holding the end of his piece of meat between his front paws, and concentrated on chewing.

Lusa finished eating and climbed up the tree. She tucked herself into a comfortable niche where two branches met the trunk and rested her head on her aching paws. Down below

she could see Toklo and Ujurak curling up to sleep. Taqqiq
clawed at the ground, circling and grumbling, and finally settled down with an enormous sigh.

Lusa wondered if Kallik was dreaming of her mother.
Qopuk's warm bulk probably reminded her of sleeping next
to Nisa, curled up in the snow. She must have felt so alone
after Nisa died. At least Lusa knew where her mother was—
safe in the Bear Bowl, well fed and surrounded by friends. She
missed her so much that it made her head hurt sometimes, but
if Ashia was dead, she would feel lonely in a totally different
way.

Lusa drifted off to sleep and dreamed of bear spirits whispering in the wind through her fur. One of them spoke with
the voice of her mother: *Sleep, little one. I am here.*

CHAPTER FOUR

Lusa

The murmur of voices woke Lusa the next morning. She peered down through the branches and saw that Qopuk was awake and talking. Kallik and Ujurak were crouched beside him. Toklo's pile of leaves was empty; she guessed he was out hunting. Taqqiq was still asleep below her. Lusa blinked at the pale pink sky overhead. It had been another short night; it felt far too early to be morning. When would the nights finally get longer again? Right now, she thought, she'd gladly give up some of the warmth of the day in exchange for more sleep.

She clambered down the tree and edged around Taqqiq, who was snoring among the tree roots.

"Lusa!" Kallik called as she trotted toward them. "Qopuk is telling us how to get to the Last Great Wilderness."

The old white bear had hauled himself onto his haunches so that he was sitting up. His eyes were brighter than they had been the day before. The remains of the hare were scattered at his paws, and the food seemed to have given him extra strength. Lusa wriggled in beside Kallik and looked up at him.

31

Qopuk nodded to her, touching the moss she had brought him.

"You were saying something about the Big River," Ujurak prompted.

"Yes," Qopuk said. "That's the first danger you have to cross to reach the Last Great Wilderness. I've seen it, but I've never crossed it myself. It's a skylength wide, and the currents are very strong. Too strong to swim, even for you, little star," he said to Kallik. The white cub looked startled. Lusa wondered why. Ashia used to call her "little blackberry," but she liked the name "little star," too. It suited Kallik.

"Then how do we get across?" Ujurak asked.

"There is one spot where it's possible," Qopuk said. "The river is shallower and calmer if you swim it from the no-claw denning place . . . but be careful, because it is still very wide and the currents are swift. If you make it across, from there you must follow the Pathway Star beyond Smoke Mountain." He lifted his nose to the far horizon.

"You mentioned the mountain last night," Lusa said. "You said it was dangerous."

"It is." Qopuk's eyes closed and he took a long, rattling breath. Finally he opened them once more and looked around in surprise, as if he couldn't remember where he was. His huge chest heaved as he struggled to breathe.

"Smoke Mountain," Lusa reminded him. "What's there? Why is it so dangerous?"

"I only know what I've been told," Qopuk rasped. His dirty white fur rippled as he stretched out one front paw and flexed his claws. "I met a bear once who said he had been to the Wilderness and back again. No one believed him ... they said if the place was so wonderful, why would he come back?" He looked down, drawing a furrow in the earth. "But I believed him. His stories were so real, with stranger things than he could have made up. He told me all about Smoke Mountain—about the rocks that burn and the fire underneath the ground. He said the sky was full of ash and smoke, stinging your eyes and leaving black powder on your fur and all over the ground, too sticky to be washed away by the rain. The dark rocks stretch for skylengths, hard and jagged underpaw. The air is choking, and it drives bears off their path. And something is lying in wait there ... something evil."

Kallik, Lusa, and Ujurak all stared at him. The frightening picture in Lusa's mind was so different from the peaceful trees around them that she could hardly believe it existed. Morning dew sparkled on the grass, and she could hear the burble of a small stream under Taqqiq's snoring. A place as terrible as Smoke Mountain seemed very far away.

"What is it?" Kallik squeaked. "The evil?"

"There is a legend," Qopuk said softly, "that speaks of a giant no-claw as tall as seven trees."

Lusa and Kallik gasped.

"He lived on Smoke Mountain many moons ago," Qopuk went on. "Every step he took was a skylength wide. The trees themselves quaked in fear when he walked by. And he was hungry—always hungry.

"Then a snow-sky came that was longer than ever before,

and fiercely cold. The no-claw had nothing to eat for many days. When the snow-sky finally passed, his hunger was so ferocious that he went into the mountains and killed every bear he could find."

"Oh, no!" Lusa cried.

"He killed *thirty bears*," Qopuk said darkly. Lusa looked down at her paws. She knew she had four of those. Was thirty a lot more? "And then he burned them the way no-claws burn their food. He hung them over a fire near a huge rock—the bear I met said he had seen the very rock, which he called Bear Rock. And then the giant no-claw ate all thirty bears."

"I didn't think no-claws *ate* bears," Kallik whispered.

"Well, this one did," Qopuk said. "And according to the legend, his spirit still haunts the mountain. They say that when the smoke thickens, the no-claw is lighting his fire and searching for bears to eat."

Lusa buried her muzzle in Kallik's fur, trying to block out the screams of bears that rang in her head.

"That's really horrible." Ujurak wrinkled his nose. "There *must* be another way to the Last Great Wilderness."

"I have heard of another path," Qopuk said, lowering his head. All three cubs leaned closer. "It is much longer. And it has its dangers, too."

"Tell us," Ujurak prompted, touching his snout to the old bear's.

"Cross the Big River and then follow it all the way to the Ice Sea," Qopuk rasped. "If you make it through the sinking sands and the waves that try to sweep you out into the ocean . . . if you can survive there . . . it is possible to reach the Last Great Wilderness along the shore." He took one long, shuddering breath and lay down. Branches and leaves crunched under his massive weight as he settled to the ground and rested his head on his paws. His eyes slowly closed.

Lusa padded closer to him and pressed her fur to his. "I am so glad you'll be with us on our journey," she whispered to him. "You can show us the way—and we can help you find the end of your path."

Qopuk didn't answer. His chest rose and fell quietly as he breathed. Lusa pawed some soft leaves around him and stepped back. Ujurak was watching her with large, dark eyes.

"We should let him sleep as long as he wants," Lusa decided, "so when he wakes up he'll be strong enough to travel."

Kallik blinked, stretching forward to sniff the old bear. "I hope he has some nice stories to tell us, as well."

Lusa picked up the moss and trotted down to the water to soak it again. After a few moments, she realized that Ujurak was right behind her. She lifted her head and looked around.

"Lusa," he said. "I'm sorry. Qopuk isn't coming with us."

"Yes, he is!" Lusa mumbled around the wad of moss. "He knows the way—and how to avoid Smoke Mountain! We need him!"

"He would come with us if he could," said Ujurak. "But this is our journey to make. Not his."

Lusa tipped her head to one side and stared at him. "You mean you won't let him come?"

"It's not like that." The breeze picked up, and a pair of

bright green leaves fluttered down between them. Ujurak
lowered his head and touched one of them with his nose. He
looked sad. "He's so old and tired, Lusa. It's time for his spirit
to go on without him."

Lusa's claws sank into the ground. "No!" she growled.
"You're wrong!" She dropped the moss and raced back to
Qopuk. The old white bear was still breathing—but his breaths
were slower and shallower now, his flank barely lifting. Lusa
felt as if she had swallowed a stone. Qopuk was tired beyond
sleep. Ujurak was right: He would never leave this place.

Kallik was leaning against the bear's shoulder, touching
one of his paws with hers. Her fur looked bright white against
Qopuk's grayer, flattened pelt, and her belly was plump and
sleek beside his hollow ribs.

"Qopuk?" Lusa whispered.

The old white bear opened one eye. It was dull and glazed.
"Please stay with me, little ones," he said in a voice that creaked
like tree branches in the wind. "It won't be long now."

"Can't *you* stay?" Lusa begged. "Stay with us. We need you.
We can go to the Last Great Wilderness together. Please."

Qopuk let out a sigh that ruffled the tufts of grass in front
of his muzzle. "You must be careful," he warned. "Smoke
Mountain is more dangerous than you will ever understand.
But the Last Great Wilderness is real . . . and you will get
there without me, brave little bears." His growl trailed off into
silence and his eyelid slid shut.

Lusa huddled beside Kallik and pressed against the old
bear's shoulder. "Qopuk," she whispered.

"He's gone," Ujurak said from behind her.

Just like that? Lusa looked up at the solid mass of white fur. It was still warm, and the hairs still wafted in the breeze. But something was different. Where there had been a feeling of tiredness and worry, there was just emptiness. It was something more than silence, more than stillness. Qopuk's spirit had gone.

She glanced around, wondering if she could see it slip into one of the trees. Surely it would take a very big tree to hold the spirit of a bear like Qopuk. But it was different for white bears, wasn't it? They weren't born under trees. What if they died, like Qopuk, so far from the frozen world that they loved? Was there room in these trees for a bear like him?

"What happens to a white bear's spirit?" Lusa asked Kallik. "Black bears go into the trees. Sometimes you can see their faces in the bark."

Kallik lowered her muzzle and met Lusa's gaze. Her eyes were troubled. "They become part of the ice," she said. "And when the ice melts, they go into the sky to join the ice spirits. But I don't know what happens if there's no ice for them. Maybe he goes straight into the sky." She glanced up at the sky, where the sun was blazing beyond the tree cover.

"That would make sense," Ujurak said.

Lusa thought so, too. "It's so sad," she said. "All his life Qopuk wanted to go to the Last Great Wilderness—and then he died on the way. He never got to see it, after dreaming about it for so long."

Kallik stood up and paced around the dead bear. "I don't

know what to do," she confessed. "I feel like we should say something, but I don't know the right words. Mother never had time to teach me." Her voice went croaky and she buried her nose in Qopuk's fur.

"Do you know, Ujurak?" Lusa asked.

He shook his head. "Brown bears cover dead bears with leaves and earth," he said, "to help their spirits find their way back to the Great Salmon River. Maybe we could do that?"

Kallik nodded. "We can't leave him like this. He looks . . . lonely."

Lusa knew what she meant. She picked up a twig that still had leaves clinging to it, and reached up to lay it on Qopuk's back.

Kallik scooped a pile of leaves up with one paw and spread them over Qopuk's front legs. "I'm sorry it isn't snow," she said softly. "I'm sorry you didn't get to see the ice again before you died."

Lusa pawed the leaves higher around Qopuk's head, but she couldn't bear to cover his face. "Good-bye," she whispered. "I hope your spirit watches over us while we finish your journey. We'll try to find the Last Great Wilderness for you."

"Go well, spirit of Qopuk," Kallik said solemnly. "I hope the ice spirits find you. I hope we see you again, dancing in the Place of the Endless Ice."

Ujurak put some moss on Qopuk's flank, where it quivered like feathers in the wind. He dipped his head. "Farewell, Qopuk," he murmured. "May your spirit travel safely, wherever it goes."

He hooked his claws in a leafy branch that had fallen to the ground and dragged it over to the white bear's body. Lusa and Kallik helped him lay it gently over Qopuk's back.

"We were so lucky to meet you, Qopuk," Lusa said.

Kallik tilted her head to the side and gave Lusa a thoughtful look. "You know, if we hadn't come down here," she said, "we wouldn't have met Qopuk. We wouldn't have heard about the Last Great Wilderness."

"True," Lusa said cautiously. She could guess where Kallik was going with this.

"So it's a *good* thing we listened to Taqqiq, isn't it?" Kallik went on. "Maybe he's meant to be with us after all?"

Lusa winced. She definitely did not want Taqqiq to start making more suggestions. If he started arguing with Ujurak over everything, this journey would become more difficult than getting honey out of her fur.

Lusa heard Toklo's pawsteps behind her and turned. The brown bear was carrying another hare in his jaws. Toklo glanced at the earth and leaves covering the old bear's fur and lowered his head. Lusa knew he recognized what they'd tried to do for Qopuk.

Beneath the tree where they'd slept, Taqqiq stretched and yawned, climbing slowly to his paws. He trotted over and blinked at the other bears.

"Is that old whale-breath dead yet?" he demanded. He peered around them at the large shape of Qopuk. "Looks like it. *Smells* like it, too."

"Taqqiq, show some respect," Kallik scolded him. "He was a

kind, wise old bear, and he told us where we need to go next."

"Old doesn't always mean wise," Taqqiq snapped. "Sometimes it means nothing but melting snowballs are left in your head."

"He knew so much about the journey," Kallik pointed out.

"We're going to listen to that mangy old rotfood eater?" Taqqiq objected.

"Can we leave Qopuk's body in peace, please?" Lusa begged. Her fur was heavy with sadness for Qopuk, and she hated hearing Taqqiq talk like that when the old bear had just died. She turned and headed down to the lakeshore.

Toklo caught up to her as she splashed into the water. He dropped his newkill on the stones and said, "Are you all right, Lusa?"

She drew her claws across the pebbly lake bottom, watching the marks disappear in a swirl of sand and water. "I just . . . I feel sad that he didn't get to finish his journey. It's hard to believe someone could die in the middle of something like that and never get to the end. It never occurred to me that any of us might not get there . . . you know?"

"We will get there," Toklo promised. "All of us together."

"But not Qopuk," Lusa pointed out. "How will his spirit know where to go? What if he never finds the ice again?" The water eddied and rippled around her paws, tinged with streaks of yellow from the sun that was peeking through the tree branches.

"At least he didn't die alone," Toklo told her. "And maybe

he was happy because he had a chance to tell *us* where to go, so we can finish his journey for him."

"Maybe," Lusa said. She waded back to shore and bumped him with her nose. "Thanks, Toklo."

As the bears ate, Kallik and Lusa explained what Qopuk had told them.

"Don't you see?" Lusa said to Toklo, her eyes shining. "We know where to go now. Qopuk told us the way to the Last Great Wilderness! This is exactly what we needed."

Taqqiq snorted. "The crazy ramblings of an old fur lump. Had he ever actually been there?" He slurped his blue-black tongue in the lake water, squinting at Lusa.

"Well . . . no," Lusa admitted. "But he told us all about it. He warned us about Smoke Mountain." She looked at Kallik, who nodded in agreement.

"Seal-brained stories and cloudfluff legends," Taqqiq growled. "No sane bear would believe any of that."

"I believe it," Ujurak said.

"Me too," Kallik said.

"Well, that's a surprise." Taqqiq snorted, scattering water droplets as he tossed his head.

"So we just have to find the Big River and then follow that to the Ice Sea and the Last Great Wilderness," Toklo said, ignoring him.

"I agree," Lusa said.

"It sounds right to me," Kallik said. "Taqqiq? Please?"

Her brother huffed loudly. "Fine. If that's what you all

want. I don't care." He ripped a large chunk of flesh off one of the hares and lay down under a tree, gnawing on it with his back hunched.

Lusa's pelt prickled with excitement. She wasn't bothered by Taqqiq. Suddenly a real path lay before them, to a place where they would be safe. Forests full of prey, enough room for all the bears, and not a flat-face in sight . . .

If only Qopuk could have lived to see it, too.

CHAPTER FIVE

Kallik

Kallik waited until Toklo, Ujurak, and Lusa had gone down to the lake to drink before padding over to her brother. Taqqiq was flopped on the ground, chewing noisily and opening his jaws unnecessarily wide.

"Rabbits are so tough," he complained as she sat down beside him. "Nothing like seals. The newkill this far from the ice is terrible. A bear would have to be stupid to actually *want* to live among dirt and trees."

Kallik glanced nervously at Toklo, who was following Ujurak to a stream that wound away from the lake. "Shh," she said. "The others might hear you."

"I don't care if they do," Taqqiq said, even louder. Lusa glanced up at them from the lake, where she was cleaning her paws.

"Taqqiq," Kallik warned, "if you don't act more respectful, they might ask us to leave—or sneak off without us. I don't want to be alone anymore! I like traveling with other bears instead of being lonely and scared and lost all the time."

"You wouldn't be alone," Taqqiq snarled. "You'd have me. And what in the name of Silaluk makes you think these bears aren't lost?"

Kallik was quiet for a moment. "But Taqqiq . . . we're going to the Place of Endless Ice. Nisa said that is the only safe place left for bears. Isn't that what you want, too?"

"Sure, fine," Taqqiq said, "but that should be *our* journey. You and me! Why would these dumb tree-living bears care about sea-ice?"

"They care about us," Kallik said, hoping that was true. "And from what Qopuk said, the Endless Ice is part of the Last Great Wilderness, where all bears can live safely. We're all going to the same place."

Taqqiq snorted and shoved aside the last of the hare. "Our journey has nothing to do with them. They're not like us. Especially that one." He jerked his head at Toklo. "And there's something weird about that other brown bear, too."

Kallik followed her brother's gaze along the lakeshore to where Ujurak was standing in the stream. The bubbling water washed over his claws while he gazed into the silver reflections. Taqqiq didn't realize just how different Ujurak was from other bears. She was suddenly very glad that her brother hadn't seen Ujurak turn into something else.

She sighed. "Well, please try to be nicer to them," she said. "For me. Okay, Taqqiq?"

He grunted and stood up. "Fine. Whatever."

They headed down the hill and joined Lusa and Toklo by the side of the stream.

"Ujurak? Is everything okay?" Kallik asked.

The brown cub looked up. "This stream," he said. "This stream will lead us to the Big River."

"Oh, really?" Taqqiq sneered. "What happened to going the other way, like you wanted to before?"

Kallik poked her brother sharply with her nose.

"If what Qopuk told us is true," Ujurak said, "this is the way we have to go."

"Oh," Taqqiq muttered. "And how can you be so sure?"

Ujurak didn't say anything. He just stared at a tree that had long branches hanging over the stream.

"I see it!" Lusa cried suddenly, making Kallik jump. The little black bear padded over to the tree. She reared up on her back paws and touched a twisting pattern on the bark of the trunk.

"What is it?" Kallik asked. All she saw was an ordinary tree. Her heart sank at the look on Taqqiq's face. This wasn't the way to make him cooperate—he'd just think the other bears were even crazier.

"Can't you see it?" Lusa prompted. She dropped to her paws again and tilted her head at the bark. "It's a bear spirit looking at us from inside the tree. That's what you saw, isn't it, Ujurak?"

Ujurak nodded.

Kallik peered at the knobby bits of wood, trying to see any sort of face in it. Beside her, Toklo had squinted, as if that would make the pattern clearer. There were lumps and whorls in the bark, but to Kallik they just looked . . . treelike.

"Here," Lusa said, touching a dark patch of the bark. "This is the face of the bear spirit that lives in this tree. I bet it's very old. And look how it's watching over the stream." She waved one paw at the long branches that hung over the burbling water. "Maybe it's a she-bear who once had cubs. Now she has something else to take care of."

Kallik stepped back, trying to see the tree the way Lusa did. It was true that the branches hanging over the stream looked a bit like a mother bear protecting her cubs. Thin green leaves trailed in the water like rippling fur. And maybe that patch of darker bark could be an eye . . . and those flecks could be whiskers . . . or more fur . . . or tufty ears.

"It's a sign," Lusa whispered. "Isn't it, Ujurak? The spirit of this bear wants us to follow this stream. She's guiding us to the Last Great Wilderness!"

Ujurak dipped his head. "I think that's what I see, too."

Taqqiq shoved Kallik aside and stalked up to the tree. He narrowed his eyes at the bear face, which was much closer to his eye level than Lusa's. Next to him, Lusa looked as small as the Arctic fox that had followed Kallik to Great Bear Lake. But Lusa didn't seem afraid. She dropped to all paws and looked up at the big white bear cub.

"You see it, don't you?" she said earnestly. "Now do you believe that we must go this way?"

Taqqiq didn't speak for a moment. Then a low growl rumbled in his throat. "There's nothing here at all," he said. "Bear spirits don't live in trees. Trees are just stupid things that get in the way when you want to run."

He stepped forward, twisted around, and started scratching his back against the tree. His lip curled back to show his teeth as he sneered at Lusa. Bits of bark flaked off and fell to the ground around him.

"No! Stop!" Lusa shrieked. "Leave it alone!" The tiny black cub threw herself at Taqqiq, battering him with her paws as she tried to push him away from the tree. It was like trying to move a mountain. He snorted as she clambered onto his back and tried to wrestle his head aside.

"Taqqiq!" Kallik barked. "Leave the tree alone!"

Toklo came running up from the stream, his teeth bared. But before he could get to them, Lusa lunged forward on Taqqiq's back and buried her teeth in one of his ears.

"Ow!" Taqqiq roared. He swung around so fast that Lusa lost her grip and went flying into a pile of leaves farther up the bank. Taqqiq reared up on his hind legs, bellowing, but Kallik threw herself in front of him before he could pounce on Lusa. With his powerful front legs, built for digging seals out of snowbanks, he could easily crush the smaller bear—whether he was trying to or not.

"Taqqiq, leave her be!" she snarled. Her fur was standing on end and her breathing was fast and angry. Why was Taqqiq always picking fights? "And don't you go near that tree again, either! Lusa wouldn't make fun of our ice spirits, and you should have some respect for her beliefs. Plus she's half your size! You won't impress anyone by hurting her!"

"And it might be the last thing you ever do," Toklo growled from behind Kallik. She turned to look at him. She had never seen a bear looking so angry, and for a moment she was scared for her brother. Toklo's long claws raked the earth as he glared at the white bear.

Taqqiq held his gaze for a moment, then dropped to all fours. He shook his shaggy head, looking disgusted. "She *bit* me," he protested.

"You deserved it!" Lusa yelped, sticking her head out from behind Kallik's leg.

"Lusa and Ujurak see the same thing in that tree," Kallik told her brother. "We'll follow this stream until we reach the Big River. *Together.* No more fighting. All right?"

Taqqiq grumbled something under his breath. He touched his paw to his ear, which wasn't even bleeding. With a snort, he turned his back on the cubs and marched down to the stream. Splashing through the water, he headed in the direction Ujurak had pointed to, out of the woods.

Ujurak breathed a sigh of relief. "Thanks, Kallik."

The brown fur on Toklo's back slowly flattened. He shook himself and trotted down to walk beside Ujurak. "Maybe next time he'll be brave enough to pick on a bear his *own* size," Toklo said, just loud enough for Taqqiq to hear. The white cub's ears twitched, but he kept pacing ahead without looking back.

"Are you all right?" Kallik asked Lusa when he was out of earshot. She craned her head around to sniff the black cub.

"I'm f-fine," Lusa said through chattering teeth. "I can't believe I attacked him! He just made me so mad! I'm sorry, Kallik. . . . I didn't mean to hurt your brother."

Kallik understood that Lusa was sorry only because it was

Kallik's brother she had bitten. If Taqqiq weren't Kallik's family, Lusa wouldn't want him here, either. Nobody liked Taqqiq, not even friendly little Lusa.

"I don't know why he's so awful sometimes." Kallik sighed. "He wasn't like this when he was a cub. We used to have fun together." She shook her head. "It must have been terrible for him when he thought Mother and I were both dead. I'm sure that's what changed him. At least I still had the hope of finding him alive to keep me going."

Lusa leaned into Kallik's side. "But he has you now," she said. "Maybe that will help him become a better bear."

"I hope so," Kallik said. "I guess we should catch up with them."

"Bye, tree," Lusa said, touching the roots lightly with her paw.

Kallik looked back up at the tree and felt something behind her eyes shifting. A dark bump on the bark suddenly looked just like a bear's nose. She followed the line of the whorl to where an eye should be and saw a delicate shape in the trunk, lined with flecks that looked like eyelashes. She felt a surge of excitement. "Lusa, I can see it! I can see the bear's face!" The nose and the eyes and the ears all seemed to emerge from the bark, and Kallik looked straight at the face watching them intently through the brown flakes rubbed off by Taqqiq.

"I hope she isn't angry with us," Lusa whispered.

"She won't be angry with *you*," Kallik pointed out. "You defended her. You were really brave!"

"We have to protect the spirits in the trees," Lusa said. "Just as the tree spirits protect black bears. We owe it to them." She looked up at the sunlit leaves. "I wish we didn't ever have to leave them. I like having the sound of leaves around me."

"There will be lots of trees in the Last Great Wilderness," Kallik said. "I'm sure of it."

Lusa wriggled. "I hope so! I hope we get there soon."

Me too, Kallik thought as the two she-bears hurried down the slope and followed the others along the stream and out of the trees.

CHAPTER SIX

Kallik

The stream widened into a small river shortly after it left the woods. The bears followed it for several days, across stretches of bare rock and then through grassy meadows dotted with purple wildflowers. Sometimes the river doubled back and they found themselves walking in the wrong direction for a day. Prey was scarce, and the leaves and berries they found to eat only left their bellies grumbling.

With each day that passed, Kallik grew more worried. They hadn't seen any other signs, or anything to suggest that Qopuk was right about where they were going. There was no Big River and no Smoke Mountain in sight. Her paws ached, but more than that, her heart ached as she saw how frustrated and prickly Taqqiq was. She'd heard him mutter more than once that it was crazy to wander blindly like this, following the advice of a dead bear.

As night fell after a day that had felt even hotter and longer than usual, she stopped to dip her paws in the river. She hated the feeling of dirt clumping in her fur, clogging up her claws.

It was nothing like the smooth, clean feeling of ice underpaw. Toklo and Ujurak were far ahead with Lusa, leading the way along the stream with Taqqiq a few bearlengths behind them, shambling grumpily by himself.

Kallik was relieved to see the sun dipping below the horizon in front of them. It felt like it had been in the sky forever. As the cooler night air moved in, her spirits rose.

She hurried forward and nudged against Taqqiq. "Aren't you glad the day is over?" she said. "It's so much cooler at night. And I like seeing the stars twinkling in the sky above us. Don't you?" She hoped she didn't sound too desperate. She wanted to remind him of their earliest days together—and of how lucky they were to have found each other again.

Taqqiq cast a scornful look at the pink-gray sky. "I don't see any stars."

"Well, they'll be out soon," Kallik persisted.

"I thought the nights would come sooner once the Longest Day had passed," Taqqiq complained. "Those old bears at Great Bear Lake went on and on about how that meant the end of the sun's power and the return of the cold and ice. But the sun still stays up in the sky forever. The nights are too short, and we barely even see the ice spots before the sun comes back and swallows them up. How do we know it will ever get cold again? What if the sun keeps eating the night until all the stars are gone?"

Kallik was shocked. "That can't happen!" she said. "The night always comes back, and so does the ice. It's just like Mother told us in the story of Silaluk and the hunters. Don't you remember?" She swerved around a jagged-looking rock in her path.

"Then why hasn't it come back yet?" Taqqiq challenged. "I haven't seen any ice in moons." He splashed his paw down hard in a puddle beside the river, soaking his fur with muddy water.

"It *will* come back," Kallik said, wishing she could sound as sure as their mother always had. "Nisa said so."

"She didn't know," Taqqiq said bitterly. "I think the ice spirits have abandoned us. They have gone into the sky and are hiding their faces behind the sun. They're ashamed because they have no power to help us and there's nothing they can do to save the ice."

"Taqqiq . . . " Kallik began, openly pleading now. She glanced at the dim shapes of the other bears up ahead, their lengthening shadows reaching across the water as they plodded forward. She hoped they couldn't hear Taqqiq's anger and despair.

"Don't *you* remember?" Taqqiq said, echoing her words, and now she could hear the deep sadness buried in his voice. "Remember the night skies when we were cubs? How bright the stars were, how dark the sky was, and how it went on forever? The snow sparkled under the moon. And we would lie curled up on the clean, cold ice, our noses buried in Mother's warm fur, listening to her stories—" His voice cracked and he turned his head away from her.

"I do remember," Kallik said softly, pressing closer to share her warmth with him. "It was beautiful and safe on the ice.

And we played in the snow while Mother watched—you would be the angry walrus chasing me."

They stopped walking, and Taqqiq twisted around to bury his nose in her fur. Kallik felt as though her heart were breaking and filling up at the same time. She had never seen him so sad—but her funny, sweet brother was still inside there somewhere.

The water gurgled over pale, flat stones beside them. With a huff, Taqqiq quickly stepped back. His large white paws splashed in the stream. "It's not like that anymore," he said gruffly. "Those days are over. The ice is gone." He hunched his shoulders and shambled away, following the other bears.

Dismayed, Kallik watched him go. Why couldn't he be glad that at least they had each other? Toklo's mother *and* brother had died; Lusa had left her family a long, long way behind to find the brown bears; and she'd never heard Ujurak talk about any family, so perhaps they were all dead, too. She and Taqqiq were lucky compared with them. And they also had friends—good friends, not like Salik and those awful cubs Taqqiq had been traveling with before. Surely now things could only get better, and they'd be together when they reached the Endless Ice?

I wish Mother were here. She'd be able to tell us if burn-sky is supposed to be this long. She started walking again, hurrying to catch up to the others.

A cool breeze ruffled Kallik's fur, bringing strange smells with it—smells of firebeasts and no-claws and their odd, burned food. A shiver of anxiety trailed through her. Nothing good came from being near no-claws. She saw that Lusa had stopped up ahead, sniffing the air with her twitching black nose. The little black bear must have recognized the scents as well.

Lusa trotted back and circled around Kallik, sniffing some more before she fell into step beside her. "I'm pretty sure there's a flat-face den nearby," the black bear huffed. "A big one—did you notice all the smells? And either some really big firebeasts or lots of them, because there's enough of that smell to make my nose hurt."

Kallik nodded. "I know what you mean. It feels like burning inside my nose."

"Yeah, exactly!" Lusa agreed. "How do flat-faces live with them? I'd want to plug my nose with leaves if I had to be that close to firebeasts all the time."

"We should figure out where the smell is coming from, so we can stay far away from it."

"Except—" Lusa broke off and started again. "Well, flat-faces have food." She wriggled, looking embarrassed. "I mean, we're all hungry, and shouldn't we eat wherever we can? Besides, it's the only kind of hunting I'm any good at."

"Lusa! Kallik!" Toklo called. Ahead of them, the stream turned left and wound around a tall, grassy hill. Ujurak and Taqqiq waded into the water and started lapping up the sparkling drops. Toklo was standing at the top of the rise above the stream. A kind of orange glow lit up the sky behind him, but it wasn't the sun, which Kallik could see going down behind the trees in the distance. She hurried up to him with Lusa close behind her.

"Look," Toklo said, pointing with his nose.

Kallik's heart leaped with mingled fright and excitement. At the edge of the sky loomed the jagged shapes of mountains, vast and tipped with snow. Even from here she thought she could see tendrils of smoke rising from them.

"Smoke Mountain," Lusa breathed. "The old bear spoke of one mountain? Look, there are loads of them!"

"Dumb old bear," Taqqiq muttered.

"Taqqiq, that's not nice," Kallik said.

"It's true, though," Taqqiq replied. "He didn't know what he was talking about."

"It doesn't matter if it was one mountain or loads of mountains, anyway," Toklo said. "We're following the river."

"Qopuk was right!" Kallik gasped. "There's the Big River!"

At the foot of the mountains, gleaming orange in the last rays of the setting sun, was a wide stretch of water. Kallik could see the shapes of no-claw dens clustered along the shore. Floating firebeasts belched smoke as they drifted down the river, and odd no-claw constructions poked out of the earth on both banks, tall and spindly but nothing like trees.

"It's so far," Lusa said. "Even to get to the Big River—and then to get to the other side where the Wilderness is . . . it looks impossible!"

"We'll do it one pawstep at a time," Toklo told her. Of all of them, he seemed the least awestruck by what stretched in front of them. "The way you found me, remember?"

Kallik's gaze drifted to the sweep of marshy brown reeds

just below them. The stream wandered through the reeds and disappeared under a large BlackPath. Only a short distance away, on the other side of the swampy terrain, was a long, low no-claw den that vibrated with noise. "First we have to get past that," she said.

The den stood by itself beside the BlackPath with no other dens anywhere nearby. Bright fire-globes shone from inside and on top of the den, lighting up the flat black earth around it. Several of the biggest firebeasts Kallik had ever seen were huddled outside, side by side, their eyes dark. They were twice the height of a full-grown bear on its hindlegs, silver like water, with tall black or red snouts. These big ones must be a different kind of firebeast than the littler ones that were all one color, Kallik thought, as different as she was from Lusa.

She stretched her neck up to see to the other side of the BlackPath. The stream emerged again in the middle of some thornbushes over there, then wandered in and out of sight between scattered scrawny trees. If they could get past the den and across the BlackPath, they could keep following the stream straight to the Big River.

An enormous firebeast came roaring along the BlackPath, its round eyes blazing. It slowed down and then pulled into the space beside the den, rumbling to a stop beside the others. A burly, long-legged no-claw climbed out of it and stomped inside the den, stretching his front legs above him. Loud no-claw noise and mouthwatering smells of meat and salt and unfamiliar food wafted out the open door.

Kallik thought about the meat she had stolen before getting

caught by the no-claws. Her mouth watered as she imagined sinking her teeth into juicy flesh, but she also remembered very clearly the sharp scratch from the no-claw stick, and then waking up in a cage in the big white den. Would these no-claws give her to a metal bird?

"It's wet and marshy down there, so we'll have to slog through some mud," Lusa said, nodding at the reeds below them, "but I think we can follow the path to the den. There are some tall clumps we can hide behind if any flat-faces come out."

Kallik shook her head. "I don't want to go anywhere near that place," she said, taking a step back. There was no way she was going to risk falling out of the sky again.

"I agree," Toklo said. "It's too dangerous."

"But they have food," Lusa pointed out. "I know you don't like it, Toklo, but we have to eat."

A white shape was moving down through the marsh, following the stream. In the fading light, at first Kallik couldn't work out what she was seeing. Then . . .

"Taqqiq!"

"Well, I guess we may not have a choice," Toklo growled. He nodded down the hill. "Unless we're going to let him risk his pelt on his own."

Taqqiq didn't hear Kallik's call, or if he did, he pretended he didn't. He kept going, straight toward the no-claw den and all those giant, hulking firebeasts.

Kallik raced after him, stumbling as the ground sloped down more steeply than she was expecting. The wind blew in her ears, and stinking water splashed around her paws, but she ignored the icky clinging feeling of the mud in her fur. Her muscles ached, but she forced them on. She had to get to Taqqiq before he reached the no-claws. What if he tried to steal their food and they shot him with a firestick?

Suddenly she felt hard black earth under her paws, the kind that smelled like burning and grew in straight lines to make BlackPaths. She'd reached the big open space around the no-claw den. Three of the large firebeasts were up ahead, glaring right at her. With a squeak of fright, Kallik shot toward a large metal box standing against the back of the no-claw den. It was swamped with strange smells, mostly of rotfood. She bundled into the shadow behind it, where the firebeasts couldn't see her, and crashed into a pile of warm fur.

"*Hey!*" the fur ball said, and she realized that it was Taqqiq.

"Oh, you're all right," she said, panting. "I was so afraid one of the firebeasts would hurt you!"

Taqqiq snorted. "I'm not afraid of them! Salik and I dealt with plenty of firebeasts," he boasted. "They're really dumb when they're asleep. You can roar right in their faces and they won't even move."

"You *tried* that?" Kallik said with a shudder. "Why would you want to do that? It's so dangerous."

"It's nothing," Taqqiq said, tossing his head. "We messed with firebeasts all the time. They never dared to hurt us."

Kallik looked around at the shadows. "So why are you hiding back here, if you're so brave?"

Taqqiq bristled. "I'm not hiding!" He shook himself so his fur fluffed out. "I was checking this tiny den for food." He nodded at the metal box beside them. "I've seen them before. Salik found good food in them, anywhere there were lots of firebeasts and no-claws together. But I can't get it open. I don't know how he did it."

"Oh." Kallik nosed the box. She'd seen ones like this behind other big no-claw dens, but she'd never tried to open one. "How does it work?"

"This top part lifts up," Taqqiq said, shoving the box with his paw.

"Maybe if we try to lift it together?" she suggested. She pressed her paws to the bit of the top that protruded from the metal box. Taqqiq leaned into it with his shoulders and heaved up. To Kallik's surprise, the box opened and the top slammed back into the wall behind it. Kallik flinched, but there weren't any sounds of no-claws coming out to see what had made the noise. She couldn't believe this much noise wouldn't bring no-claws running, but then again, the noise coming from inside the big den was loud enough to drown out anything.

"There's nothing here!" Taqqiq snarled, digging through piles of shiny, soft, flabby stuff and broken no-claw things. He dropped to all paws and scraped his claws along the ground in a frustrated gesture.

"It's all right," Kallik said. "We'll find something."

"Hrrmph," Taqqiq grumbled. He looked around at the den and the firebeasts, then back at her. "I'm not just a useless lump of fur, you know."

Kallik blinked at him, surprised. "I know that."

"You think those other bears are so great, like they're the only ones who can find food and figure out which way to go." He swiped the metal box with his paw. "I survived on my own for a while, just like you did, remember? But you treat me like you think I can't do anything."

"That's not true!" Kallik said with a pang of guilt. "I mean . . . this isn't the right world for us—of course it's harder for us to hunt when we're off the ice."

"And all you do is complain about my friends," Taqqiq persisted, "and then drag me off on some other bears' journey, and then get all mad when I complain about *your* friends. They're not even white bears! What do they care about the Endless Ice? Sometimes I think you've forgotten that *you're* a white bear."

Kallik glanced at the reeds near the edge of the denning place. The light from the den was blindingly bright, making it hard to see into the darkness, but she thought she saw the gleam of the other bears' eyes watching them. She hoped they couldn't hear this conversation from where they were.

"See!" Taqqiq snarled. "You're not even listening to me! You're thinking about *them*!"

"I'm sorry!" Kallik protested. "I am listening, really."

"You say you came all this way to look for me, but now that you've found me you ignore me and act like I'm some stupid nuisance."

"Taqqiq," Kallik said. She stepped forward to press her nose into his fur, but he jumped away from her, glaring. "I'm sorry you feel that way. I don't mean to treat you badly. I really do want you on this journey with me—and I'm sure our mother does, too."

Taqqiq snorted. "Nisa is dead," he growled. "We don't know what she would think."

"I think she would like them," Kallik said, jerking her head at the shadows where her friends were waiting. "They're brave, like she was."

This was the wrong thing to say. Taqqiq's fur fluffed up all across his shoulders and he bared his teeth. "You keep saying how brave they are! How great and perfect and wonderful they are! Well, I'm just as good as them! I'm brave, too! Here, I'll prove it!"

"No, don't!" Kallik cried, trying to hold him back, but he marched out of the shadows and headed for the nearest firebeast. Kallik peeked out to watch him go. "Taqqiq, come back! Leave them alone!" She looked at the firebeasts' enormous round black paws and thought how easily they could crush her brother if they wanted to.

She looked back toward the others again. Were those Lusa's bright eyes watching from the tall reeds? Were the other bears scared for her brother? Or were they secretly glad that he might not be able to travel with them anymore if he got hurt by a firebeast?

It didn't matter. She couldn't let Taqqiq face the firebeasts on his own. He was wrong if he thought they couldn't guess what Nisa would want. She most definitely wouldn't want Kallik to abandon her brother now. Digging up every bit of courage she had, she crept after him.

Taqqiq was standing almost nose-to-nose with the nearest firebeast. It loomed over him, all shiny and hulking and dreadful-smelling. Its two round, blank eyes stared back at Taqqiq.

Kallik edged up beside him, sniffing the air. The firebeast didn't move. "Is it dead?" she whispered. "But if it's dead, why doesn't it fall over?"

"You don't know anything," Taqqiq scoffed. "It's sleeping. That's what they look like when they sleep. Hey, firebeast! Where's your fur? Did something claw it off while you were sleeping? You're so stupid, maybe you haven't even noticed that you don't have any fur!"

"Oh, shhh, don't make it mad!" Kallik cried.

"It doesn't even notice," Taqqiq said. "Firebeasts are so dumb, a seal could probably trick them." He said this really loudly, but the firebeast didn't blink. It stayed perfectly still.

"Okay, I believe you, Taqqiq," Kallik said. "You're very brave." Her paws were trembling. A crash from the den behind them made her jump. She could hear the constant murmur of no-claw noises through the open door. Even if the firebeast stayed asleep, she knew that no-claws could come out with firesticks at any moment. They had to get out of this open space.

"You think *that's* brave," Taqqiq said. "Watch *this*." To Kallik's horror, he reared up on his hind legs and slammed his front paws into the firebeast's face.

"ARRF ARRF ARRF ARRF ARRF ARRF ARRF!"
the firebeast bellowed.

Kallik pelted back behind the metal box. Her fur felt as if
it were about to fly off her skin, and her heart was thundering
almost as loudly as the firebeast. She crouched there, shivering, for a long moment. Slowly she realized that Taqqiq was
huddled up with her, his nose pressed into her fur. He was
shaking as badly as she was.

She could still hear the firebeast roaring, but it didn't seem
to have come any closer. "Is it going to find us and eat us?" she
asked.

Taqqiq jumped away from her and took a deep breath. "I've
never heard a firebeast do that before," he said. His voice was
wobbly and high-pitched. "They never woke up when Salik
hit them."

"Why isn't it coming after us?" Kallik whispered.

Taqqiq shook himself. "Maybe it's scared of us, too," he
said. His voice was lower now, as if he were getting over being
startled.

"I don't think that's it," Kallik said. "We didn't look very
scary when we were running away."

Taqqiq slid over to the edge of the box and poked his nose
around the corner. Kallik held her breath. Would the firebeast spot him?

Her brother sat down with a thud. "We're seal-brains," he
said.

"We are?" Kallik said. Seal-brain or not, Taqqiq wasn't
about to persuade her that firebeasts were safe.

"It's not the firebeast making that noise. Come on, look."
He stood up and trotted back out into the open. Reluctantly,
Kallik followed him.

"ARRF ARRF ARRF ARRF ARRF!" The fierce roaring
certainly *sounded* as though it were coming from the firebeast.
But the enormous creature was still and unmoving. Its eyes
weren't even lit up, the way they were when they ran along the
BlackPaths at night.

"Look, up there," Taqqiq said, jerking his snout at a clear
square in the front of the firebeast. Something was jumping
up and down *inside* the firebeast. Kallik suddenly remembered
the white firebeast she had seen on the beach. It had been full
of no-claws trapped inside. This one had something inside it,
too—two somethings—but they weren't no-claws.

"Oh!" she said. "I've seen those kinds of animals before.
They look like wolves, but they live with no-claws."

"I know," Taqqiq said. "They're called dogs. You didn't
know that?"

"How would I know that?" Kallik argued. "I've been by
myself for moons, remember? No one told me anything. I had
to figure it all out myself."

Taqqiq shifted uncomfortably. "Well, Salik said they were
dogs," he said. "Some of them bite, but mostly they're all
noise."

He strutted around to the side of the firebeast, where he
could see the dogs more clearly. They were as big as Lusa,
both black and brown, with fat snouts and small ears and very
sharp teeth. They threw themselves against the inside of the

firebeast, barking and howling at the white bear cub. One of them shoved his nose against a small crack in the side of the firebeast, sniffing the air furiously.

"What's the matter?" Taqqiq taunted them. "Are you stuck in there? You have to do what the no-claws tell you to, don't you? You're no better than a newborn cub, mewling and whining for food. I bet you couldn't catch your own, not even if you tripped over a dead seal."

"Taqqiq, let's get out of here," Kallik said, taking a step backward. "They look really angry."

"They can't do anything," Taqqiq sneered. "They're trapped in there like snails in a shell. All noise and no fight. Salik and I have scared off dogs bigger than these two before. I bet even if they could get out, they'd be too scared to—"

One of the dogs slipped and hit something on the inside of the firebeast. All at once a whole piece of the firebeast popped open, like it had opened its mouth. As it slowly swung wide, Kallik realized that there was nothing to keep the dogs inside the firebeast.

And the dogs were really, really big. Saliva dripped from their jaws, and their sharp white teeth glistened as they snarled.

With a roar of fury, the two dogs leaped out of the firebeast and hurled themselves at Taqqiq.

CHAPTER SEVEN

Toklo

"Toklo!" Lusa shrieked. "Do something! They're going to kill Taqqiq!"

We should be so lucky, Toklo thought, but already his paws were sprinting across the hard black stuff toward the two white cubs. From their spot hidden in the bushes, he and Lusa had watched Taqqiq strutting around the firebeast. Toklo didn't know where Ujurak had gone off to, but he was glad he was well away from the danger here. Toklo wasn't a bit surprised that Taqqiq had gotten himself in trouble. He just wondered if he was doing the right thing by going to his rescue.

One dog had sunk its teeth into Taqqiq's front leg while the other went for his head, snarling. Taqqiq stood up with a roar, flinging the first dog off him and clawing at the second one with his other paw. The dog dodged his attack and lunged forward again. Its teeth snapped shut only a hairbreadth away from Taqqiq's nose.

The first dog rolled back onto its paws and charged at Taqqiq again. This time Kallik jumped forward and slammed into the dog with her body. It yelped as it fell over, but quickly twisted around and tried to bite her leg. Kallik stumbled back and it missed, but only barely.

Toklo didn't know which dog to fend off first. Which cub was in more trouble? Then he saw the second dog lunge for Taqqiq's neck. Taqqiq was still reeling from the last attack and didn't see it coming fast enough to dodge away.

Just before the dog's jaws closed on white fur, Toklo's massive paw slammed into the side of its head. The dog was knocked several bearlengths across the black earth. At the same moment, Toklo whirled and sliced at the other dog as it leaped toward him. The dog tumbled to the ground. With a whimper, it climbed to its paws and limped away.

Toklo turned and saw that the first dog was also on its paws, shaking its head as if it were stunned. He took one step toward it, and the dog fled into the flat-face den.

"We've got to go," Lusa urged, racing from the bushes to his side. "The flat-faces will be out here with their firesticks any moment!"

"Come on!" Toklo ordered the white bear cubs. Kallik started to limp toward him, but Taqqiq just glared at him.

"I could have taken care of those dogs myself," he snarled.

"Yeah, you were doing a great job!" Toklo retorted.

There was a clatter from inside the flat-face den, and the sound of their high-pitched noises got louder.

"Quick!" Lusa cried. "Run!" She pelted away into the marsh.

"Come on, Taqqiq!" Kallik said, ramming her brother in the side.

Well, I don't care if the flat-faces get him, Toklo thought. He turned his back and ran after Lusa. His paws squished heavily in the mud as he dived off the flat black earth. *Ungrateful, selfish, stupid . . .*

Lusa tore through the swampy grassland ahead of him. Toklo would have preferred to run straight across the Black-Path, in the direction of the Big River, but he had to follow her so they didn't lose her. He realized she was heading for a thin grove of trees several bearlengths away, beside the Black-Path. *Typical black bear response, running for trees,* he thought, but it wasn't a bad idea. Hopefully the trees would hide the bears from flat-face eyes—as would the growing darkness now that the sun was all the way down.

He caught up to her as they dived between the first few tree trunks. A firebeast roared as it charged by on the Black-Path, only a bearlength away. Lusa shot up the nearest tree and clung to a branch, panting. As the noise of the firebeast faded, there was a thundering of paws, and Toklo realized that both white bears had followed him after all. Kallik and Taqqiq ran into the trees and collapsed beside a clump of leafy bushes. Toklo spun around, looking anxiously for Ujurak. There was no sign of the other brown bear.

He peered out between the bushes and saw flat-faces running around the den with the dogs, pointing at the big firebeast and shouting. But they weren't looking toward the trees. Perhaps they hadn't seen the bears.

An odd chittering noise startled him, and he turned to see a squirrel staring at him from the roots of the nearest tree. Its eyes were very bright, like little berries, and instead of running, it stood there looking at him.

"Ujurak?" he asked. Had he changed shape to hide better?

Suddenly a flash of white fur flew past him. Taqqiq snatched the squirrel up in one huge paw. Before Toklo could move, Taqqiq's jaws closed over the squirrel's head with a devastating crunch.

"*No!*" Toklo howled. He threw himself at Taqqiq. "No! Stop!" It was bad enough risking his fur to rescue the dumb white bear from the dogs, but there was no way he was going to watch him eat Ujurak.

Startled, Taqqiq dropped the squirrel and spun around, roaring and lashing out at Toklo with his claws. The squirrel fell onto the ground and lay there without moving. Then Taqqiq's claws raked across Toklo's snout and Toklo lunged to bury his teeth in the other cub's neck. Taqqiq's powerful shoulder muscles knocked him over, and Toklo lashed out with his back paws, leaving streaks of blood on Taqqiq's white fur.

He could hear Lusa and Kallik roaring at them, but their voices were only a buzz in his ears. Rage pounded through him. If Taqqiq had killed Ujurak . . . *if he had killed Ujurak* . . . His despair and anger rose to a frenzy. He slashed and bit and tore into Taqqiq as if the white bear were the reason for every terrible thing that had happened in Toklo's life.

"Toklo! Taqqiq!" Lusa screamed from the tree branch. "Stop it! Stop!"

Hot pain seared through Toklo's skin as Taqqiq's claws

sank into his back. He rolled free and kicked, smashing Taqqiq's skull into a tree with a vicious thud. The white bear bellowed and cuffed Toklo across the ears. It felt as if a firebeast had slammed into his head. Ears ringing, Toklo crouched and tensed to spring with his claws extended. If he could pin down Taqqiq, just one swift bite to his neck would end this battle.

Kallik threw herself between them, and for one moment Toklo, blinded by rage, thought he was seeing two of Taqqiq. But before he could pounce, a cold bear nose shoved his snout aside, and somebody muscled into his way. Somebody bigger and heavier than Lusa, with brown fur . . .

"Toklo, what are you doing?" Ujurak barked. "Why are you fighting? What happened?"

"Ujurak!" Toklo yelped. Exhausted, he collapsed on a pile of leaves. "You're alive!"

"Alive?" Ujurak echoed, looking puzzled. "Why wouldn't I be? I was just scouting ahead."

Over by the tree, Kallik was holding her brother back, standing in his way and murmuring in a low voice. Taqqiq's eyes were still blazing with anger.

Toklo's muscles ached all over, and he could feel trails of sharp pain where Taqqiq had clawed him. But Ujurak was alive, and that was the only thing that mattered.

"I thought . . . I thought . . ." he stammered. He glanced up, searching for a way to explain, and saw Lusa's bright, horrified eyes watching from a high branch. She looked terrified, as if Toklo had suddenly turned into a firebeast.

"You could have had the stupid squirrel!" Taqqiq yelled. "I would have shared it with you!"

"He just . . . The dogs got you both angry," Kallik said. "It's all right; it's over now." She laid one paw on Taqqiq's shoulder, but he shrugged her off.

"And that's another thing!" Taqqiq shouted. "I could have handled those dogs! I would have smashed them and clawed them and torn them to shreds without you getting in the way! You don't always have to interfere! Always telling us what to do and where to go and acting like we don't know anything. Bossing everyone around like you're the king of all the bears— who made you so special? You're not even a white bear. You're just a stupid brown bear!"

Guilt prickled through Toklo's pelt. He could see the dead squirrel lying on the ground nearby; it hadn't been Ujurak after all.

But anger flared up in him, too. How had he gotten into this mess? No other bear had to constantly watch out that he didn't eat his best friend!

"I thought it was Ujurak, all right?" he snapped. "I thought you had killed Ujurak."

Taqqiq glared at him for a long moment, his sides heaving. Then, very slowly, as if he really thought Toklo had no brain at all, Taqqiq said, "What . . . are . . . you . . . talking about?"

Toklo nodded at the squirrel. He didn't know how to even start explaining.

"That is a *squirrel*," Taqqiq said. "Not a bear. *Squir-rel*. Small, noisy, edible? Nothing *like* Ujurak!"

"I know!" Toklo growled.

"Taqqiq," Kallik said, "there's something we haven't told you about Ujurak."

Her brother turned his head toward her. "What?" he snarled sarcastically. "Sometimes he looks like a squirrel?"

There was an awkward pause.

"Well . . . yes," Lusa's voice said from above them.

"Not often," Ujurak offered helpfully.

"Sometimes he's a bird. Or another kind of bear. Or a flat-face," Toklo said. He was almost enjoying the baffled look on Taqqiq's face. "Once he was a mosquito. That was probably my least favorite."

"Mine, too," Ujurak agreed.

Taqqiq hunched his shoulders, his hackles rising. "You are all out of your minds," he said. "Bears don't turn into other animals."

Kallik looked pleadingly at Ujurak and Toklo. "We don't know that for sure, right?" she said. "We haven't met *that* many bears. Maybe there are lots of others like Ujurak."

"I doubt it," Toklo muttered.

"But *why*?" Taqqiq demanded. "Why would you turn into anything else? Why would you want to be anything but a bear?" He pawed at his nose. "And if you *can* be anything in the world, why wouldn't you be a white bear?"

"Hey," Toklo growled.

"I don't know why," Ujurak said. "It just started happening. At first I didn't do it on purpose. . . . Now I only try to change when it'll be helpful."

"Is that what you were doing just now?" Toklo asked.

"No, I was still a bear. I was following the stream to see if we could crawl under the BlackPath with it," Ujurak said, pointing with his snout at the spot where the stream disappeared under the BlackPath. "But it's barely a trickle clogged with thornbushes under there. There's not enough room for us to squeeze through. We have to cross over the top instead."

"We should do that soon," Toklo said, "while it's still dark. The firebeasts are more active in the day."

"Wait," Taqqiq snarled. "This doesn't make any sense. I think you're all lying to me about Ujurak."

"Taqqiq, we wouldn't do that," Kallik said.

"Just show him, Ujurak," Lusa said, inching down the tree. "It'll be faster than talking about it."

That was true, but Toklo didn't like it. Every time Ujurak changed, Toklo was afraid he'd forget about being a bear and never change back. Being a bear could be so hard; they were all tired, and hungry, and dirty. What if it was easier being something else?

Ujurak raised his head, thinking. All at once his fur started to ripple, like wind blowing across grass, and black speckled patterns appeared as the fur turned to feathers. He lifted his front paws, and wings sprouted along his forelegs. His neck stretched longer and longer while his body shrank. A beak appeared where his nose had been, and suddenly Ujurak was gone. A long-necked goose blinked dark, beady eyes at them.

With a loud honk, the Ujurak-goose flapped its wings and soared into the air. Much too fast for Toklo, the goose disappeared into the dusk-colored clouds.

Kallik and Lusa watched him go with their eyes shining. They clearly thought Ujurak's abilities were amazing, but Toklo just wanted to jump on the goose and sit on him until he was a normal bear again. He clawed at the earth. Why couldn't Ujurak just stay a bear?

Taqqiq had his back pressed against a tree. His lips were curled in a snarl, and he kept whipping around as if he thought Ujurak was going to pop out and scare him.

"I don't like it," he growled. "Why do you all stay with him?"

"What do you mean?" Kallik asked. "Don't you see how wonderful it is? Ujurak's special. That's why he's the right bear to lead us to the Place of Endless Ice."

He's special, all right, Toklo thought. *Specially irritating.* But deep down he agreed with Kallik. He just wanted Ujurak to come back so they could get on with their journey.

"It's unnatural," Taqqiq said, shaking his head. "It's wrong and it's creepy. What if he turned into a walrus and attacked us?"

"He wouldn't do that," Toklo said, adding pointedly, "just like we wouldn't harm him while he's a squirrel."

Taqqiq snorted. "Well, I think someone might have *warned* me instead of trying to claw my ears off for no apparent reason."

There was a fluttering sound overhead and Ujurak landed in the clearing, turning into a bear again as he rolled across the grass. He shook himself, panting. A few long goose feathers lay on the leaves where he had landed. Taqqiq sniffed them, then glowered at Ujurak.

"They just smell like goose," he said accusingly. "How are we supposed to know it's you when you're not being a bear?"

"I'll try not to change again unless I have to," Ujurak promised.

"And we'll just be careful whenever he does," Kallik said.

"Let's get moving," Toklo growled. He could hear one of the firebeasts by the den rumbling. The farther they could get from that den and this BlackPath, the better Toklo would feel.

Lusa slid down the tree to join them as they all padded out of the woods. "Are you okay?" she asked Toklo quietly.

"Yeah," he said with a wince, feeling a stab of pain in his shoulder. A trickle of blood was running down his neck, but he didn't want to stop and lick his wounds. He didn't want Taqqiq to know that he was hurt. The white bear cub was pacing along briskly, as if he couldn't feel any of the marks Toklo had left on him.

Toklo was also determined to stay in front. He didn't want Taqqiq getting any ideas about who could lead this group. That meant he had to trot faster than he wanted to, to stay ahead of the white bear cub, but he pressed on, ignoring his aching muscles.

He stopped at the edge of the BlackPath, waiting for everyone to catch up. An enormous firebeast whipped by, bellowing and roaring the way they always did. Toklo had to shield his eyes from the bright light blazing from the firebeast's eyes.

They were able to light up the ground in front of him, like a harsh yellow stream that picked out the BlackPath as clearly as day. *How do they do that?* he wondered.

Ujurak bumped him lightly as they stood there, and Toklo knew that his friend was trying to tell him that he wasn't mad at him for jumping on Taqqiq.

"Can you turn into a firebeast?" Lusa suddenly asked Ujurak. "That would be amazing! Then you could tell us what they're thinking and what they eat—gosh, I hope it's not bears—and why they stay on the BlackPaths all the time and how to keep really, really far away from them and—"

"Oh, shush," Taqqiq snapped. "Don't encourage him. We don't want a firebeast appearing in the middle of us."

Toklo hated agreeing with him, but he did not want to see Ujurak turn into a firebeast, either.

"I-I don't think I can anyway," Ujurak said, thinking it over. "It's like . . . it's as if they're not really *alive*. I can't get any life-feeling from them at all."

"Not alive!" Taqqiq barked. "Well, that's plain stupid, isn't it? Obviously they're alive! They run and roar and attack just like bears do!"

"Not just like bears do," Ujurak said. "I don't know how to explain it."

"Well, I'm still not afraid of them!" Taqqiq announced. He bounded out onto the BlackPath and trotted to the other side.

"Come on," Toklo said to the others. He sniffed the Black-Path carefully and listened with an ear close to the ground.

He couldn't hear any rumbling.

"Lusa, you first," he said.

Lusa set one paw cautiously on the BlackPath, and then, taking a deep breath, she sprinted across at full speed. She tumbled into a patch of weeds and lay there, catching her breath. She covered her nose with her paws. "I really hate BlackPaths," she called back. "They smell horrible! And you can always tell that firebeasts have killed other animals there. They're like paths of death. I wish the spirits could get rid of them!"

Taqqiq snorted. "Like any spirits have that kind of power." He shifted his paws at the edge of the hard black earth.

"Wait a moment," Toklo warned Ujurak and Kallik. "I think a firebeast is coming." He could feel the earth quivering under his paws. The bear cubs ducked back into the bushes. Toklo saw Kallik's eyes gleaming in the light from the firebeast's eyes as it hurtled past.

"All right, come on!" he called once it was gone.

Ujurak, Kallik, and Toklo bolted out of the bushes. Ujurak made it across first, and Lusa butted him happily with her head.

Toklo kept an eye on Kallik; he wasn't sure how many BlackPaths she'd crossed when she was traveling alone, or whether this one would frighten her. He was pleased to see that she ran steadily beside him, barely flinching when a firebeast roared in the distance.

They stumbled onto the grass on the far side, rejoining the others.

"Good job," Toklo said to Kallik. "You stayed so calm. I guess you're really one of us now."

"What about Taqqiq?" she asked. "Is he one of us, too?"

Toklo didn't answer. He wanted to be patient, for the sake of the others, but the wounds on his shoulder ached, and anger still burned inside him when he looked at Taqqiq. No matter what the others said, Toklo would never believe that Taqqiq belonged with them.

He stared past Kallik and blinked in shock. Ahead of them, half a skylength away, lay a whole cluster of flat-face dens, burning with sharp yellow lights like firebeasts' eyes. The dens had been partly hidden by a dip in the land, but now he could see that an entire denning place lay between the cubs and the Big River.

He'd thought the big firebeasts and their noisy den and dogs were the worst danger they'd face before the river . . . but it was only the beginning.

CHAPTER EIGHT

Kallik

Night had fallen completely now, although the sky was still glowing from the lights of the no-claw dens up ahead. Kallik blinked and squinted, trying to see into the distance beyond the dens. Smoke Mountain was just a ridge of black blotting out half the sky.

Toklo led the way along the stream to a spot with a few trees and several scrubby bushes. Kallik's stomach growled. She watched Lusa snap a branch off one of the bushes and try to chew on it.

"Blech," Lusa said, spitting out bits of bark.

"Let's stay here for the night," Toklo suggested. "We should rest. We can head toward the flat-face dens in the morning." From the way he stood on three legs, with one hind leg crooked under his belly, Kallik guessed he was hurting. She felt a stab of guilt, knowing her brother was responsible. Part of her didn't want to face the no-claw dens in daylight, but she also didn't want to argue with Toklo when he perhaps needed rest more than any of them.

Lusa flopped down on the grass immediately. Within moments she was snoring. Taqqiq shambled off to curl up by himself, his shaggy white shoulders hunched. He shot angry glares at all of them. Kallik could tell that he was still seething about the fight and the Ujurak secret they'd all been keeping from him.

Toklo waded into the stream, gingerly washing his paws in the cool, flowing water. Kallik followed him, guessing that he was trying to clean the wounds her brother had inflicted. In a way, Toklo was as bad as Taqqiq: too proud to admit that he was hurt and might need help.

Ujurak emerged from the shadows with a bundle of herbs in his mouth. He dropped them on the bank near Toklo. "For you," he said quietly to the brown bear cub. "Rub them on the cuts after you've finished washing."

Toklo made a rough grumbling noise and shot an angry glance at Taqqiq. Kallik looked from Toklo to her brother, Taqqiq. She thought how alike they were: two stubborn, troubled bears trying to survive in a world that seemed to be against them. Couldn't they see it, too?

As Ujurak began nosing Toklo's fur, examining his wounds, Kallik dragged herself up onto the grass and lay down close to Taqqiq, but not touching him. She didn't know if he'd like it if she tried to curl up together, the way they had when they were younger. But she wanted to be as close to him as possible.

The bright lights from the denning place up ahead turned the night sky pale orange over the river. Kallik could just make out a scattering of stars twinkling far, far away in the heavens.

She didn't feel close to the ice spirits now. The hot air crackled like the sky before a storm. Kallik's fur felt heavy and prickly. She wriggled and shifted, trying to get comfortable, but it was hard to fall asleep, despite being so tired that her paws felt like stones. The glow from the dens was always there beyond her closed eyes.

Giving up trying to sleep, Kallik rolled over and stared up at the sky, searching for the tiny stars glittering like faraway pieces of ice. She wondered if her mother could see Kallik and Taqqiq from wherever she was. Was Nisa proud that Kallik had found her brother? She wondered if Nisa would be sad about how mean Taqqiq had become. This hostile, angry bear was so different from the little cub she'd been raising. It worried Kallik that Taqqiq couldn't see how amazing Ujurak was.

Her thoughts were muddled as she finally drifted into sleep. She dreamed of dogs and geese and Ujurak turning into a firebeast, his fur covered in hard, shiny stuff and eyes glowing in that bright, eerie, terrifying way.

The light woke Kallik early, bringing the too-short night to an end. The sun was already climbing over the trees, shining into her eyes. A few stars were still sparkling in the sky, and a chill morning dew sparkled on the grass. She could feel a warm body pressed against her back, and she lay still for a long moment, just being happy that she wasn't alone anymore.

The other cub grunted and shifted. One paw flopped sideways so Kallik could see Taqqiq's white fur. Feeling warm and cozy for the first time in moons, even though they were sleeping on a patch of grass out in the open, Kallik snuggled closer to him.

"Hrrrrft," Taqqiq mumbled. "Hrrrmmmble."

Those were his waking-up noises—she remembered them from their BirthDen. *Oh, Taqqiq,* she wailed silently. *What happened to you? Why did you have to change so much?*

With a long yawn, Taqqiq rolled away from her. She sat up and watched him stretch, reaching each paw out as far as he could. He shook out his fur and glanced around. The other three bears were still asleep.

Taqqiq gave Kallik a bright-eyed look. "Want to go hunting?"

"Really? Out here?"

"Sure," he said. "Just the two of us. Like old times."

Not like old times, Kallik thought. *Back then we had Mother to show us what to do.* But she didn't want to remind him of Nisa. Bounding to her paws, she sniffed the air. "Where should we start?"

"Follow me," he said. He turned his back on the denning place in the distance and began to walk back the way they'd come last night, but swerving away from the stream to avoid the BlackPath. He walked quickly, as if his wounds had healed overnight.

Kallik's paws felt light as air as she trotted after him. She was hunting with her brother again! Maybe things would be different now. Maybe he really wanted to change, starting with

catching food for all of them. Perhaps Taqqiq even wanted
to apologize to Toklo for hurting him? *Hmmm, maybe he won't
change that much.*

She sniffed at the bushes they went past, trying to catch a
scent of prey, but Taqqiq barely paused. His eyes were focused
on the distant edge of the sky. He seemed to be trotting faster
the farther they went.

"I think I smelled something," she said, panting, then
stopped and lifted her nose. "I think it was a rabbit. Did you
smell it?"

Taqqiq swung his head around but didn't stop walking.
"No," he said. "Anyway, it's too open out here. We won't catch
anything. We should keep going and find some better cover."

Kallik thought he was wrong—she was sure she smelled
rabbit—but she didn't want to argue with him when he was
finally being nice, so she scrambled to keep up with him.

"Remember hunting for seals?" Taqqiq said over his shoulder. "Nothing tastes better in the whole world. All these little
land animals are nowhere near as satisfying. Remember how
fast Mother was? I thought I'd never be that big or that fast.
But I bet I could keep pace with her now!"

"I bet you could, too," Kallik agreed. "I haven't eaten seal in
so long. Not since . . . "

They both fell silent, remembering their last meal with
their mother.

"If you're right, and the sea-ice does come back," Taqqiq
said, "I'll catch you lots and lots of seals."

Kallik hoped she could catch her own seals, too, but she

nosed him gratefully. "That'll be much better than berries and birds' eggs."

"I tried to swipe a bird's egg once," Taqqiq said. "I nearly got pecked to death!"

"Me too!" Kallik cried. "I didn't know birds had such sharp muzzles! It was awful. My head hurt for ages afterward."

"One time I found some food inside a firebeast," Taqqiq told her. "That's how I met Salik. We were both trying to figure out how to get the food out without waking up the firebeast. That's when we learned that they sleep so deeply." He paused. "I know you didn't like Salik, but I didn't want to travel by myself. Not when I thought you and Nisa were dead."

"I understand," Kallik said. "Really I do. I was lonely, too."

"At least you knew I was alive somewhere," Taqqiq said. "I was sure you were dead. I thought I was completely alone."

"I would have done the same thing you did," Kallik said. *Although maybe not with Salik.* "I wish I'd met other bears who would let me travel with them. Actually, I did, but . . . she died."

"What happened to her?" asked Taqqiq.

Kallik told him about Nanuk and the metal bird that had carried them, and how it had crashed out of the sky in flames. It was so lovely to have someone she could talk to—her own brother, blood of her blood, someone who knew the same BirthDen stories she did. She forgot all about hunting, until her paws stumbled in a small bog and she stopped to look around.

The BlackPath, the no-claw dens, and the stream were out of sight, far behind them. A bleak plain of scrubby bushes stretched around their paws.

"Wow, look how far we've come," Kallik said. "We should go back." She started to turn around, but Taqqiq jumped in front of her and blocked her way.

"What if we didn't?" he said. "Great Bear Lake is only a day or two in this direction—we could get there much faster without all those other cubs holding us back. We could find the white bears again and travel with them to the Melting Sea, where we used to live."

Kallik stared at him in surprise. "But what about the Place of Endless Ice? Don't you remember all the things Nisa told us about it?"

"I do remember," Taqqiq said, "but what if those were just stories? She also told us about stars with bird names chasing one another in circles. You don't think *that's* real, do you?"

"Of course I do!" Kallik cried. "The Great Bear, Silaluk, is always watching over us. Even during burn-sky, while the hunters are chasing her. And the Place of Endless Ice *is* real, Taqqiq—I've heard about it from lots of other bears." *Well, a few.*

Taqqiq snorted. "Old bears with seal-holes in their brains. Even if it does exist, how do you know you'll ever find it? What makes you trust these bears you want to travel with? They aren't interested in finding a place that's made of ice and snow." He stepped toward her, his eyes pleading. "We don't belong with brown and black bears, Kallik. And we definitely don't belong with freaky shape-changing bears who might not even be bears at all."

"Ujurak has the heart and spirit of a bear!" Kallik protested. "As much as any of us, if not more."

"You barely know him!" Taqqiq snarled. "You barely know any of them, but you want to risk your life and run off into the wilderness with them instead of going home, where you belong, with your own kind?"

Kallik struggled to find the right words for what she was feeling. It did sound crazy when Taqqiq said it that way. But she knew . . . she *knew* that this was the path to the place where the bear spirits danced. She knew she was meant to go there, and she knew she should go with these bears. How could she explain that if Taqqiq didn't feel it himself?

"Please, Kallik," Taqqiq said, and his eyes were gentle now, and pleading. "Come with me. It'll be like it was before. We'll go back to where we were born and hunt seals together and tell stories about Mother, and it'll be the way it should be. Besides, you've come this far already. We may as well keep going to Great Bear Lake."

"Because you tricked me!" Kallik said, anger flaring in her chest. "You knew I wouldn't come with you if you told me what we were doing!" She looked around, fighting back panic. Their trail was disappearing fast into the marshy ground. What if she couldn't find her way back to the others?

"But you *should* come with me," Taqqiq insisted. "You should be with other white bears—with *me*."

Kallik thought about her mother's stories and the light in

Nisa's eyes when she talked about the Everlasting Ice. Nisa had believed that they would need to travel there someday, because the ice was melting earlier every year. Surely she would want Kallik to go in search of it?

But then, Nisa's spirit had been guiding her to Taqqiq all this time. Kallik had heard her voice and seen her shape in dreams and fog and reflections. What if her mother did want them to stay together? Did that mean Kallik had to return to the Melting Sea?

Please send me another sign, Kallik begged. She stretched her head up to look at the sky, wishing an ice spirit would come down and tell her what to do.

Suddenly she gasped. One of the ice spots was still visible in the dawn sky. But it wasn't an ordinary star. It was blinking, like an eye opening and closing. And it was *moving.*

"Taqqiq, look!" she said, standing up on her hind legs to stare at it. The flickering star was definitely moving . . . and it was moving away from Great Bear Lake and the Melting Sea. The strange blinking light headed steadily toward the Big River and the Last Great Wilderness, the same way Ujurak was leading them.

"It *has* to be a sign," Kallik said, dropping to all four paws again. "Don't you see, Taqqiq? The spirits want us to go on with the other bears. I think . . . I think it's Nisa sending me a message. She doesn't want me to go back to the Melting Sea."

Taqqiq sighed. "I think you're wrong. It just looks like a star to me; I don't care if it is moving. But there's nothing I can say, is there?"

Kallik's fur felt heavy with her sadness. "And there's no way I can convince you."

Taqqiq shook his head. "I'm going home," he said. "I want to be with other white bears."

"And I have to keep going," she said. "I have to find the Place of Endless Ice." Her claws sank into the damp earth underpaw. "Oh, Taqqiq! I don't want to lose you again!"

Taqqiq stretched forward and bumped her nose with his. "But this time you know that I'm alive—and I know you are, too. I'll be okay, I promise."

"I'm so glad I found you," Kallik said. Her heart was too full for her to know what to say. She knew the truth was that they would probably never see each other again. She could also see that Taqqiq was right, and this journey wasn't for him. But at least she had found him; at least she knew he'd survived.

"I'll think of you all the time," Taqqiq said.

"I will, too," Kallik said.

With a playful growl, Taqqiq shouldered into her and knocked her over.

"Walrus attack!" she cried, leaping up and bowling him over in return.

They both rumbled small purrs of happiness, remembering. *If only Taqqiq had been like this all along!*

"Are you sure about this?" she asked, gazing up into his dark eyes.

Taqqiq nodded. "I'm not like those bears," he said. "You know I'm not. But you're one of them now. I know they'll look after you."

"Yes, they will," she said. "I'm sorry for taking you away from your friends, Taqqiq."

"It's all right," Taqqiq said. "I found them before. I'll find them again. Or better ones, maybe. Good-bye, Kallik."

"Maybe we can make it work," she tried one last time. "I promise I'll listen to you more. Maybe . . . maybe there's a way for us all to get along, if you stay. Taqqiq, it'll be lonely on the Endless Ice without you."

"I'll miss you, too," he said, nuzzling her shoulder. "But it isn't working. You know that. It doesn't feel right for me."

Kallik sighed. "If you're really sure . . . "

"I am," he said. "Good luck, Kallik."

"Good luck to you, too," she said sadly.

Touching noses one more time, they both stepped back and turned, heading in their own directions.

Kallik glanced back once and saw that Taqqiq was galloping across the plain, leaping over the scrubby bushes. He still leaned a little to the side as he ran, giving him the funny rambling gait he'd had when he was a cub. She wondered if she would ever know that much about any other bear. Then she turned and fixed her eyes on the far horizon, where the hulking shape of Smoke Mountain loomed. There was a long way to go. They still had to get through the no-claws' denning place, and then there were all the dangers that Qopuk had warned them about. It would be a hard journey.

For a moment she thought about how easy it would be to turn and follow Taqqiq. But she'd had her sign. The message of the moving star was clear. Her paws carried her on, back to where Lusa and Toklo and Ujurak were sleeping. She had to keep going, to find the place where the ice spirits came down to the earth and danced.

CHAPTER NINE

Lusa

"Lusa, wake up."

Somebody poked her with his nose.

"Go 'way," Lusa mumbled. This was why it was better to sleep in trees. Brown bears couldn't climb up and poke you there. They'd have to sit and wait until you woke up at a more reasonable time. But she'd been too exhausted to climb a tree last night, and the trees by the stream didn't look particularly comfortable anyway, with all those thorns. A patch of soft grass under the branches had been good enough.

"Lusa," the voice said again, and this time she realized it was Toklo. "Lusa, Kallik and Taqqiq are missing." Lusa rolled to her paws and shook the sleep out of her eyes.

"Missing?" she echoed, craning her neck to see past him. She could see the mashed and flattened patches of grass where the two white bears had slept. "Where did they go?"

"I don't know," Toklo said. "They were gone when I woke up."

"Same here," Ujurak said, splashing through the stream

behind her with water droplets dripping from his muzzle. "I didn't hear them go."

Lusa padded over to the hollow where the white cubs had curled up to sleep. There were two indentations in the grass the size of Taqqiq and Kallik. She could still smell their scent, a faint smell of fish and ice. Lusa sniffed around the hollow and found the spot where the scent began to move away. They'd set off in the opposite direction from the Big River and Smoke Mountain.

Lusa felt a pang of worry shiver through her fur. She took a few steps along their trail, her nose pressed to the ground.

"I already did that," Toklo said. "They went that way." He jerked his head toward the rising sun.

"But that doesn't lead to the Big River!" Lusa exclaimed.

"No. I know," Toklo said. He sighed, dabbing one paw in the river. He couldn't meet Lusa's eyes. "They went back the way we came—to Great Bear Lake. To the other white bears."

"No!" Lusa said. "They wouldn't do that! Kallik wouldn't just leave me!" She paced around the white bears' sleeping spot, clawing at the grass in frustration.

"Maybe she would, if she was really mad," Toklo growled. "I'm sorry, Lusa. It's my fault. I didn't mean to drive Kallik away." He lifted his head, squinting at the line of pale gold sunlight on the horizon.

"But why would she go without saying good-bye?" Ujurak said. "I don't think Kallik would do that." He looked genuinely puzzled.

Lusa sniffed the trail again, hoping to find that Kallik's

scent split off and went another way, but the bears had clearly left the trees together.

"You're wrong, Toklo," she said. Even if the white bears were angry at Toklo for attacking Taqqiq, Kallik would have stayed to talk about it, not run away while they were all sleeping. And surely Kallik could understand—she knew about Ujurak changing. Couldn't she see that Taqqiq might have eaten Ujurak? Lusa knew why it had made Toklo so upset and angry . . . she thought Kallik did, too.

"Lusa—" Toklo began, hunching his shoulders as if he were bracing himself for an argument.

"No," she interrupted him. "Kallik wouldn't just leave us. She wants to find the Endless Ice more than anyone! You saw how excited she was about what Qopuk told us. And she's my *friend.*"

"We're your friends," Toklo growled. He turned his head toward the dark ridge of mountains that lay in wait for them. "Come on—we've got to keep going."

"We can't go!" Lusa protested. "What if they just went hunting? What if they're on their way back right now?"

"What if they're not?" Toklo countered. "How long will we wait?"

Lusa planted her paws firmly on the earth. "I'm not leaving without Kallik."

Toklo gave her an incredulous look. "What if she doesn't come back?"

"She will come back," Lusa insisted. "We can at least wait until the sun is all the way up. I'd wait for *you,*

Toklo. Forever, if I had to."

"Maybe they haven't been gone very long," Ujurak interjected, wading out of the stream to stand beside Toklo. "It wouldn't hurt to wait and give them a chance to return."

Toklo sighed. "Fine." He splashed into the stream and started licking his wounds. His fur was green in places where he'd used Ujurak's herbs; it looked as if moss were trying to grow on his pelt.

Lusa padded over to the stream beside him and lapped up some of the water. This close to the BlackPath, it tasted sooty and kind of gross, but she was thirsty.

"I'll go find us something to eat," Toklo said after a while. He heaved himself up and paced away, his shoulders still hunched.

A bird was chirping in one of the crooked trees, breaking the stillness of the dawn. Lusa breathed in the smell of the grass and the river, knowing that the air would be clogged with flat-face and firebeast scents the closer they moved to the denning place. "We will make it, won't we, Ujurak?" she said, turning to the little brown bear. "We'll get to the Last Great Wilderness?"

Ujurak stopped wiping his paws on the grass and looked at her.

He's so small, Lusa thought. *No bigger than me. And younger than I am. Are we crazy to be following him?*

No. There's something different about Ujurak. There's a reason we believe in him.

"I hope so," Ujurak said. "I hope we'll get there."

"Thanks for agreeing to wait," Lusa added.

"I think you're right about Kallik," Ujurak said, flopping down in the shade of a thorny bush.

"I think Toklo secretly agrees, too," Lusa said.

Ujurak chuffed with laughter. "He's all prickles on the outside, like a porcupine," he said. "But inside he's like a snail when you dig it out of its shell."

"That's so true!" Lusa said. She thought for a second. "Wait, what's a porcupine?"

A twig crackled behind her, and she spun around. Kallik was standing on the other side of the stream, looking tired and filthy. Mud was caked in the white fur on her paws.

"Kallik!" Lusa cried. She leaped out of the water and nuzzled her friend. Kallik pressed her nose into Lusa's fur, blinking.

"Where's Taqqiq?" Ujurak asked.

Lusa lifted her head and looked around at the quiet marsh that surrounded them. Kallik was alone.

"He's decided to go back to the Melting Sea," Kallik said in a very small voice.

"Oh, Kallik," Lusa said. "I'm so sorry. I know how much you wanted to be with him."

"I thought finding him would make everything all right again," Kallik said with a sigh. She dipped her paws in the river, letting muddy rivulets stream away. "Now I don't know what to think. I just know I'll miss him."

Lusa couldn't pretend that anyone else would miss the surly white bear, but she felt a deep pang of sadness for her friend. "Well, I'm pleased that *you* stayed with us," she said.

"Me too," Ujurak agreed.

Toklo padded up with a squirrel dangling from his mouth. His dark eyes went from Lusa to Kallik and then scanned the empty landscape around them. He dropped the squirrel next to Lusa's damp paws.

"I'm glad you came back," he said, dipping his head to Kallik. "I . . . I'm sorry about your brother. I know I . . . I mean, I could have been—"

"It wasn't your fault," said Kallik. "This journey wasn't for Taqqiq. He belongs with his own friends now."

Lusa looked at the warm, shaggy bulk of Toklo beside her. She would be so heartbroken if he left like Taqqiq had. Lusa hoped they didn't lose anyone else. The ominous shape of Smoke Mountain looming ahead made her feel very small.

"Let's keep going," Kallik said. "I'll feel better once we're on our way again."

They shared the squirrel and a small fish that Ujurak caught, and then together they set off toward the Big River. Lusa noticed that Kallik turned to look back once. Her eyes were full of sadness and her ears pricked forward hopefully. But she shook herself and kept walking, away from her brother and the other white bears. Lusa wondered if she could be that strong.

Toklo took the lead, as usual, with Ujurak right behind him. Lusa padded next to Kallik. They were quiet for a long time. Lusa wasn't sure what to say. The smells and sounds of the denning place grew stronger as they drew closer.

"Ujurak's been trying to teach me to read the signs that

lead us on our path," Lusa said finally. "I think finding you was a sign, actually. Don't you? I mean, if we're going to find the place where all bears can live happily, then we should have one of each kind of bear—one black, one brown, one white—and now we do."

"I didn't even know there *were* brown and black bears until I met you all," Kallik admitted. "I only knew about white bears. What if there are other kinds of bears we haven't met yet?"

"Other kinds of bears!" Lusa exclaimed. "Like what—green bears? Pink bears?"

"Maybe bears that are black *and* white!" Kallik said.

"I think that would look very elegant," Lusa teased.

"Would you two hush up back there?" Toklo called. "Chatter, chatter, chatter! Are you bears or are you magpies?"

Lusa and Kallik exchanged amused looks. Then Kallik's eyes darkened. "Lusa, *I* saw a sign. I'm sure of it."

"You did?" Lusa stared at her in amazement. "When?"

"This morning," Kallik said. "One of the stars in the sky was blinking. And it was *moving*—in the same direction we're going! I think it was a message from the spirits to tell us we're going the right way."

Lusa bounced on her paws. "I bet you're right! That sounds exactly like a sign!"

It was getting close to sunhigh when they reached a Black-Path on the outskirts of the flat-face denning place. This cluster of dens was much smaller than the one around the Bear Bowl where Lusa had grown up. But it smelled strongly of flat-faces and firebeasts, and they could hear the clatter and hum of sounds that always came from flat-face dens. Lusa's fur felt as if it were crackling from the sharp energy in the air. She shook herself from nose to tail.

They stopped in the shadow of a tree that was surrounded by bramble bushes. Lusa touched her nose to the bark, wondering if the spirit inside was bothered by having the flat-face denning place so near by. There were several trees on this side of the BlackPath, but not many on the other side, around the dens.

"Let's hide in here until it gets darker," Toklo suggested, clawing some of the brambles aside. "It'll be easier to get through to the Big River when more of the flat-faces and fire-beasts are sleeping."

"If only it stayed darker for longer," Ujurak said nervously. "I hope we can get across the river before they all wake up."

Lusa's belly rumbled as she crawled into the dark space under the bushes. She felt hot and grubby and absolutely starving. Kallik's heavy fur pressed against hers as they squeezed out of sight of the BlackPath, and Lusa wished briefly that she could throw herself into Great Bear Lake just for a moment. Then her fur might not be so dusty and itchy.

There's plenty of swimming ahead, she reminded herself, thinking of what Qopuk had said about the vast, dangerous Big River. *Be careful what you wish for.*

CHAPTER TEN

Lusa

The four bears settled down, and Lusa drowsed with her head on her paws, listening to the rumble of firebeasts a few bearlengths away. Their smell muddled all her senses, and her half-waking dreams were full of their glowing eyes as they prowled. Every so often, she peeped out from the bush; it seemed the sun was stuck in the sky, trapping the bears in their prickly hiding place forever.

Slowly, the shadows lengthened and the sky darkened. Bright fire-globes began to blink on in the flat-face dens across the BlackPath, one after another. A twilight gloom settled over the denning place.

Toklo got to his paws and stretched. He started turning over rocks and scratching in the dirt, looking for grubs to eat. "Let's get far away from these smelly, noisy, firestick-popping flat-faces as quickly as we can," he growled.

"Not all flat-faces are *all* bad," Lusa said, thinking of the kind, friendly ones who had fed her in the Bear Bowl. Her friends gave her astonished looks. "Well, I guess most of them are," she amended.

"It's not that they're bad," Ujurak said with a thoughtful look, as if he were trying to puzzle it out. "They just don't think about what they do."

"Sounds bad to me," Toklo grumbled. "Let's go."

"Maybe Lusa should lead us," Ujurak said, nodding at her.

"Me?" Lusa squeaked.

"You traveled through a place like this when you escaped the Bear Bowl, right?" Ujurak said.

Lusa looked at the other two cubs. Toklo lowered his head to her, and Kallik nodded, too. Her friends really trusted her. She hoped they were right. Leaving the Bear Bowl seemed like forever ago. Somehow that flat-face place had seemed more familiar than this one. Perhaps that was because she'd seen part of it from the top of Old Bear's tree.

Lusa scrambled out of the bushes and braced her shoulders. She just had to concentrate. She remembered the dens and BlackPaths she'd run through after leaving the Bear Bowl. One thing she had certainly learned—to trust her nose. She looked up and down the BlackPath, lifting her nose to the wind.

The breeze coming from one direction was thick with tangled scents of firebeasts and food: piles and piles of flat-face food being burned, in that funny way flat-faces had of setting everything on fire before they ate it. Her belly growled, and part of her longed to go that way. Perhaps if the bears were careful, some of that food could be theirs.

But she knew that where there were lots of firebeasts

and lots of food in one place, there would also be lots of flat-faces—lots of *awake* flat-faces. It would be safer to sneak behind some of the quieter dens and search those big cans of rotfood they kept outside. The bears needed to get through the denning place without being noticed; that was the most important thing. If flat-faces saw them, they might loose firebeasts on them, or try to hurt them, or worst of all, catch her and take her back to the Bear Bowl. Lusa didn't want to give up on her journey when she'd come so far. And she especially didn't want to lose her friends.

In the gloom, she led the others across the BlackPath and turned the other way, following the curve of the BlackPath past big, glowing dens until she found a smaller BlackPath branching off in the direction of the river. Here the smells and noises were more muted and the dens were smaller, with soft grass and leafy green trees between them.

The little BlackPath had raised stone paths on either side, shadowed by tall bushes with tiny purple or pink or blue flowers that ran around the edges of the dens. The ground felt hard and strangely flat under Lusa's paws as they slunk along, pressing close to these bushes. It was easier than walking through grass, because it didn't trip her up, but it was hot and sticky, and her paws started to itch.

She sniffed each firebeast as they crept past, but almost all the ones they saw seemed to be slumbering outside the dens. Their hard pelts were silver or red or green or bright blue or black—Lusa even saw one that was yellow like sunlight. She wondered if they got along or if they were friends only with firebeasts of their own color.

The bears saw no flat-faces outside. A few firebeasts crawled past on the BlackPath, but it was so quiet that Lusa heard them coming from far away and could duck into the bushes with the others close behind her.

Light spilled from holes in many of the dens, and if Lusa strained her ears, now and then she could hear flat-face voices murmuring. Often the light had a bluish tinge, and sometimes she spotted flat-faces inside staring at tiny flat-faces inside a brightly lit box.

She waited until they came to a den that was dark. There was no firebeast outside, and no sound coming from the den. Cautiously she crept over the short grass in front of the den and followed the faint scent of food around to the side, where a small space separated the den from the fence running alongside. Here she found what she was looking for: three tall silver cans standing outside a door.

"Shhh," she cautioned the others as they joined her. Toklo wrinkled his nose at the can.

"Flat-face food," he grumbled. "I thought we talked about how real bears don't need to steal food from flat-faces."

Lusa was about to retort sharply when, to her surprise, Kallik spoke up.

"I'd rather eat than starve," the white bear said. "And we need our strength to cross the Big River. Besides, no-claws have so much food that they just throw it away. I think it's all right to eat it—if we're really, really careful. I once stole some meat from a no-claw den, and that's how they caught me." Her eyes were huge with fear, in spite of her brave words, and her fur quivered as if she were trying not to shake. Lusa blinked at her friend, hoping she could tell how much she appreciated her support.

"We'll be careful. Kallik's right; we have to eat where we can. It'll be better this time," Lusa reassured Toklo. "I don't think there are any flat-faces in this den right now."

Toklo swung his head around, his gaze darting across the unnaturally short grass. "Well, hurry up then."

Lusa slid her claws under the lid of the can and pried it off, grabbing it in her mouth so it wouldn't clatter on the hard ground. She stuck her nose inside and found two shiny black skins stuffed full of flat-face rubbish. She dragged one out into the open, tipping over the can but pressing her body against it so it made only a small hollow thud when it hit the ground.

She sliced open the skin with her claws, and all four bear cubs examined what fell out. There were some squashed blueberries in a clear container. Lusa clawed it away from the rest of the rubbish and licked up half the blueberries, then offered the rest to Kallik. The white bear's eyes widened as she ate them. The berries left little dark blue smears on the fur around her mouth.

"Yum," she whispered. "I didn't know that no-claws ate berries."

"They eat *everything*," Lusa said.

"How about this?" Ujurak asked, nosing something over to Lusa. "Can we eat it?"

It looked like a fluffy bit of crust with part of it chewed off.

Lusa had eaten lots of these while she was raiding metal cans. "Yes, they're good," she said. "Usually a little salty."

She found a few more in the skin, which they all shared. In the second skin they lucked into several half-eaten bits of meat. Some of it was long and round like a stick, and covered in salty red sauce that tasted faintly like tomatoes, which Lusa had eaten a lot in the Bear Bowl. Some of it was flat and brown and stuck between two pieces of bread, also covered in the same red sauce. Lusa remembered finding that sauce on the potato sticks she liked, but there weren't any potato sticks in these cans.

"Why does their meat taste so funny?" Toklo growled.

"Because they burn it before they eat it," Lusa said. "I don't know why."

Toklo huffed. "I would rather catch a fish."

"Or a seal," Kallik said wistfully. "But at least I'm not so hungry anymore. Thanks, Lusa."

Lusa wriggled with pleasure. If they *had* to deal with flat-face dens, she thought it was only fair to take the food the flat-faces didn't seem to want. If Toklo wanted to wait until he could catch a salmon, he was welcome.

There weren't many fences around the flat-face dens here, so for a while Lusa led them behind the dens, out of sight of the BlackPath. The grass was soft and springy under their paws. They didn't have to climb to get from one den to the next, which was a relief to Lusa—she wasn't sure how good a climber Kallik would be, and it was easier to escape when you weren't surrounded by a fence.

They were creeping behind a large white den that looked empty when suddenly there was a roar, and a bright beam of light sliced through the dark in front of them. Lusa squeaked and bundled backward, shoving the others into the shadows up against the den. The light swept up the tiny BlackPath beside the den as a firebeast charged off the bigger BlackPath onto the smaller hard, flat surface.

"Did it see us?" Kallik whispered in Lusa's ear. "Is it coming for us?"

"Shh," Toklo hissed. "Stay very still." Lusa held her breath and closed her eyes. *Please don't eat us. Please don't eat us.*

With a coughing sputter, the firebeast stopped beside the den. The light blazing out of its eyes vanished, and its roar dwindled into a murmur, then silence.

"What happened?" Ujurak whispered. Lusa peeked out between her paws.

A flat-face male climbed out of the side of the firebeast. He hurried up to the den and disappeared inside. The door slammed behind him.

Everything was still.

"It didn't see us," Lusa breathed. "And now it's asleep."

Her ears were ringing from the noise of the firebeast. As they started to clear, she heard something else. She stood on her hind legs and pricked her big round ears.

"Water!" she cried. "I hear the river!"

She squeezed past the slumbering firebeast, being careful not to brush against it, and down to the BlackPath, which crossed another BlackPath where the dens were pressed closer together. Lusa sped up, hoping to get through to the river before they were spotted. She heard the rumble of a firebeast and broke into a run to get away before it reached them, leading the others around a den and into the grassy space behind it.

As they tumbled into the dimly lit area enclosed by bushes with neat, even edges, a ferocious noise split the quiet night. Lusa saw the glint of fangs as a massive dog leaped out of the shadows, barking madly. Kallik yelped and turned to run. Toklo's fur fluffed up, and he stood with his paws braced, snarling and ready to fight.

"Wait!" Lusa barked at both of them. She had spotted something the others hadn't. Her heart thudded as she hoped she was right. She stood her ground, her eyes shut tight, as the dog hurtled toward her. His jaws snapped at the air, but just before he reached her, something jerked him back with a clanking sound. The dog's barks were cut off with a yelp. Lusa slowly opened her eyes.

"See? It's chained to that tree," she said, nodding at the long metal vine that held the dog out of reach. Its eyes rolled and its tongue hung out as it strained to get to her, but it couldn't move any nearer. She took a long, shuddering breath. *Phew.*

"Wow," Toklo said, and he actually sounded impressed.

A light came on inside the den. Lusa shoved her friends back into the bushes, where they crouched, holding their breath, as a flat-face stormed out the back door and shouted at the dog.

"Poor thing," Ujurak said. "He was just trying to warn the flat-face about us."

"I say it serves him right." Toklo snorted. "Picking a fight with me! I'd like to see him try!"

Lusa's ears perked up as the dog stopped barking and the flat-face went back inside. There was a rushing, bubbling noise very nearby. "Do you hear that?" she whispered. "I think we're close to the river!"

She pushed through the bushes to the other side and ran across the grass behind the next den. The others followed her as she ducked under a low-hanging branch, slipped between two dens, trotted across a small BlackPath, and darted around a big square patch of BlackPath that smelled like firebeasts had been hulking there all day.

Lusa came to a halt when her paws hit wet sand and stared down the slope that stretched below her. Just as the other cubs crowded up behind her, the clouds parted and a thin, pale moon came out, glimmering on the river right in front of them. They'd reached the Big River that Qopuk had told them about! Now they just had to follow it to the Ice Sea, and they'd be well on their way to the Last Great Wilderness.

"Good job finding it, Lusa," Kallik said. "I'd have gotten all turned around in the middle of those no-claw dens."

"Yeah," Toklo rumbled. "Well done."

Lusa glowed with pride. They had made it through the flat-face denning place.

But her happiness drained away as she looked down at the dark, fast-flowing water only a few bearlengths from her paws. She swallowed hard. This *had* to be the Big River . . . there couldn't be any rivers bigger than this!

"It's *huge!*" she squeaked.

They all stared at the vast stretch of water. It was too dark to see the other side. Lusa didn't think she'd ever seen anything like it—Great Bear Lake was enormous, too, but that was a lake; it was supposed to be big, and lakes didn't have strong currents that could wash a bear away. She thought of rivers as being a sensible size that a bear could swim across without drowning. Kind of like watery Black-Paths—dangerous, but not impossible to cross.

But this . . . this was terrifying!

CHAPTER ELEVEN

Toklo

It was eerily quiet on the mudflats. Toklo could hear the faint hum of firebeasts in the distance and an occasional sharp, lonely bark that he thought might be the dog they'd passed. Smoke Mountain loomed on the far side of the river.

"Are we sure this *is* a river?" Lusa said. "I mean . . . it's so . . . it's so . . . *big*." She stood up on her hind legs and stretched her neck up, trying to see the opposite bank.

Kallik sludged forward through the wet, clingy mud and tentatively lapped up a mouthful of water. She looked back at the others and nodded. "It's not salty. It tastes yucky, but it's not the sea or anything."

"And from the current you can tell it's a river," Ujurak pointed out. "Just a really . . . really big one."

Toklo was no longer afraid of swimming. His fear of water spirits was gone after Great Bear Lake, where he heard the voices of his mother, Oka, and brother, Tobi. But that didn't mean he'd lost all his fear of drowning. The dark river in front of him stretched as far as he could see. And it wasn't still like the lake when he'd swum out to Paw Print Island. The cubs would have to fight hard to avoid being swept away by the currents. He wondered if there were any brown bear spirits in the river. . . . Even if there were, he wouldn't count on their being any help.

He could just make out branches and bits of flat-face debris floating down the river, faster than a bear could run. Farther out, he glimpsed some kind of structure rising from the water, silhouetted in the pale moonlight. *Is that a tree?* he wondered.

"Are you sure we have to cross this river?" he asked Ujurak. "You said the old white bear told you to follow the river to the Ice Sea. Can't we do that on this side?"

Ujurak shook his head. "The Last Great Wilderness is on that side," he said. "We will have to cross this river somewhere to get to it, and Qopuk said this was the only place where we could."

Toklo stared at the thick black water. "There's got to be an easier way," he muttered.

"We have to trust Qopuk," Ujurak said in a voice that sounded strangely high and squawky. Toklo turned and saw that gray and white feathers were popping out through Ujurak's fur. His limbs shrank into his torso, and wings sprouted as his snout turned into a beak.

"I thought you said you'd try not to change," Toklo growled.

"Going to scout," Ujurak managed to croak before his bear features disappeared completely. A scrawny, bedraggled seagull now stood on the sandy shore beside them. With a vigorous flap, Ujurak launched himself into the air and soared away over the river.

"Gosh," Kallik said, watching him go. "I wish we could all do that!"

"It'd be a lot easier than swimming!" Lusa agreed.

Toklo wasn't sure. Flying didn't look particularly easy or safe to him. He would much rather keep all his paws on the ground, thank you very much.

They waited uneasily on the exposed bank of the river. Toklo swiveled his head from side to side, jumping at every small sound. He wished there were somewhere to hide. If something came at them, there was nowhere to go except back up to the dens—or straight into the river.

Normally Toklo was comfortable beside rivers. He liked the speeding rush of water and smooth river stones under his paws, and he loved fishing—and eating fish—more than anything. Perhaps tomorrow he would catch a fish in the river as they followed it to the sea. But this river, or at least this part of the river, felt strange and unfriendly to him. Instead of the murmur of bear spirits, he heard the sucking and slapping of water against flat-face constructions. Its scent was grimy and metallic, not sweet and fishy and clean, the way it should be.

Toklo spotted a grayish shape in the sky, growing bigger as it got closer. He lost it for a moment in the shadow of Smoke Mountain, and then it reappeared as the Ujurak-gull swooped down and landed next to them. His feathers quivered as they turned brown and smoothed out into fur again. He waved his growing snout, eager to talk.

"Qopuk was right," he burst out as soon as he could. "This spot is different from the rest of the river. I flew up and down a long way to see if there was anywhere else. But this is the spot." He stretched his forelegs stiffly. "Flying is tiring."

"How do you know this is the right place?" Toklo asked.

"There are small islands all the way across," Ujurak said, pointing with his snout out at the river.

"There are?" Lusa said, squinting to see them through the darkness. "Are there any flat-face dens on them? Or fire-beasts?"

"No, they're empty. There are some flat-face metal things, but they aren't doing anything. We can use the islands to rest, so we don't have to swim the whole way without stopping," Ujurak explained.

"Hmmph," Toklo grumbled. "It still sounds weasel-brained to me."

"We can do it," Kallik said. "I'm a strong swimmer. I'll stay near Lusa and make sure she doesn't get swept away."

"You should change back into a seagull and fly across," Toklo said gruffly to Ujurak. As much as he hated his friend's changes, he wanted him to be safe. "Then you can keep an eye on us and warn us if anyone gets caught in the current."

"Good idea," Ujurak said, dipping his head. "Will you be all right?"

"We will," Lusa said. "Right, Toklo? Let's go before the flat-faces wake up and see us."

Ujurak slipped back into the gull's feathers and lifted off

into the sky. Toklo led the other two cubs down to the water's edge.

The river smelled sharp and dirty, as if there were fire-beasts swimming in it. Toklo shuddered. *That* was a horrible thought—firebeasts lurking in the dark water. He'd never seen any orcas like the ones in Kallik's story of her mother's death, but he pictured them like big, wet firebeasts with teeth. He shoved that image aside as he waded into the water. Their journey—wherever they were going—continued on the other side, so they had to cross.

He glanced back to make sure the other two cubs were right behind him. Taking a deep breath, he launched himself forward until his paws struck off the bottom and he began paddling. The force of the current took his breath away. It seemed to grab his fur with strong, hooked claws as it tried to haul him downriver. His paws churned as he drove forward. A gull swooped overhead, and he nearly snarled at it before he realized it was Ujurak, pointing the way to the first island. Squinting and snorting to keep water out of his nose, Toklo lifted his snout and realized he could see a bulky shape loom-ing out of the water below the seagull. The island!

He barked to let the others know, hoping they could hear him and that they would spot the island up ahead. He tried to twist about in the water to see them, but he only caught a glimpse of Kallik's white fur before the current yanked him around and he had to focus on swimming again. Lusa was too small and dark to spot, he told himself; that was why he couldn't see her. But surely she was back there.

At first glance the island didn't seem so far away, but the more he paddled, the farther it seemed to be. So much of his strength was used up simply not being swept away, but he kept swimming, forcing himself across the surging waves until his paws stubbed against gritty sand. He dragged himself up on the island's shore and collapsed on the pebbles. Sticky black liquid was splattered over the stones, smelling of firebeasts. A huge, square flat-face construction loomed over him, bigger than their dens, with long limbs like bones reaching into the sky. Toklo remembered the story of the giant flat-face and shuddered, even as he reminded himself that he didn't believe in that kind of cloudfluff.

Catching his breath, he hauled himself to his feet and spotted Kallik stumbling through the shallow water. Bobbing in the water beside her was a small, dark shape that he guessed was Lusa's head. Kallik nudged her shoulder under Lusa's paws, supporting her up onto the shore. The two cubs crawled out of the river and flopped down beside him. Water streamed from Lusa's fur, soaking the sand underneath her.

"Brrrrr," she muttered. "Kallik, you don't even look wet!"

It was true; the water seemed to run right off Kallik's fur. The bigger bear shook herself vigorously. "That's just how white-bear fur is," Kallik said.

The Ujurak-gull landed nearby.

"How many more islands?" Lusa asked, panting.

The gull turned one beady, bright eye on her, then the other. It flapped its wings as if to say either, *I don't know*, or, *Lots and lots*. Neither answer made Toklo feel better. He looked back at the shore where the flat-face dens glowed. Then he looked ahead and spotted the same tall metal bones rising over the next island. It was reassuring to be able to see it . . . but daunting to see how far it was. He just wanted to lie down and fall asleep.

They rested for as long as they dared. The nights were so short that Toklo kept glancing at the sky expecting to see the first rays of dawn, especially since getting through the denning place had taken so much of the brief time of darkness. He didn't want to be caught by flat-faces on one of these islands. They smelled of flat-face things, and he was afraid the flat-faces might decide to protect those things with firesticks. Better to get safely across, away from the flat-faces altogether. And there was no food or water on the island, nothing but strange metal flat-face towers and the sharp smell of that sticky black liquid coating everything. They picked their way around the towers and slipped down to the shore on the far side of the island.

Ujurak flew overhead again as the cubs waded into the water. River water flooded into Toklo's mouth and he spit, losing his rhythm for a moment. It tasted bitter and disgusting, nothing like the streams in the woods where he grew up. He couldn't taste or smell any signs of fish nor hear the murmurs of the bear spirits. The river was as empty and dead as the islands. Oka wasn't here, and nor was Tobi. Toklo felt a pang of loneliness. After all these moons being scared of their spirits, now he missed them with something that felt like pain.

His muscles were all aching by the time he dragged himself

onto the second island, and the scratches that Taqqiq had given him stung. A few of them had started seeping blood again, and he licked them while he waited for Kallik and Lusa to catch up. They were farther behind this time, which worried him. Kallik swam with broad, powerful strokes, and she kept herself on the downstream side of Lusa so the smaller bear wouldn't be swept away. But Toklo could tell that it was tiring her to swim as slowly as the black bear.

"I can swim with Lusa this time," he offered as they dragged themselves across the second island. He ducked under a low-hanging branch of the flat-face construction. The islands were so strange and evenly spaced. Was it possible the flat-faces had built the islands, too? Could they make islands sprout from rivers like that?

"I'm *fine*," Lusa protested. "I like swimming; really, I do." But Toklo could see her paws trembling with exhaustion.

"It's all right," Kallik said. "You go on ahead, Toklo. It's easier to follow you than to keep my eyes on Ujurak."

So Toklo led the way again as they swam to the third island. His head felt as if it were full of sodden thistles. He couldn't think of anything except keeping his nose above water and paddling his paws as hard as he could. Ujurak circled overhead, letting out sharp cries to call them forward when they drifted off course or lost sight of the island in the waves.

On the third island they were all too exhausted to speak at first. The Ujurak-gull strutted around them, poking at their fur as they huddled together, their eyes drooping.

"Give us a moment, Ujurak," Toklo said irritably.

"Can we sleep just for a little while?" Lusa asked.

Toklo could see she was exhausted. He nodded and leaned into her wet fur, trying to warm her with his bulk as she dozed. He felt himself slipping in and out of sleep, restlessly half dreaming of flat-faces and of drowning.

Soon the Ujurak-gull was poking them again. Toklo blinked awake and realized that the sky above the flat-face denning place was already turning gray as the night shifted toward dawn. The short night was nearly over. Ujurak impatiently flapped his wings.

"All right, all right." Toklo sighed. He heaved himself down to the water and turned to make sure Kallik and Lusa were right behind him.

The next swim was a blur of aching muscles and bitter water sloshing over his head. A large tree branch covered in scummy yellow foam came barreling down along the current and whammed into his side before he could avoid it. Pain blossomed along all his wounds, and a part of him wished he could just give up—stop swimming and let the current take him wherever it wanted to. Maybe he'd find his mother and his brother at the end of the river. . . .

As the water rolled him right over, Toklo caught a glimpse of the dawn-gray sky through the surging waves and spotted the last star still glimmering up there. He remembered Oka's story of the lonely bear being chased by the other stars. But maybe he wasn't being chased . . . maybe he was being followed, the way Toklo was followed by Kallik and Lusa.

He couldn't give up. The other two were counting on him.

They needed him to lead the way through the river. With a new surge of energy he forced himself forward until he felt sand under his paws. He'd reached the fourth island.

While he waited for the others he paced forward to look for the next island. The light was bright enough now that he could see clearly across the water to a long shore, much bigger than the other islands. . . .

It was the other side of the river! They were nearly there!

"Lusa!" he called as Kallik nudged her out onto the pebbly bank. "Kallik, look! We're almost there! We're going to make it!"

"Bawwrk!" Ujurak squawked from overhead. Toklo guessed he was trying to say, *Hurry!* The first gleam of the rising sun was peeking up at the edge of the sky.

Lusa was too tired to speak, but her eyes shone as she leaned against Kallik.

"Just one more swim," Kallik urged her.

Toklo stayed close to the she-bears this time as they swam. They could all see the distant bank; they didn't need him to lead the way. A few slanting beams of sunlight glinted on eddies in the brown water around them.

Lusa was struggling to swim. Her back paws were dragging behind her, and her nose kept dipping under the water. Kallik tried to support her, but the current was fast and strong, and Toklo could see that they were all drifting downriver from the islands. He paddled around and took Kallik's place beside Lusa, nudging the small black bear to the surface and kicking his back paws to shove her forward.

At last the three exhausted bears reached the shore. They were coughing and spitting water, and rough, sticky sand clung to Toklo's paws as he staggered out of the river. Ujurak was waiting for them, a bear once more, looking dry and tireless. He pressed his nose into Toklo's fur, almost holding him up. "You've made it," he said. "We're on the other side of the Big River."

Toklo blinked slowly, looking around. Smoke Mountain towered overhead, suddenly much closer. In the gray dawn, he could make out the distinct shapes of separate mountains, though their peaks were still hidden in shadow.

There were only a few flat-face dens here, small with shiny silver sides, scattered across the churned-up earth. But there were more flat-face constructions with limbs like the ones on the islands, blossoming out of the ground every few bearlengths. He saw strange new firebeasts slumbering everywhere, all enormous and oddly shaped, many of them bright yellow, like dandelions.

He was too tired to explore. The important thing was that the river flowed behind him and he was safe. He'd never have to set paw in the Big River again.

Ujurak hurried to Kallik and Lusa at the water's edge. The little black cub lay listlessly on the ground, rubbing water from her eyes. "Why does it still smell like flat-faces?" she mumbled. "I thought we'd gotten away from them."

"Not yet," Ujurak said. "There's a huge gash in the earth just over that rise—it runs along the riverside. At the bottom is a long, silver flat-face thing that smells like the black stuff we saw spattered on the islands. I think we should cross the trench and then stay near the tree line while we follow the river to the Ice Sea."

"What are those awful things?" Lusa asked without sitting up. She pointed with her snout at the enormous misshapen firebeasts that were sitting up the slope from them.

"I think they eat the earth," Ujurak said. "From the air I saw some of them sitting in the trench with their claws full of dirt."

"Why would they do that?" Kallik asked. She lay down right where she was, letting the clay turn her belly fur a muddy brownish red.

"I don't know," Ujurak said. He turned to Toklo. "But the birds don't come anymore. They used to feed in the mud by the river. I talked to an old gull—he told me the flat-faces have been spreading farther across the land on both sides of the river. They dig and dig and build strange things into the earth. They're taking something sticky and black out of the ground that clogs the birds' feathers and gets on everything they eat and makes them sick. There's nothing here for the gulls anymore."

Toklo huffed. What did it matter about the birds? He felt as though he were ready for the longsleep that was supposed to come only with the end of fishleap. He thought he might sleep straight through until *next* year's fishleap.

"We should keep going," Ujurak urged. "We're still too close to all these flat-face things."

"There's no way," Toklo said. Even if he could keep going,

he could tell from the way Lusa was panting that she needed to rest. "We can barely walk. We need to sleep a little."

Ujurak hesitated, glancing at the hazy orange band of sky above the flat-face denning place. "All right," he said. "But only for a short time. We must move on before the flat-faces wake up."

The bears dragged their paws to a patch of ground half-enclosed by leafy bushes, the best shelter they could find at a short distance from the river. From here they had a clear view of the flat-face diggers, which were too close for comfort, but at least they weren't moving. And, Toklo reasoned, this way the bears could see them coming if necessary.

He took a moment to glance down the river before curling up to rest. All he could see along the shore in either direction were flat-face dens and diggers and hills of earth and rocks. His heart felt as heavy as his limbs. Qopuk had told them to follow the river down to the Ice Sea. But how would they ever make it? Wherever they went, it seemed they couldn't escape the flat-faces.

He rested his chin on his paws and drifted into sleep, but in his dreams he was running, running, dodging firebeasts, and tumbling into holes dug by the flat-faces, smelling nothing but burning and death, no matter how far or how fast he went.

CHAPTER TWELVE

Kallik

Something shrieked, a long, piercing wail, and in Kallik's muddled sleep she thought for a moment it was the metal bird crashing down out of the sky again, taking Nanuk to her death. Then it shrieked again, followed by roaring and growling and rumbling, as if all the bears at the Longest Day Gathering were shouting at one another, but with no words. She blinked and rubbed her nose, slowly coming awake. Perhaps she was still lying by the Great Bear Lake, and everything since then had been a dream. . . .

She looked up and saw an enormous yellow claw, twice the size of the biggest white bear, falling out of the sky toward her.

Kallik yelled with terror, springing to her paws. Beside her, the other three cubs were still waking up. Desperately, Kallik slammed her head into Toklo's side.

"Wake up! We're being attacked!" she roared.

Toklo leaped up, snarling. Ujurak and Lusa struggled to their paws behind him. Kallik could see that Lusa's paws were still wobbly with exhaustion. It didn't feel like they had slept for long, but when they woke the sun was high in the sky and the no-claws had woken. So had all their giant beasts.

Kallik bundled into Lusa, shoving her away from the claw in the sky. "Run!" she howled. "Run!"

The claw paused above them with another shriek as the bears scattered, diving into the bushes. Now Kallik could hear no-claws yelling above the other sounds. They had spotted the bear cubs!

She swerved, staying close to Lusa as they burst out on the other side of the bushes. More beasts and no-claws and burning smells waited for them here. Kallik scrambled to a stop at a line of firebeasts that blocked the way forward. Beyond them she could see the trench Ujurak had told them about. It looked like a huge claw had sliced through the earth from one end of the sky to the other. Bare tree trunks lay abandoned where they'd been cut down. Thick streams of brown and black water trickled from the mud churned up by the firebeasts' paws. Kallik spotted something long and silvery lying at the bottom, like a giant dead snake running the length of the trench.

"We can't go this way!" she cried. "We have to find a way around the firebeasts!"

Lusa tried to dart away, but she got turned around and started running back toward the river. Kallik knew she'd be trapped there; none of them was strong enough to swim any farther. They needed to cross the trench and run up the slope into the woods she could see on the far side, where the no-claws might not follow.

She chased after Lusa and headed her off, driving her back up the shore. Lusa's eyes were huge and frantic; Kallik wasn't even sure the little black bear knew that Kallik was trying to help. She was just running in blind panic.

"This way!" Toklo called. He was racing toward a gap in the firebeasts with Ujurak on his heels. Kallik pushed Lusa toward them. As the bears sprinted between the firebeasts, suddenly the ground seemed to fall away. Kallik felt herself tumbling head over paws down a slippery, muddy slope. She crashed into the silvery snake thing at the bottom with a bone-jarring thud, and then Lusa tumbled right into her.

"Oof!" Kallik grunted.

Toklo and Ujurak landed a short way off, in a heap of brown fur and flailing paws. Kallik wriggled out from underneath Lusa and shook herself. Her white fur was caked with red mud, dragging her down. She shoved Lusa to her paws and they scrambled after Toklo, slipping and sliding. The brown bears had already picked themselves up and were floundering along beside the silvery tube, which loomed higher than their heads. Fortunately, it was still and quiet.

The walls of the trench rose up on either side of them, steep and slick with wet mud. Kallik wondered desperately how they would get out. Toklo and Ujurak stopped to wait for them, their flanks heaving and their eyes huge with fear. Kallik looked past them and spotted that a part of the trench had collapsed against the silver snake. The heap of red earth blocked their way along the bottom of the snake—but it could offer a way out. . . .

"Toklo!" she barked. "Look up there!"

Toklo spun around, wiping mud out of his eyes.

"If we climb up that pile of earth, we could get on top of the snake and make it across to the other side of the trench," Kallik explained breathlessly.

Toklo nodded. "It's worth a try. We might be able to jump from the snake to the top of the slope. I'll help Ujurak; you take Lusa!"

Without waiting for an answer, he shoved the smaller brown bear ahead of him until they came to the collapsed mud. Ujurak scrambled up, his belly dragging in the sticky soil, and Toklo followed in a couple of giant leaps. Then he nudged Ujurak onto the top of the snake. The little bear's paws slid from under him and he flopped to his belly. It would have looked funny if they hadn't been running for their lives. Toklo buried his nose in Ujurak's flank and heaved him toward the bank on the other side.

Legs flailing wildly, Ujurak sank his claws into the wall and grabbed a tree root between his teeth. With Toklo pushing from behind, he scrambled up and over the top of the trench. He crouched there, panting, while Toklo braced his slippery paws on the snake and turned to help Lusa.

The black bear's climbing skills proved useful as she scrabbled up the pile of earth and jumped on top of the snake. She wobbled for a moment, then balanced herself before stepping carefully toward Toklo. He gave her a shove, and she flew through the air to land close to the top of the slope. Ujurak was waiting for her, ready to sink his teeth into her scruff and haul her up beside him.

Toklo jumped next, his powerful hind legs pushing him off the snake. His paws left brown smears across the silver surface. When he was at the top, he turned and called down to Kallik: "Come on! Quick!"

From the anxious glance he gave behind her, Kallik guessed that the no-claws were coming along her side of the trench. She dug her front paws into the pile of earth and heaved herself up. The silver snake was slippery as ice—but Kallik quickly sank her weight evenly through her paws and kept herself low, just as she had done on the frozen sea. She ran along the top of the snake and sprang into the air. Her muddy pelt flapped wet and heavy against her belly, pulling her down, but her front claws sank into the side of the trench, and a moment later Toklo's face appeared at the top. He leaned down to bury his teeth in her neck fur and drag her up.

"Go!" Kallik gasped as she tumbled onto flat earth. She scrambled to her paws and looked around. On this side of the trench, the trees were close enough for her to see each trunk, with the mountains looming black and misty beyond them. A short row of firebeasts stood in their way, but they were all quiet, and there were no signs of no-claws.

Ujurak was already running toward them. On the far side of the silver snake, no-claws were standing in a line, staring and shouting, but none of them tried to cross. Toklo raced after Ujurak, his paws skimming over the bare, ruined earth. Kallik nudged Lusa to her paws and they sprinted away from the trench, leaping holes and splashing through puddles.

Up ahead, Kallik could see that Toklo and Ujurak had made it safely through the sleeping firebeasts and were nearly at the tree line. She put on a burst of speed and darted right between two of the huge yellow creatures. *Can't catch me!* she thought triumphantly.

Suddenly there was a rumble, which quickly built to a roar. The ground trembled, and there was a bitter, choking smell in the air. One of the firebeasts was waking up! Kallik looked over her shoulder to make sure Lusa was close behind her. To her horror, the little black bear was heading for the gap beside the firebeast that was awake. Maybe Lusa hadn't heard the noise above the splash of her paws and the thudding of her heart. Her head was down and she was running, running, running.

Kallik held her breath. *Please let her get past.* From the position of its big round eyes, the firebeast was facing the other way, so it couldn't see Lusa. But just as Lusa darted through the gap, the firebeast let out a bellow and rolled backward. The little black cub howled with pain as the beast struck her, and she crashed down onto her side.

"Stop! Get off her!" Kallik roared. The beast didn't seem to hear. It rolled a few more paces, and Kallik couldn't see Lusa anymore. Had it crushed her under its massive black paws?

"Lusa!" Kallik wailed.

She spun around, calling for Ujurak and Toklo, but the brown bears were too far away to hear. Kallik didn't know what to do. Should she chase after them? There wasn't time.

Lusa needed help now. There was a harsh scraping noise, and the firebeast started rolling forward, heading out of the line toward the trench. As the beast lumbered away, Kallik saw Lusa's limp body lying in the dirt. No-claws were jumping out of the other firebeasts and running toward her.

She tore across the bare earth, roaring at the top of her voice. The no-claws took one look at her and started running in the other direction. *That's right,* she thought. *Fear my teeth! And my claws! I won't let you hurt my friend!*

She skidded to a stop beside Lusa. Her heart lurched when she saw how still the little cub was. Blood puddled around her friend's paws, and her eyes were closed. Kallik crouched closer, trying to listen for a sign of life. Was that . . . was that a soft breath? Kallik prayed to Nisa and all the ice spirits, hoping there were still some in the sky to help her. *Please save her. Lusa's done nothing wrong. She's a good, kind bear. Please let her live.*

Lusa let out a tiny whimper. She was alive! Kallik sprang up and carefully fastened her teeth in the scruff of Lusa's neck. She hated moving her when she was so hurt, but the no-claws were already creeping back toward them—slowly, as if they thought Kallik might not notice.

Kallik took a step back, and then another, dragging Lusa along as gently as she could. Lusa whimpered again, sending claws of agony into Kallik's heart. *I'm sorry, Lusa. I'm trying not to hurt you.* She was surprised by how heavy the black bear was. She always looked so tiny next to the other cubs. But Kallik had gone only a few steps, and already her legs were shaking with the effort. How would she get Lusa to safety on her own?

Plus she still had to frighten off the no-claws. She let go of Lusa for a moment and bellowed at them, sending them stumbling backward. But not far enough . . . they seemed more confident now and came forward again, pointing and chattering to one another. Why couldn't they just leave the bears alone?

Desperately, Kallik grabbed Lusa's scruff and dragged her another few steps. Her jaw ached, and she winced every time Lusa's body bounced over the uneven dirt and rocks.

Suddenly a no-claw broke away from the others and came running at her. He was waving something long and silver—longer than a firestick, but Kallik didn't know what it was. He moved faster than she expected, darting forward while she was looking down at Lusa.

"Get away from them!" Toklo bellowed, charging up behind Kallik. He leaped at the no-claw with his teeth bared, knocking him to the ground. Toklo reared up on his hind legs over the no-claw and opened his jaws wide to roar his fury. The no-claw scrambled away and fled, leaving the silver stick where it fell.

Toklo roared again, and this time there was an answering call from Ujurak. The other brown bear came bounding up on Kallik's other side and galloped at the crowd of no-claws. With screams that sounded like bird cries, the no-claws scattered, most of them running for the river while others leaped inside their beasts.

"Help me!" Kallik called to Toklo. He ran over to her and skidded to a halt, staring down at Lusa.

"Is she alive?"

"Barely," Kallik said. "We have to get her out of here." She fastened her teeth in Lusa's scruff again and pulled. Lusa let out another soft whimper without opening her eyes. Kallik let go of her and shuffled her paws. "I'm afraid that I'm making her injuries worse."

Toklo paced around Lusa, growling. "There must be another way to move her," he said. "Maybe . . . " He stopped and crouched low to the ground. Inching forward, he gently worked his nose under Lusa's body, then the rest of his head.

Kallik realized that he was trying to get Lusa on his back so he could carry her. She slid her paws under Lusa and helped to keep her steady until Toklo had crawled halfway under her. Very slowly, he rose to his paws. Lusa was draped across his back like a white bear cub resting on her mother. Kallik had a vivid flash of Taqqiq riding on Nisa's back as the three of them padded across the ice.

But Lusa was more than half Toklo's size. She must be very heavy on his back. Kallik pressed close to him, making sure Lusa didn't slide off.

"Are you sure you can carry her?" she asked.

"Yes," Toklo rumbled stubbornly. He took a wavering step forward, then another and another.

"Ujurak!" Kallik called, and he came bounding up after them. She didn't have to say anything; he went instinctively to Toklo's other side. Together they tried to take a bit of Lusa's weight, pressing their fur close to Toklo's. Their paws padded in a steady rhythm as the cubs hurried away from the no-claws and into the woods.

Kallik felt her shoulders relaxing as the shadow of the trees fell over their group. "Hey, look over there," she said, spotting a track that cut through the trees. "I see a path. It might be easier to follow that."

"It's a flat-face path," Toklo spit. He turned in the other direction and stumbled over a fallen tree. Lusa's limp body slid sideways and nearly fell off.

"Toklo!" Kallik said, catching the black bear cub and rebalancing her. "Be smart! The path will be clearer, and you'll be able to walk without falling over anything."

Toklo growled, but he didn't argue anymore as Ujurak led the way onto the winding trail. It slanted up over a rise and then down beside a gully where the trees were thinner. As they struggled forward, heavy clouds rolled in, casting a dark greenish gray light over the sharp-edged peaks above them.

"Where are we going?" Kallik asked, panting.

"As far away from the flat-faces as we can get," Toklo answered. He was breathing heavily, and his words came in short bursts. "We can't go back to the river. Too many flat-faces. We'd never make it."

Kallik's ears twitched. "I think I hear water," she said, and all three bears stopped to listen. She tried to smell it, but it was hard to pick out above the powerful scents of clay, river grime, and blood that clung to their fur.

"There must be a stream down there," Ujurak said, nodding down into the gully. A glimmer of water trickled at the bottom, nearly hidden by the undergrowth.

They staggered down the scrubby earth and pushed through prickly thornbushes until they found the stream. Toklo began to follow the stream uphill, lowering his head and using his broad shoulders to shove aside the branches in his way.

As he stepped into the stream to get around one gnarled, crooked tree trunk, his paws slipped on the wet stones. For a heart-wrenching moment Kallik thought Lusa was going to tumble off his back and crash down the hill. But Ujurak jumped in the way and nudged her into place, her tiny paws dangling limply against Toklo's thick fur.

The stream was fast-flowing and clear as it rushed down the gully, splashing over the roots of the bushes. They pushed their way up as the sky grew darker and a drizzly rain began to fall on them. Kallik couldn't see any more trees over the top of the gully, only gray sky. The water gushed around her muddy white fur, surprisingly strong. It smelled of snow, but it also had an undercurrent of a darker, bitter scent, like the islands in the river.

Kallik's paws stung as sharp pebbles stabbed her with every step. Her fur felt sticky and heavy, and she could barely keep her eyes open. After the long swim the night before, hardly any sleep, and the encounter with no-claws this morning, she wasn't sure how much farther any of them could walk.

Toklo was struggling beneath Lusa's weight. His head was bent, and he stared at the ground as he walked. The little black bear still hadn't woken up, and her blood was leaving matted trails through Toklo's fur.

The gully ended abruptly at a small waterfall. A cold spray

of water soaked their fur as they looked up the sheer rock wall
in front of them.

"Oh, no. Do we have to go all the way back?" Kallik murmured, glancing over her shoulder at the long walls of the
gully behind them.

"I think there's a way up over here," Ujurak suggested.

He led the way as they scrambled over the boulders, hook-
ing their claws in the scraggly bushes to pull themselves up.
Kallik climbed behind Toklo, reaching up to help him balance and keep Lusa in place when he shifted his weight. Her
paws itched at how agonizingly slowly they had to move, and
her heart pounded every time Lusa's paws started to slide
toward her.

Finally they reached the top, where Ujurak was waiting to
guide Toklo over the edge. Kallik blinked the rain out of her
eyes and gazed at a steep rise of wet black rocks that loomed
ahead of them. Her heart sank as she thought of struggling
on in this weather, with their paws aching and Lusa bleeding
to death.

"I see a cave!" Ujurak cried, bumping her side with his
muzzle.

Kallik lifted her head and spotted the dark opening in the
rock ahead of them, overlooking the stream a few bearlengths
before it cascaded into the waterfall and the gully below. She
hoped the cave was empty. She didn't have enough strength
left to chase off any other animals that might be sheltering
there.

Following Ujurak, she padded out of the rain. The cave

was dry, and big enough for all of them. Its cold stone walls were covered in patches of moss and messy remnants of birds' nests. Toklo collapsed to the sandy floor as soon as he stepped inside. Kallik and Ujurak gently slid Lusa off him and onto the hard sand.

Toklo bent over Lusa, sniffing her. Ujurak crouched on her other side, studying the wide gash in Lusa's back leg and the bleeding scratches in her side. All of them were covered in mud from nose to tail.

Toklo looked up at Kallik, his eyes bleak. "I know this smell," he said. "My brother, Tobi, smelled like this before he died."

Kallik shook her head. They couldn't lose Lusa, not here, not like this. "But . . . we brought her so far," she whispered. "You carried her all this way . . . and she came so far by herself. . . . " She knew that what she was saying didn't make sense. A bear could die at any moment, especially on a journey as dangerous as this one. And the gash in Lusa's leg looked as bad as the wounds on Nanuk after the metal bird crashed.

But it still shouldn't be Lusa. It *couldn't* be Lusa. The little black bear had come farther than any of them: from a life in the Bear Bowl to being in the wild. It wasn't fair.

"I know this smell," Toklo said again.

Kallik lay down next to Lusa and snuggled close to her, ignoring the sticky warmth of the black cub's blood trickling from her cuts and grazes into Kallik's fur. "No," she murmured. "No, Lusa. You can't die."

"She isn't dead yet," Ujurak said quietly. "Come on, Toklo.

We'll go look for herbs. I'm going to try to heal her."

Toklo followed him without arguing. Left alone in the cave with Lusa, Kallik listened to the patter of raindrops and the blowing wind outside. She wanted to have hope, but part of her knew that Toklo was right. She knew this smell, too. It was the same smell Nanuk had before *she* died.

"Kallik!" Toklo called from outside the cave.

She pushed herself upright again and dragged her paws to the mouth of the cave. Toklo and Ujurak were staring up at the low-hanging clouds above them. The mist had parted for a moment, revealing sharp black peaks looming overhead.

Kallik turned to look back down where they had come from. They were much higher than she'd realized. Far below, the Big River twisted across the landscape like a flat brown snake.

All around them, dark wisps of smoke hung in the mist, as if they'd risen from the rocks themselves.

Toklo's dark eyes met hers. "We're on Smoke Mountain."

CHAPTER THIRTEEN

Lusa

Fluffy, sun-filled clouds scudded across the bright blue sky, carried by the warm breeze. Leaves rustled in the trees, and the scent of blueberries and pears hung in the air. Far in the distance, the chatter of flat-face voices sounded like laughing birds.

Lusa blinked. Bark scraped under her paws, and she twisted around to see that she was perched on the highest branch of a tree.

A very familiar-looking tree.

Lusa caught her breath. She had seen the winding stone paths below her before, and the enclosures full of odd-looking animals. The funny ones were called monkeys, and the leggy pink birds were flamingos.

She was sitting in the tallest tree of the Forest, back in the Bear Bowl.

Quickly she scrambled off the branch and climbed down the tree. Every bump and twist of the branches and bark seemed to fit naturally into her paws. At the bottom of the tree she jumped off and turned around.

She was surrounded by black bears. Not just any black bears—her family.

"Lusa!" Yogi cried. He charged forward and knocked her over. They rolled on the grass, batting at each other with their paws. He felt heavier to Lusa, but she was bigger now, too. She ducked under one of his paws and popped up behind him, tumbling him onto his back.

"Ha!" she cried, pouncing on him triumphantly. "I win!"

"No fair!" Yogi said. "You used wild bear tricks on me."

Lusa shrugged. "I'm a wild bear now," she said. "I'm allowed to."

"You *are* a wild bear," Stella said admiringly, poking Lusa in the side with her nose. "You even smell like a wild bear."

"Do I?" Lusa asked. She didn't know her smell had changed.

"And you weigh as much as *four* wild bears," Yogi protested, wriggling underneath her. Lusa hopped off and poked him playfully.

"Oh, little blackberry," Ashia said, pacing up and burying her nose in Lusa's fur. "We miss you so much."

"I miss you, too," Lusa said, cuddling close to her mother. "The wild is *so big*! You'd never believe it!"

"I know it is," Lusa's father, King, rumbled. He'd been born in the wild. He stalked in a circle around Lusa and Ashia, sniffing suspiciously. Ashia ignored him, licking Lusa's ears.

"You're so thin," Lusa's mother fretted. "What have you been eating? Do you get enough sleep?"

"Not nearly," Lusa admitted. "But I've met the most

wonderful friends. Yogi, guess what? I'm traveling with grizzlies!"

His mouth dropped open. "No way! Brown bears? And they haven't eaten you yet?"

"No, they like me!" Lusa said. "And they're not that bad, actually. Well, they don't smell as nice as black bears." She leaned into her mother, inhaling the warm honey-berry-milk scent of her. "And guess what else? My best friend is a white bear! She's not *nearly* as grumpy as the ones in the Bear Bowl. I like her very much. We're going to the Last Great Wilderness."

Suddenly Lusa stopped. The bears around her seemed to freeze, and even the wind fell still. She blinked, looking around at their staring faces.

"Except . . . I'm not going to make it," she whispered. She knew what was happening. She wasn't really back in the Bear Bowl.

She was dying.

There was a pause as the other bears gazed at her. Finally King shook his graying pelt. "You'd better make it," he said sternly. "I won't have the legends say that a brown bear and a white bear got to the place where the spirits dance, but the black bear gave up halfway!"

"Legends?" Lusa echoed.

"Stella tells stories about you all the time already," Yogi chimed in.

The she-bear nodded. "You're much more interesting than my 'Old Bear in the tree' story," she said. "I can't believe you really escaped! King thought you were dead."

"But I knew you weren't," Ashia said, nuzzling Lusa.

"I'm sorry, Mother," Lusa said. "I think I am." She took a deep breath, inhaling the scent of the leaves and feeling the wind brush her fur. "I'm going to join the bear spirits in the trees." She fought to sound brave. "I must be here to say good-bye to you." She hoped her tree would be something big and beautiful, maybe with blossoms on it, like the one she'd seen when she first reached the wild.

King growled, but it was Ashia who spoke.

"No, little blackberry," she said. "It is not your time yet."

Lusa felt the vision wobble, as if the Bear Bowl might disappear if she closed her eyes for too long. "What do you mean?" she asked. "I can feel them calling me—the tree bears."

"Don't listen to them!" Yogi blurted. "Don't you go to them, Lusa! Tell them you're not ready yet!"

"There's something important you still have to do," Ashia said.

"Me?" Lusa asked. "What is it?"

"You must save the wild."

Lusa gazed up at her mother, then at the other bears. They were watching her intently, as if they all knew what that meant.

"I don't understand," Lusa said. "Save the wild? From what? I'm only looking for a place to live safely with my friends."

"No," Ashia said, shaking her head. She stepped away from Lusa. Her eyes were sad but hopeful. "You must save the wild."

"Wait," Lusa said. The bears and the Bowl behind them were starting to fade and get fuzzy. "Don't go yet. Tell me what that means! I don't understand!" She tried to force her eyes open, to keep her family in front of her, but finally she had to blink.

When she opened her eyes again, the Bear Bowl was gone. The sunshine, the warmth, and the breeze were gone. Yogi, Stella, Ashia, and King—all gone. Lusa was lying on damp, scratchy sand. Stone walls curved overhead. The sound of rain reached her from somewhere nearby, mingled with the dark smell of smoke and snow.

Ujurak was bending over her. Lusa felt a pang of longing for her family. She missed cuddling with Ashia, playing with Yogi, listening to Stella's stories—even getting growled at by King.

Ujurak saw her eyes open, and his face lit up. "You're alive!"

"Ujurak," Lusa whispered hoarsely. "I had a dream."

"Shhh, just rest," he said.

She felt as if it were terribly urgent to tell him about it, even though her throat hurt when she spoke. "It was so strange," she said. "I thought I was going to die, and then my mother told me—"

"You must save the wild," Ujurak said. "I know. I've had that dream, too." He pressed a mixture of herbs onto her leg.

"Ow!"

Lusa tried to wriggle around to see it and felt a fierce slashing pain all through her body. Just then, paws thudded on the cave floor as Kallik and Toklo galloped in.

"You're awake!" Kallik cried. "Lusa, you're alive!"

Kallik's face went blurry as Lusa's eyes drooped shut. When she opened them again, her friends were still there, but she must have fallen asleep for a while. The light from outside was different, and the sound of the rain had ebbed.

Kallik crept closer and offered Lusa a pawful of wet moss. Lusa lapped up the moisture gratefully. Her mouth felt dry as bark.

"You scared us *so much*," Kallik said. "I'm so glad you woke up."

Toklo just stared at her.

"Where are we?" Lusa asked. The last thing she remembered was running away from flat-faces by the Big River.

Toklo and Kallik exchanged uneasy glances. "We're on Smoke Mountain," Kallik said. "We couldn't stay by the river. We have to go this way instead."

Lusa shivered, which made her wound flare with pain. She couldn't stop herself from letting out a small whimper. All three of her friends looked concerned.

"It's okay," Lusa squeaked, trying to be brave. "I'm okay." She'd never felt anything as bad as this pain in her whole life. She could barely breathe without wanting to shriek with agony. She couldn't imagine walking ever again.

"We'll rest here until you're better," Toklo said gruffly. He pawed at his nose, avoiding her eyes. "Glad you're okay. Come on, Kallik; let's go hunting." He shuffled to the front of the cave and ducked out into the rain.

"Toklo thought you were going to die," Kallik whispered. "He carried you all the way up here from the river."

"He did?" Lusa said. Ujurak nodded.

"Kallik!" Toklo called.

"We'll be back soon," Kallik promised. "With food! I hope!" She turned and bounded out of the cave to join Toklo.

"Rest now," Ujurak said. "Save your strength."

"So that I'll be strong enough to save the wild?" Lusa asked, half joking, but when Ujurak simply nodded before padding away, she felt too weak to ask again. Lusa's vision grew blurry. What exactly was she supposed to save the wild from, anyway? Her head started to swim, and she let her eyelids droop and her muzzle rest on her paws. Her sleep was fitful and broken, and she woke in the half dark of the cave several times, confused and upset, her head filled with fading dream images—rivers with no fish, starving bears, burned forests and fallen trees, and water that made animals sick. *Save the wild,* she thought. She couldn't even run away from flat-faces without getting hurt. What was a little bear cub like her supposed to do?

CHAPTER FOURTEEN

Toklo

The next morning, Toklo was lying nearby, watching Lusa, when she opened her eyes and looked at him.

"Stop scowling at me, you old grumpus," she said.

"I'm not scowling!" he huffed.

"Oh, my mistake," Lusa teased. "That's just your regular face."

"It *is*," he grumbled. "I was just making sure you didn't *die* in your *sleep* or anything."

"Nope," Lusa said. She pushed herself to a sitting position, wincing. "Too bad for you guys. Looks like you saved my life."

Toklo scraped his claws along the rocks. "That's not bad," he muttered. "That's fine."

"Oh, good," Lusa said. "I'm glad you don't *mind* that I'm alive." He looked at her, confused, and she opened her jaws wide in amusement. "I'm only teasing, Toklo!" She dipped her head in his direction. "I'm just . . . I mean, I'm grateful that you all didn't go on without me. I know it must be hard, waiting here."

"We wouldn't leave you," Toklo said.

When Kallik came back from hunting with a squirrel, Lusa shared it with Toklo. And that night she wriggled closer until their pelts were touching before she fell asleep.

Toklo felt his fur settling for the first time in almost a moon. He let his relief overpower his worries, and slept a peaceful, dreamless sleep.

The rain tapered off into a slow drizzle as Toklo and Kallik climbed away from the cave, following the stream up into the mountains. Toklo hoped it would lead to more bushes or even trees—anywhere prey might live. He hadn't scented any below, but perhaps the flat-faces had scared it away.

His pelt was still prickling with worry for Lusa. Their first sleep in the cave he had tossed and turned, his dreams a muddle of Lusa and Tobi dying, Lusa's and Tobi's spirits sweeping away downriver, Lusa and Tobi gone forever. He hadn't thought she would make it, and by morning he'd already started building a thick shell around himself of not caring, trying to prepare himself for losing her. But now she was back, and he realized that he did care after all.

Kallik was silent as they walked, their paws squelching over the brittle, soaked grass. They avoided talking about the gray wisps of smoke rising from the rocks, and when they found a smaller stream leading away from the main one, Toklo inhaled deeply, searching for scents of prey. Though the smell of smoke lay over everything, he thought he picked up a faint hint of wet fur on the breeze.

"Let's follow this," he said, nodding at the smaller stream. It led them across a sharp, pebbly plain and then disappeared between two high cliffs.

"All right," Kallik said. She shivered as they stepped over the flat river stones. "Toklo, do you think we'll see the giant no-claw?"

Toklo snorted. "A flat-face as tall as seven trees?" he said.

"But Qopuk was right about the smoke," Kallik said, glancing up at the hazy mountain peak. "Remember? He said it was from the fire the no-claw builds for the dead bears, and that it means the giant no-claw is out hunting. What if Qopuk was right? What if these mountains *are* evil?"

Toklo looked up at the top of the cliffs, which seemed to be scraping the sky high above them. The rain had stopped, but still the dark gray clouds huddled overhead, hiding the sun.

"I'm not going to be afraid of stories," he growled. "We'll face the dangers here like all the others we've run into."

His nose twitched. He could smell burning, but there was no fire to be seen in any direction. He peered into the mist, watching for flickers of flame. His eyes stung, and he realized that the smoke was getting thicker as they slipped into a canyon between the cliffs.

A few pawsteps into the gully, Kallik started coughing and pawed at her eyes, leaving streaks of black down her face. Toklo looked down and realized that the soil underpaw here was black and gritty.

"Ow!" Kallik yelped, blinking and shaking her head. "My eyes hurt."

"Here, wash your paws," Toklo suggested, nudging her into the stream. Even in the clear water he could see flecks of black ash dancing along in the current. Kallik held her paw underwater until it was washed clean, and then dabbed at her face again.

"Where is the smoke coming from?" she asked, still coughing.

Toklo peered into the thick gray fog ahead of them. His eyes burned and he squinted, trying to shut out the smoke. He could barely see the dark mass of the cliff walls on either side of them.

Something was glowing near the base of the cliff wall to his right. He inched toward it, lowering his head to peer at the rocks. They felt strangely warm under his paws.

"What is it?" Kallik said in a frightened voice. "Toklo? Don't go too far."

There was a crack in the rocks at the bottom of the cliff. Toklo peered down and saw black lumps of rock inside the mountain. Some of them were glowing orange.

The mountain was on fire! But it was burning from the *inside*. Toklo backed away. There were no flames. It puzzled and unsettled him; he didn't know whether they needed to run away or not.

"We should go back," Kallik said. "I don't like this. What if the giant no-claw is out there hunting us?"

"We need to find food," Toklo insisted. "For Lusa."

Suddenly something darted across his path. It was small and brown, and it wasn't moving terribly fast. Beaver!

"Kallik!" he called, his voice a harsh croak from the black mist.

The white bear splashed out of the stream and pressed up close beside him. He pointed with his snout in the direction the prey had gone, hoping she'd understand. His throat hurt too much to speak again. She nodded and they followed after it, crouching low to the ground.

Toklo's head ached, and his paws felt as though they weren't attached to his body anymore. He had a strong feeling that the cliffs on either side were creeping in closer, like they were about to smash him and Kallik flat between them. No, that couldn't be right. He shook his head, but now it seemed as though the cliff walls were leaning away, like they didn't want to get too close to the bears. The smoke thinned, swirling around their paws like ground mist, and then thickened into a heavy gray-yellow fog. He tried to veer to the left to feel the stream below his paws, but it seemed to have vanished.

He saw the flash of brown again, and this time he caught a glimpse of a flat tail. He sped up, his paws padding quickly over the ash-covered rocks. His heart plunged as he saw the cliff walls closing in ahead of him. *We'll be crushed!* In a panic, Toklo turned to run and hurtled into Kallik.

"Toklo!" she cried, steadying him. "What is it? What's wrong?"

Toklo blinked. "Nothing." The smoke was clearing. The walls narrowed to a gap in front of them, but they weren't moving. It was a trick of the smoke.

The beaver's tail flashed on the other side of the gap, and

Toklo hurried after it, bounding through the pass between the cliffs. The beaver was heading for a grove of pine trees up the slope from the stream, and Toklo followed.

He scrambled up the slope and dove into the trees. He could hear Kallik's paws thudding behind him. Thin pine needles slipped and scattered under his feet.

The beaver ducked behind a tree, and Toklo leaped after it. But when his paws hit the dirt, there was no sign of the prey. His nose and chest seemed to be so full of smoke, he couldn't smell anything else.

"This way!" Kallik called from a few bearlengths away. But that couldn't be right—surely the beaver had gone in the other direction? The white bear cub was already disappearing through the leaves. Toklo bounded after her, wondering if his senses were deceiving him.

They ran, ducking and weaving through the trees, not trying to be quiet anymore.

Then Toklo saw a flash of brown off to one side. "Over there!" he yelled.

"No, it's over there!" Kallik insisted, charging straight through a bush in the opposite direction.

Frustrated, Toklo turned away from her and ran after the prey he was *sure* he had seen. Just a few more pawsteps . . . it would be right there in front of him . . .

He crashed into a tree with a bone-jarring thud. Shaking his head, he jumped back and snarled at it. It was as if the tree had leaped out of the mist into his path. Was he going crazy?

"Toklo!" he heard Kallik shouting. "Toklo, where are you?"

He turned and blundered back into the maze of smoke and trees. His eyes watered and he pawed at his snout, blinking and trying to clear his mind.

"Kallik!" he called.

"Toklo!" she called back. Only now her voice was coming from a different direction. He tried to go that way and suddenly found himself snared in a tangle of brambles.

"Kallik!" he shouted frantically. "Kallik!" Thorns snagged his fur and pricked his skin. It got worse the more he struggled. *Ow!*

Suddenly he saw Kallik bounding out of the mist. Her eyes were glazed with fear.

"Kallik!" he barked. She skidded to a stop and looked around. "Over here!"

Her eyes widened in surprise as she spotted him in the brambles. "Toklo!" she yelped with relief.

"I'm stuck," Toklo said grumpily.

Kallik took some of the brambles in her teeth and tugged. Toklo shoved with his paws and wriggled, wishing for a moment that he were as small as Lusa. His fur felt as though it were being ripped off him, and when he finally struggled free, several brown tufts were left on the branches.

"Why did you go that way?" he barked.

"I was hunting! What were *you* doing?"

"*I* was hunting!"

"I don't like this place," Kallik said.

"Wait, there it goes!" Toklo cried, spotting the beaver again. This time they both saw it, and they sprang to their paws. Toklo was determined not to let it get away this time. He led the way as they raced through the trees, bounding between rocks and bushes. Up ahead he saw daylight shining through the tree trunks. Clear sky! The beaver ran toward the light, but Toklo was gaining. The scent was stronger now, warm flesh and fur. . . .

Toklo burst out of the trees, and the ground suddenly disappeared in front of him. He skidded to a stop with his front paws nearly over the edge. Pebbles shot out from under his feet and bounced down the cliff. Toklo stared in horror. He was standing on the edge of a precipice, looking down at jagged rocks like black teeth, many bearlengths below.

With a massive thud, Kallik crashed into him from behind. Toklo stumbled forward, knocked off balance, and felt the world tipping around him.

He was falling over the edge of the cliff!

CHAPTER FIFTEEN

Kallik

"No!" Kallik cried as Toklo's paws slipped over the precipice.

She lunged forward and sank her teeth into the fur on Toklo's haunches. She hauled herself backward, dragging Toklo pawstep by pawstep over the top of the cliff. He scrabbled with his hind paws, trying to push himself away from the edge. Kallik gave a final heave, and they both tumbled to the ground on a bed of pine needles.

Toklo rolled to his paws and shook himself. Kallik could see that one of the wounds Taqqiq had given him had opened up. Blood was rolling down his shoulder, leaving a sticky dark red trail through his fur.

"I'm sorry," she said. "I didn't see that you had stopped—I didn't see the cliff there—"

"Neither did I," Toklo said tersely. He licked his shoulder. "It's not your fault."

"It's these mountains," Kallik said. "I told you they were evil. There are spirits here trying to lead us to our deaths."

"Spirits?" Toklo scoffed. "Surely they have better things to do. Why would they want to kill us?"

"Maybe they're angry about what the flat-faces are doing by the river," Kallik said. She remembered the horrible gash in the earth and all the fallen trees lying in the mud. "Maybe the black bear spirits from those trees have lost their homes and are looking for revenge."

"On us?" Toklo said. "That's dumb. These are just mountains. Come on; we should get back to Lusa."

Kallik couldn't see the cliffs they'd come through, or the stream they'd been following. She could smell smoke and pine trees, but no prey. The cliff yawned on one side and the pine forest stretched off on the other. Normally Kallik could detect bear scent from skylengths away, but now when she sniffed the air, she just became more confused.

"I think we're lost," she said softly.

"We're not lost," Toklo snapped. "Brown bears are never lost." But he looked uneasy, too. His head whipped around at every small sound.

Kallik closed her eyes. "Ice spirits, please guide us," she whispered. "Please take us safely back to Lusa and Ujurak. Please, spirits of the ice, protect us from these mountains."

"*What* ice?" Toklo muttered.

Kallik ignored him and kept whispering to the spirits. It was the only thing she could think of to do. With an irritated growl, Toklo shoved his way in front of her and padded off through the trees.

Kallik climbed to her paws and followed him. She didn't want to lose sight of him again.

They had gone only a few pawsteps when it started to rain, a drenching downpour that soaked Toklo and Kallik in moments.

"Perfect," Toklo grumbled. He walked faster, his paws sloshing and splashing in the wet mud that quickly formed underpaw. Kallik could feel the mud sticking to her white fur.

She remembered what Lusa had said about reading signs. Perhaps if there were bad spirits in these mountains, there might be good spirits, too. She stopped and looked around. The trees were thinner here, and she could see bare rocks off to the right. The rain made everything look blurred and slick. *Ice spirits? Are you there?*

Her eyes opened wide and she gasped. "Toklo!"

The brown bear came galloping back, skidding on the wet pine needles. "What? What is it?"

"I think we should go that way," Kallik said, pointing to the rocks.

Toklo stared at the slick gray stones. "Why?"

"Look here, at this tree," Kallik said, nudging it with her snout. "Do you see it?"

"See what?" Toklo growled.

"The sign!"

Toklo huffed. "You're getting as bad as Lusa, seeing signs in everything!"

Kallik shook her head impatiently. "Look at these four branches. They're all new little branches, and they're all growing off the tree trunk in the same direction—pointing toward those rocks!"

"What?" Toklo spluttered. "That makes as much sense as trying to follow a butterfly!"

"No, it does make sense," Kallik insisted. "Don't you see? The four branches are us—we're cubs, so we're like new branches, and we're all traveling together. It's pointing the way back so we can be together again."

"Who told you that?" Toklo challenged. "Your ice spirits?"

"No, it must have been Lusa's spirits—the spirits of the black bears who live in these trees," Kallik said. She had felt so sure, but after she explained herself to Toklo, her fur prickled with doubts. Would the black bear spirits really speak to her?

Well, there was no ice here—this was the best she could do.

Toklo opened his mouth to argue some more, but Kallik cut him off. "Just trust me," she said. "I'll get us back to the cave." She bounded in front of him, leading the way out of the pine forest and onto the wide, flat rocks. She hoped she sounded confident. *Thank you, tree spirits. I put my faith in you.*

The rocks were slippery underpaw, and the bears had to move carefully, stepping from boulder to boulder. Kallik kept searching the blank rocky terrain in front of her for more signs. *Help me, please.* She was beginning to worry that she'd gone the wrong way when she spotted something else.

"Aha! See that?"

"No," said Toklo.

"That little black stone!" Kallik said. Tucked in among the giant gray boulders was a tiny, perfectly round, dark black stone. It looked as if it were sparkling with speckles of starlight—as if an ice spirit were trapped inside. Kallik trotted up to it and pointed with her nose. "Don't you get it? That's *Lusa*. She's a little black bear, but she isn't like any other bear around her. It's like she's sparkling on the inside."

Toklo rolled his eyes. "So we go that way."

"We go that way," Kallik agreed. It was encouraging that "that way" was downhill, since they'd gone uphill from the cave. She picked up the stone in her mouth and brought it with her. She wanted to show Lusa. If they got back safely, Kallik thought it would be a powerful sign that the good spirits here were stronger than the bad spirits, as long as bears were willing to listen to them.

The rocks ended at a scrabbly stretch of earth and dry grass with ragged bushes clinging to it. Tall peaks surrounded them, and wind whistled up from the canyons, driving the rain into their eyes. A few lone trees were scattered near the cliff walls.

Kallik squinted at the cliffs rising up some distance to their right. Were those the ones they'd followed the stream through? She put the little black stone on the ground to speak. "I think—"

"Hang on!" Toklo said. And suddenly he was bounding away, racing across the dirt toward one of the trees. His powerful shoulders propelled him forward at a startling speed. Kallik blinked after him in surprise.

Then she saw what he'd spotted: a moving ball of fur pelting across the rocks to the safety of a tree. She held her breath as Toklo got closer and closer. And then . . . he pounced!

When he turned around, she saw the animal hanging limply from his jaws. It looked like a long, low fox with a bushy tail and a face like a weasel. Kallik padded closer. "Nice catch," she said. "What is it?"

He gave her an odd look and put the animal down to say, "It's a pine marten, of course."

"Don't you 'of course' me," Kallik said. "We don't have pine martens on the ice."

Toklo snorted. "At least we have something to take back for Lusa."

"We're going this way," Kallik said, pointing with her nose to a gully that led downhill and dipped between two large, blocky boulders. Rainwater was running along the bottom of it, but they could follow it along the top.

"Why?" Toklo asked. "Because there are four big rocks over there?"

"Well . . . yes," Kallik said. "But not just any four rocks! Look how they're leaning against one another. It's like the way the four of us have to support one another, too." *Right, spirits? Is that what you're trying to tell me?*

Toklo heaved a sigh. "I hope you're right about this." Toklo picked up the pine marten again. Kallik could tell he thought she was being seal-brained. She sent another prayer to the spirits. *Please let this work.*

They edged along the lip of the gully, peeking down at the river that was starting to form below them. Suddenly Kallik felt the mud crumbling under her paws. The ground was giving way underneath her! She let out a yelp of terror, dropping the black stone from her jaws as she scrabbled for a pawhold. Toklo dropped the newkill, lunged forward, and sank his teeth into her scruff as the bank collapsed into the stream and her paws were left dangling in space.

With a heave, Toklo dragged her back to safety. Kallik was shaking.

"I dropped Lusa's stone," she said. "Maybe we're going the wrong way. This could be a bad sign."

"Don't think like that," Toklo said quietly. He picked up the marten again and poked her side with his snout. "Let's keep going," he mumbled.

Kallik plodded on, staying on the rocks now, even though their hard surface scratched the pads of her paws. Doubt churned inside her. She shouldn't have lost Lusa's stone! Was she taking them the wrong way?

But a few steps later, the ravine turned and slanted downward, and the water raced through it to merge with a fast-flowing stream that ran down the mountain. Kallik lifted her nose. *Now* she smelled familiar scents. She even thought she could pick up the warm, furry smells of Lusa and Ujurak.

"That's our stream!" she said. "That's the one that runs by the cave! Come on, Toklo; we're almost there!" She wasn't being led by bad spirits after all!

She sprinted ahead, slipping and sliding down the muddy slope with the rain pattering around her. Sure enough, soon she spotted the dark mouth of the cave overlooking the river.

Kallik stumbled into the semidarkness and inhaled the comforting scents of Lusa and Ujurak. The brown bear trotted forward to greet her.

"You made it back!" Ujurak said. "We were worried when the storm got so bad."

Toklo crowded in behind Kallik and dropped the pine marten on the floor of the cave. "For Lusa," he mumbled. His stomach growled loudly, as if it were arguing with him.

"She's asleep, but I'll wake her," Ujurak said. "And then we can share this." He dragged the newkill to the back of the cave.

Toklo and Kallik stood in the entranceway for a moment, catching their breath. Kallik realized how exhausted she was. Her heavy fur seemed to be pulling her down to the ground.

"You believe me now, don't you?" she said to Toklo. "There are spirits looking out for us. Lusa's tree spirits rescued us from the evil spirits of the mountains."

Toklo grunted. "Well, I guess something worked," he admitted, and stalked after Ujurak.

Despite her tiredness, Kallik felt a flutter of happiness in her chest. The spirits had brought them home to Lusa and Ujurak. Maybe they'd even helped to save Lusa's life.

Will they be strong enough to help us cross Smoke Mountain?

CHAPTER SIXTEEN

Toklo

It rained for days. Toklo lost track of time; it was hard to tell what was morning and what was night, between the constant gray fog of the storm and the dripping, still darkness of the cave. Whenever he went hunting with Kallik, they were swallowed up by a blur of smoke and strange shapes in the mist, although they were careful not to go as far as they had the first time.

Lusa was awake more often now, but Toklo felt as though something were missing. She didn't tease him the way she had before, and he kept finding her staring into space with a tired, thoughtful look.

Kallik had noticed, too. "I'm worried about Lusa," she said as they picked their way back to the cave one evening.

Two rabbits were dangling from Toklo's jaws; the bears had had a lucky hunt. "Why?" Toklo mumbled around the prey.

"She's just not the same. I'm afraid the firebeast hurt her more badly than we can tell. It's like something is still hurting her."

"Maybe it's just her leg," Toklo put down the rabbits to say. "I'm sure she'll be fine."

He picked up the rabbits and followed Kallik into the cave and padded to the back, where Lusa was resting on a pile of leaves. He dropped one of the rabbits at her paws.

"Thanks, Toklo," Lusa said quietly. She didn't lift her head off the floor or reach for the rabbit. Toklo glanced around at Ujurak, who was scraping herbs into piles nearby, and put down the other rabbit.

"How's your leg?" Toklo asked Lusa.

"All right," Lusa said. "I mean . . . it still hurts." She shifted on the leaves and peeked back at the wound. Toklo hated seeing the sharp cut like a lightning strike through her fur.

Ujurak shook his head. "I can't find anything wrong with it. It should be feeling better."

"You need to exercise it," Toklo said. "Come on; I'll exercise with you."

"Oh, dear," Lusa said, wrinkling her snout at him. "That sounds like a bunch of fun."

Toklo was encouraged by even this faint glimmer of her old sense of humor. "Here we go!" he said. "Stretch your front toes!" He slid his front paws far out in front of him and wiggled his claws.

"Hmm," said Lusa, but she heaved herself up to a sitting position and did the same thing.

"All right, now your back toes," Toklo said, flexing his hind paws.

Lusa copied him and winced. Toklo felt a stab of guilt,

but he was sure she needed to get her leg moving again. It was the only way to heal it.

"Now lie down and kick your paws like you're swimming," he said.

Lusa looked at him as if feathers had just sprouted from his nose. "Without any water?"

"Yes," Toklo said. "Like this." He lay down on his belly and began paddling in the air.

When he looked up, he caught Kallik and Ujurak exchanging amused glances. "Go ahead and laugh," he grumbled. "But it might help! Go on, Lusa."

Reluctantly, Lusa lay down and imitated his movements. "Ow," she grunted between clenched teeth. "That hurts."

"It won't if you keep doing it," Toklo said encouragingly.

"I'm tired," Lusa complained.

"Okay, when did you two switch brains?" Kallik asked.

That made Lusa chuff with laughter a little bit, and Toklo decided that was enough for the day.

But he tried again the next day and the next. He couldn't understand why sweet, enthusiastic Lusa was resisting so hard. He nudged her to her paws and helped her take a few pawsteps, leaning against him. They took a few more each night before Lusa had to lie down again. He was sure she was getting stronger. But she wasn't getting happier, and that was what worried him the most.

Several days later, shortly after sunrise, Ujurak padded back from the front of the cave and sniffed Lusa from ears to tail. Toklo watched him anxiously.

"Is she all right?" he asked. Lusa looked up at Ujurak with bright eyes.

"Yes," Ujurak said. "I think it's healed. You should be okay to travel, Lusa."

"No!" she said with such force that Toklo blinked in surprise. "It's not healed, Ujurak; really it's not. I think . . . I think you all should go on without me." She looked down at her claws.

"No way!" Toklo said.

"We're not going anywhere without you," Kallik said, sitting up from her sleeping spot and shaking off the moss that clung to her fur.

"You're one of us, Lusa," Ujurak said. "If you don't think you're ready, we'll wait some more."

Lusa scuffed her front paws on the cave floor and didn't say anything.

That night, Toklo woke up in pitch-darkness. He sat up, pawing at his face and wondering what had woken him. A cool breeze drifted in through the cave opening; the rain had slowed to a delicate drizzle. He glanced around, and a shock ran through his fur when he realized that Lusa's pile of leaves was empty. Lusa was gone!

He jumped to his paws and hurried outside, hoping she hadn't fallen into the gully. He snuffled at the ground outside the cave and picked up her scent, heading back down the mountain. Where could she be going?

Padding soundlessly across the rocks, he followed her scent trail along the stream for a few bearlengths, but then it disappeared. Toklo glanced around. A few stars twinkled through the clouds above him. Tiny water droplets clung to his fur and chilled his nose.

A few steps from the stream was a large bush with wide green leaves. Toklo peered at it and realized there was a small shape huddled under the shelter of the leaves.

"Lusa?" he whispered, creeping closer.

She jumped, and he saw the gleam of her bright eyes as she peered out at him. "Oh, no," she said, and her voice broke. "Oh, Toklo. I can't even run away properly."

"Run away!" Toklo stared at her in disbelief. "Why would you do that?" He crawled under the bush and pressed himself close to her. He felt the warmth of her tiny shape leaning against his fur and realized that she was trembling with fear. Lusa turned her head and buried her nose in his thick neck fur. Toklo touched her paw with his, awkwardly trying to comfort her.

"Lusa, what's wrong?"

"I can't do it," Lusa said. "I can't save the wild."

Toklo tipped his head to one side. "Save the wild?"

"I had this dream before I woke up, after the firebeast crushed me," Lusa said. Words spilled out of her as if she was relieved to finally be telling someone the truth. "I saw my mother, Toklo—I saw Ashia. And she told me that I have to save the wild. Me!"

"It was just a dream," Toklo said.

Lusa shook her head. "No, Ujurak said it wasn't. He said it's true. But he won't tell me what it means! I'm not sure he even knows. Toklo, I'm scared. I—I'm sorry—the truth is, my leg is better. I'm sure I could keep going. But I don't know what I'm supposed to do, and Kallik told me about the bad spirits and everything that happened to you while you were hunting, and all about the burning rocks, and what am I supposed to do about any of that? And what if we're not supposed to keep going through the mountains—Qopuk said it was dangerous! I'm afraid we're making all the wrong choices, and I'm afraid I'll fail, whatever I decide to do, and mostly I'm afraid something will happen to you . . . all of you, I mean—"

Toklo touched her snout with his. "Listen, you know I don't believe in these stories about evil spirits. But if there were bad spirits trying to hurt me and Kallik, they didn't succeed, did they? The good spirits helped us back to the cave. If you believe in the bad ones, you have to believe in those, too. Right?"

The branches pressed closely around them. Toklo wondered if black bears believed that there were spirits in the bushes as well. Could Lusa hear voices in the whisper of the rain on the leaves?

"I'm just one cub," Lusa said softly. "A useless little black bear cub. I can't save the wild."

"You're not useless," Toklo said. "You came all the way into the wild to find me, even though you'd never been outside the Bear Bowl before and you had no idea where you were going. And you're not alone. We're all on this journey with you—if you need to save the wild, or whatever, we'll be there to help you. Isn't that better than running away and trying to do it on your own?"

Lusa rested her head on his paws. "I . . . I guess you're right."

"Come back, Lusa," Toklo said. "Come with us."

"Okay." She wriggled closer to him for a moment, and the warm scent of her, smelling like honey even though they hadn't seen any in moons, filled his nose. "Thank you, Toklo. I'm not sure I could have left you anyway. I was lying here wondering if I really wanted to go. I'm so glad you came to get me."

They climbed out from under the bush and padded back through the rain the way they'd come. Ujurak and Kallik were standing in the mouth of the cave, wide awake, peering anxiously into the darkness and rain.

"We woke up and you were gone!" Kallik exclaimed, stepping aside to let them hurry into the dry cave.

"Sorry," Lusa said. "That was my fault. I-I woke up feeling restless and decided to go for a walk to see if my leg was okay." She glanced at Toklo, blinking nervously. He gave his head a tiny shake, letting her know that he wasn't about to tell them what really happened. "Toklo came looking for me, that's all. But guess what? My leg does feel stronger." She turned to Ujurak. "Thanks to you, Ujurak. I think you're right. I'm ready to move on."

Ujurak's eyes sparkled. "Then we'll leave in the morning," he said, poking his nose outside the cave and blinking as raindrops splashed in his eyes.

Toklo wasn't sure how to feel as he settled back down to sleep on the sandy floor with Lusa curled up beside him. He was very, very relieved that Lusa hadn't left them. But it worried him that she was talking about dreams. She was sounding more and more like Ujurak every day. And *one* Ujurak was enough for any journey. More than enough. It was the smoke, he thought, putting thoughts into their minds. The sooner they were out of these mountains, the better for everyone.

He slept badly that night. He could tell that Kallik was also having bad dreams, because whenever he woke up her claws were flexing and she was growling in her sleep. Once when he jerked awake, he saw Ujurak sitting silently at the mouth of the cave, staring out at the smoke-clouds covering the moon.

The mountains seemed to loom higher at night. He thought about the journey ahead, and dread prickled his fur. He shook his head, then rolled onto his side, facing the back of the cave. He must have smoke in his brain, too.

Giant flat-faces eating bears, he thought. *It's just a stupid story.*

CHAPTER SEVENTEEN

Toklo

When Toklo woke up the next morning, he couldn't feel Lusa curled beside him. Cold with worry, he sat up and glanced around the cave. Had she run away again?

Then he heard her voice outside the cave, chattering to Kallik down by the stream. Ujurak was just waking up, too. He stretched and nodded to Toklo as they padded outside.

The rain had stopped, and glints of sunshine were peeking through the heavy clouds. For the first time since they'd come to Smoke Mountain, the breeze smelled fresh. It ruffled their fur, and Toklo could detect only a faint scent of smoke in the air. *A good sign,* he thought wryly, glancing at Lusa. She was wading in the stream with Kallik, pouncing on the tiny flickers of fish that shot past their paws.

Toklo looked sideways at Ujurak. "When you said that we'd leave this morning, did you know the rain was going to stop?" he asked.

Ujurak shrugged. "Maybe." He headed off, trotting along the stream.

Toklo huffed.

"Are you ready?" Kallik asked Lusa, splashing in a circle around her. "Are you sure your leg will be all right?"

"Oh, my goodness," Lusa huffed. "I'm just a big pile of wet, useless fur, aren't I?"

"No, you're not," Kallik said, bumping Lusa's shoulder with her nose. "You're our ray of sunshine. See, you came outside, and the sun just had to come back out." She looked up at Toklo, and he dipped his head in agreement.

"Hmm—a heavy, dopey, limping ray of sunshine," Lusa said with a sigh.

"You *are* surprisingly heavy," Toklo teased. "I think you must've been sneaking blueberries when we weren't looking."

"Hey!" Lusa yelped, batting a spray of water at him. "I wish!"

"Come on, let's catch up to Ujurak," Toklo said, his spirits feeling lighter than he'd expected after the long, fretful night.

They climbed all morning, stopping often so that Lusa could rest. The days of rain had damped down the smoke, so the air smelled clearer than it had in a while. For a long time they stayed by the stream, but when it wandered off between some tall cliffs, Ujurak insisted on leaving it. They needed to keep going straight ahead; he was sure of it. They scrambled away up some sharp rocks, beneath trees that were twisted by the wind. Toklo kept a sharp eye out for prey, but the only thing he caught was a mouse, which was barely a mouthful for Lusa.

When the sun was high, they stopped in the shade of an enormous boulder and lay down to rest. They had climbed to a point where they could see a wide view of the ridge stretching ahead of them. To Toklo's surprise, he could see swaths of tall green trees and swaying grasses in the valley meadows. Not all of Smoke Mountain was as dark and rocky as Qopuk had described.

He sat down beside Lusa and noticed she was breathing heavily. "You're sure you're okay?" he murmured.

"I am," Lusa said, resting her head on her paws. "Truly."

Toklo wasn't convinced. "Can we stop to hunt?" he called up to Ujurak. The smaller brown bear was pacing along the edge of the boulder, staring out at the mountains. He looked down at Toklo with a startled expression, as if he'd forgotten about eating. *He probably did just that,* Toklo thought.

"Oh . . . sure," Ujurak said. "I was just trying to remember where the Pathway Star is. Qopuk said to follow it beyond the mountain." He lapsed into silence again, gazing at the sky.

Toklo shrugged, deciding to leave Ujurak to it. He sniffed the air for prey. The scent of smoke was coming back now that the rains had passed.

"Toklo!" Kallik called from behind the boulder. "What's this over here?"

He traipsed over the rattling pebbles to the white bear, who was sniffing along a trail. Something had come through here, something big enough to leave prints and flattened grass behind it, and Toklo could tell that it had gone up the steep, rocky slope to their left.

"Is it prey?" Kallik asked, her ears pricked. "I don't recognize the smell."

Toklo shook his head. "That's the scent of lynx," he told her. "They're too big for us to eat, and they've probably eaten what little prey there is around here."

Pebbles crunched underpaw as Ujurak trotted over to join them. He lowered his head and sniffed along the trail.

"We'll hunt somewhere else," Toklo said. He glanced at Ujurak and saw two odd tufts of black fur fluttering at the top of his ears. "Ujurak," he said, "there's something wrong with your ears."

Then he realized that Ujurak's ears were also getting longer and pointier. His face was getting flatter, and his eyes were turning yellow and catlike.

Toklo sighed. "Again?" he said.

"*Mrrrrrowrt*," Ujurak answered. He picked up one furry paw and studied it with interest as the rest of him changed into a large gray wildcat.

"What is that?" Kallik asked curiously, looking Ujurak up and down.

"It's a lynx," Toklo said. "I mean he—he's a lynx."

Ujurak blinked and crouched low, glaring at the bears as if he didn't recognize them. Then he spun around and disappeared up the slope into the rocks, sprinting on silent paws.

"Well, that's useful," Toklo grumbled, stamping his feet. "What is he *doing*?"

"Should we wait for him?" Kallik asked.

"No, let's keep looking for food," Toklo said, heading back

around the boulder to Lusa. "Ujurak can follow our scent trail—it's not like there's much else to smell around here."

"Except smoke," Kallik said, coughing as a breeze brought the acrid smell up from the rocks behind them.

"Lusa? Are you ready to go on?"

The black bear got to her paws and stretched. "I've been doing my exercises," she said. "See?" She wiggled her toes at him, and he chuffed with amusement.

"I think our best chance is to head down into a valley," Toklo said. "Where there's grass and trees, there's more likely to be prey."

"There are trees down there," Lusa said, nodding at the slope below them. Toklo could see a small stand of dark pine trees huddled close together near the center of a yellow meadow.

"And it doesn't smell like smoke in that direction," Kallik pointed out.

"Maybe that's because the fire is inside the rocks," Toklo said, trying to puzzle it out. "So there's less smoke in the grassy parts of the mountain."

Lusa shivered. "Rocks burning under the ground. I guess I'd rather have that than a giant flat-face setting bears on fire, but it still seems spooky and wrong."

The smoke was definitely getting stronger from the rocky slope behind them, as the mysterious fires came back to life after the rains.

"Come on," Toklo said, jerking his head at the clear meadow ahead. He started forward down the hill, bracing himself so he didn't slip on the loose rocks underpaw. Overhead, once they left the smoke and the boulders on the ridge, the sky was a startling bright blue. Toklo had almost forgotten the sky could be so blue, after so many days of rain and smoke.

A rocky streambed wound toward the trees, and after all the rain it was filled nearly to overflowing with a gurgling rush of water. Toklo studied the bubbles as they followed it, looking for signs of fish. His stomach was rumbling painfully. Lusa padded in front of him when he paused to pounce in the river, but he caught nothing but shadows and splashed back out, angrily shaking his pelt dry.

Suddenly Lusa came to an abrupt halt. She reared up on her hind legs, her ears and nose twitching. "I smell flat-face food," she said.

"Flat-faces!" Kallik exclaimed. "Here?"

"Why would they bring their food all the way out here?" Toklo asked.

"Some flat-faces like to eat and sleep in the woods," Lusa said. "I've seen them putting up little dens with sticks. Then they build fires, burn their food, eat it, fall asleep in these fluffy sacks inside the dens, and the next day they take everything and leave again." She shook her head. "I have no idea why. Flat-faces are weird."

"Making a fire on purpose," Kallik said with a shudder. "I'll never understand no-claws."

The three bears stood beside the stream for a moment, letting the strange smell of burning food waft across their noses. Toklo could tell that it was coming from the stand of trees—exactly where they'd been going to search for prey.

"We have to eat," Kallik pointed out.

"Let's get closer and have a look," Toklo agreed. He dropped low to the ground and crept forward, trying to move as if he were stalking prey. The she-bears followed close behind him. He slipped along the bank of the stream until he was in the shade of the trees and then crawled up through the bushes toward the sound of flat-face voices.

There were three flat-faces gathered around a tiny fire in a clearing, clattering pots and tearing open packages that smelled like food. Behind them were two of the dens, one bright blue and one bright red. They looked flimsy, like large leaves stretched over a couple of sticks. Toklo thought they seemed as if they would blow away in a strong gust of wind.

"Head for the dens," Lusa whispered. "They're the easiest place to find food. If we're quiet, the flat-faces won't even notice us. They always miss things that are right under their noses."

"Those are *very* small noses." Kallik sniffed.

"The walls of the den are really thin," Lusa added, "like the skins they put their garbage in, so you can slice right through the back and stick your head in."

"How do you know all this?" Toklo asked suspiciously. If it was something that happened in the woods, he thought he ought to be the expert on it, not Lusa.

"I had to steal from flat-faces while I was looking for you," Lusa said. "I didn't know how to hunt . . . and then I found some flat-faces like this in the woods."

"So you've done this how many times?" Toklo demanded.

"Um . . . just once," Lusa admitted. "But it'll work! Trust me!"

"You're not going," Toklo said. "You're not strong enough to run away if you need to. I'll go see what I can find." As much as he didn't like the idea of stealing flat-face food, he would rather do it himself than risk Lusa's fur.

"Are you sure?" Lusa said. "Can you be really quiet?"

Toklo snorted at her.

"I don't see any firesticks," Kallik said, peeking out at the clearing. "If the flat-faces see you, just run really fast."

"Great plan," Toklo grumbled. "All right, stay here. *Don't move.*"

He set off through the trees, padding lightly around the clearing with his nose to the ground. He glanced back and saw the other two watching as he crept up to the back of the dens. The skin of the blue den flapped and billowed a little bit in front of him. With a long, sharp claw, he sliced through the back of it. Lusa was right; it peeled open easily.

Toklo poked his head through the gash. The den was very small and confined, with that odd blue skin on all sides. It made the light inside the den blue as well. He saw two long green things that were probably the fluffy sacks Lusa had been talking about, which the flat-faces used for sleeping. A little red-and-white box sat in between them.

Toklo shoved and wriggled, making the hole wider until he could climb inside the den. He trotted over to the box. After a moment of sniffing, he realized that the top could lift up.

He slid his claws into the cracks in the box and the top of it popped right off.

He paused to listen. Outside, the flat-faces were making their high-pitched yabbering noises around the fire. They had no idea that a brown bear cub was rooting through their stuff right behind them.

Inside the box were some silver-and-blue cans the same shape as the ones behind flat-face dens, but much smaller. Toklo scrabbled at them with his claws, but they were too difficult to pick up and felt cold and hard under his teeth. This wasn't food.

Disappointed, he crawled out of the hole again and crept over to the red den. When he ripped open the back of this one, there was a small *zzzzzt!* sound, and Toklo froze. The noise from the flat-faces didn't change. After a moment, Toklo wriggled into the second den.

This looked more promising. The den was full of bags and piles of stuff. It had only one of the green sacks in it. Toklo nosed through the bags, following the smell of food. He stepped onto the green sack and stood up on his hind legs to reach a delicious-smelling bag on top of a pile of boxes.

Suddenly the sack slipped out from under his back paws. Toklo lunged to the side, trying to grab something to stay upright, and all the boxes and bags collapsed on him with an enormous crash.

Outside he heard the flat-faces yelling with alarm. As he struggled to his paws again, one of them ran over and yanked open the front of the red den. Toklo poked his shaggy head out of the opening and blinked at the flat-face. The flat-face blinked at him.

Toklo braced himself. It was time to fight.

CHAPTER EIGHTEEN

Lusa

"*Yaaaaaaaaaaaaaaaaaaaaaaaaaaaaaaah!*" *the flat-face* screamed. It spun around and pelted back across the clearing to the others, who were also screaming and running in circles.

Toklo rolled out of the den and flailed his paws in the air. A long green sack was wrapped around one leg, and a shiny silver bowl was stuck on one front paw. He jumped and danced and wriggled, trying to shake them off.

"*Yaaaaaaaaaaaaaah!*" the flat-faces screamed again, and all four of them ran off into the forest. Lusa could hear them crashing and thumping through the trees in the direction of the BlackPath.

"Nice work, Toklo," Kallik barked.

"You looked terrifying!" Lusa squeaked, bounding over to untangle Toklo from the flat-face things.

Toklo shook a strip of feathery white stuff from his shoulder. "We'd better leave before they come back with firesticks and more flat-faces," he said.

"Did you see that?" Kallik said. "They were afraid of you!"

"I think it was your ferocious, bewildered expression," Lusa teased. Her heart was still racing in her chest.

"Let's get what we came for," Toklo growled, pawing through the stuff the flat-faces had dropped near the fire. Lusa nosed her way into the red den and found some flat bars that smelled delicious. They had colorful skins, but once she chewed those off, there was sweet brown stuff inside, sweeter than any fruit she'd ever tasted.

Back by the fire, Toklo and Kallik had found a packet of thin slabs of meat. Lusa joined them as they ripped it apart and shared the meat between them.

"We should save some for Ujurak," she said.

Kallik pawed a few strips of meat aside. "I'll carry these for him," she said.

"All right, let's go," Toklo said after they'd wolfed down what they could find. "Quick, before they come back."

The cubs ran through the trees, putting as much distance between them and the flat-faces as they could before they stopped to rest. The meat dangled from Kallik's mouth, which she held high in the air to keep the strips off the dirt. Toklo led the way out of the pine trees and across the meadow. He deliberately crossed a few streams, wading along in the water to hide their scent.

Lusa knew it was smart to hide their scent from the flat-faces, but she worried about Ujurak. Would he still be able to find them? But Toklo's face was set and determined, so she didn't say anything. They climbed onto another rocky slope leading up the side of a mountain. Lusa's paws hurt as she struggled across the sharp rocks, and her leg felt as if a giant bear were raking her with his claws, but she didn't want to slow the others down.

Dark clouds were rolling in over the blue sky. A chilly, damp wind swept through their fur as they traipsed across a pebbly slope, then into a dense patch of trees. On the other side of the trees, Kallik lifted her head and tilted it to the side, listening. Her black nose twitched. "Do you hear that?" she asked, putting down the meat for a moment. "I hear rumbling."

Toklo pricked up his ears. "I hear it, too," he said.

Lusa stared up at the ridge ahead of them. It sounded like a giant bear growling in the distance, or a giant flat-face. She hoped it was neither, as they crept forward and poked their noses over the boulders.

They were high on the side of the mountain, overlooking a vast pine forest. Winding through the forest was a Black-Path. Crawling along it were long silver firebeasts, roaring and skulking in a row, belching black fumes into the air. Beside the BlackPath, large yellow firebeasts like the ones they'd seen at the Big River were digging up earth from another giant trench. They rumbled and roared as their huge metal claws sliced into the ground. The same smell of the black, sticky liquid hung in the air, and Lusa could see another silver snake at the bottom of the trench.

Toklo paced along the ridge, glowering down at the firebeasts on the BlackPath. Several of them were even larger than the ones they'd seen by the trench and dragged huge things behind them—sometimes entire trees. Lusa could see flat-faces inside, hunched over near the front of the firebeasts.

She jumped when she heard branches cracking nearby. An odd-looking animal was pacing up the slope toward them, and it took her a moment to realize it was Ujurak. His fur was already shifting from gray to brown, and he shook himself as he slowly transformed back into a bear.

"Where did you go?" Kallik asked eagerly, after bounding up to Ujurak and dropping the meat at his paws.

Ujurak didn't answer. He ate the meat, then looked down at the BlackPath. "It was quiet and peaceful here not long ago," he murmured. "Then the flat-faces came with their firebeasts and started tearing up the dirt. They keep taking what they want from the earth—the black stuff, and the trees, and anything else they think they need."

"Just our luck," Toklo said.

"The lynxes are really worried," Ujurak went on. "There are so few of them left." His eyes clouded with pain.

Lusa wished she could say something to make him feel better.

After a long pause, Ujurak shook himself and spoke again. "Let's rest here until moonhigh," he suggested. "There's a caribou trail that crosses the BlackPath at its highest point. If we can find that, it might be an easy, direct route through the mountains."

"You figured that out as a lynx?" Kallik asked. "That's amazing."

"I can just . . . sense what they know," Ujurak said. "I don't know why."

They all curled up in the pine needles. Lusa saw Toklo watching her.

"Aren't you going to climb the tree to sleep?" he asked.

"Oh, no, I'm all right down here," she said. She didn't want to put the strain on her injury, and she could tell Toklo guessed that.

"Okay, sleep well," he said, touching his nose to her snout. He paced a short distance away, hunched his shoulders, and sat staring out at the forest, keeping guard while the others slept.

Lusa woke up when darkness had fallen, or at least, the dusky twilight that passed for darkness during leaftime. The moon was a misty glimmer high above, and the rumbling of the firebeasts below had stopped. Ujurak was pacing in circles, and Toklo was snoozing next to Kallik.

"I think the BlackPath is safer now," Ujurak said when he saw Lusa sit up and stretch. He nodded down the mountain. "We should follow it while we can."

Lusa nudged Kallik and Toklo awake, and they all trudged sleepily downhill through the trees until they came to the BlackPath. Up close the damage to the earth around it was even clearer. Lusa was used to hard black stone paths running for skylengths straight through forests and plains and over mountains and even over water. But next to this BlackPath was a muddy, gaping hole torn open by the yellow firebeasts. Uprooted trees and bushes lay beside it in broken heaps.

The four cubs stopped to peer down into the trench. Lusa's

heart pounded when she saw a firebeast that looked like the one that had hurt her. But this one was silent and unmoving, and she turned away quickly before it woke up and saw her.

The BlackPath was still and eerie in the half-light, with only distant rumbles to indicate that faraway firebeasts were still awake somewhere. Ujurak took the lead, padding along the side of the BlackPath as it headed uphill.

They climbed higher and higher, passing several more sleeping firebeasts, all of them huge. Lusa peered down at the trench and thought it looked like her leg injury, only much bigger. She gazed at the fallen trees and hoped the tree spirits had found a new home in time. Then she hurried forward to Ujurak. He was looking in the trench, too, as he padded along.

"Do you know why the flat-faces are doing this, Ujurak?" she asked him.

"No," he said. He lifted his snout, gazing up at the peaks above them. The bears were nearly at the highest point of the path. "I think the caribou trail is somewhere up there."

Gratefully, Lusa followed him away from the trench. Kallik trotted behind her, and Lusa could hear Toklo's paws crunching over scrubby grass as he brought up the rear. They scrambled up a muddy slope studded with big rocks, slippery pebbles, and tough, scraggly bushes. Above the BlackPath was a flat outcropping of rock. Ujurak heaved himself onto it, and the other three clambered up to join him.

Lusa turned to look back. They were high up, looking down over a white layer of fog. Here and there she could see the tips of pine trees poking out of it, and all around were dark mountain peaks.

But the best part was that, up this high, they could see the stars.

Lusa sat down with a happy sigh a bearlength away from the BlackPath, looking up at the twinkling lights above her.

"Isn't it beautiful?" Kallik said to Lusa, following her gaze to the sky. "Look, there's the Pathway Star."

"We call it the Bear Watcher," Lusa said. "Black bears, I mean. At least, my family did. I think we all do."

"I like thinking about the ice spirits all together up there," Kallik said.

"Me too," Lusa said, leaning into her friend's fur. "Mother and Stella always said that all those stars were animals that keep Arcturus—that's the Bear Watcher—company."

"That's not what I see," Toklo said.

"What do you see, Toklo?" Lusa asked.

"I see a bear who's all alone," he replied. "He did something bad, so he's being punished. He's alone in the coldest, loneliest part of the sky, and the other animals dance around mocking him."

Lusa remembered Toklo's mother on the other side of the Fence in the Bear Bowl. Oka had told her the same story of a sad and lonely bear in the sky. Poor Toklo. Even the sky made him feel alone and frightened.

"He's a brave bear, though," she told him. "He stays up there leading the way for us. I bet some of the animals like him more than he knows."

Toklo dropped his gaze to look at his paws. "Well, it's just a stupid story," he said, scratching at the mud.

"There it is!" Ujurak yelped. He jumped to his paws and leaned forward. "I see the caribou trail. Come on!"

Lusa slid off the wide rock and followed Ujurak. Now she could pick up the strong, musky scent of caribou. It wasn't the smell of prey that had recently gone by; instead, it smelled like it had been drummed into the ground by many hooves over a long, long time.

They followed the trail down into the smoky pine forest, leaving the Black Path behind them. Stars glittered beyond the canopy of thick needles overhead. Lusa had her ears pricked, listening for the whisper of spirits, when they came to a bend in the trail. *What was that?* She stopped with a gasp.

"Can you see that?" she hissed.

The other bears stopped and stared into the dimness ahead of them.

A short way ahead, not far from the caribou trail, was a hulking shape, bigger than a full-grown brown bear. It sat there, glinting ominously in the moonlight, and didn't move. Lusa thought she caught a flash of eyes staring at them, but although they stood frozen for several long moments, it stayed perfectly still.

Toklo took in a long breath. "I think it's dead," he whispered.

"Or asleep," Kallik said.

"Or waiting for us," Lusa whimpered.

They fell silent again, staring at it.

"We can't stay here forever," Ujurak pointed out.

"I'm going to see what it is," Toklo decided. "Stay here." He strode forward.

"Toklo!" Lusa cried. He stopped and looked back over his shoulder at her. "Um . . . be careful."

The brown bear nodded and kept going. His pawsteps became slower and slower as he approached the dark shape. Lusa felt as if she were about to burst. All of her fur was tingling with fear. What if it sprang on Toklo and killed him?

Toklo slid up to the shape and sniffed it. After another long moment, he touched it lightly with his nose.

Nothing happened.

"Okay, come on," he called in a loud whisper.

Lusa's heart thudded in her chest as she padded up to him. As she got closer, the shape became clearer.

"Oh," she said. "It's a firebeast!"

"How did a firebeast get all the way out here in the woods?" Kallik asked.

It was a firebeast, but it didn't look like the roaring ones they'd seen earlier that day. This one was smaller and had lots of holes in it, and its large black paws were flat and saggy. Lusa paced around it carefully and saw that its eyes looked broken, like someone had poked them out. Strange sharp shards were left where the eyes had been.

"Is it . . . is it sleeping, like the ones we saw before?" she asked Toklo.

"I think it's dead," he said.

Kallik crept closer, smelling the air, and then poked her

head into one of the holes.

"Oh, Kallik, don't!" Lusa yelped.

"It's all right," Kallik said. "Toklo's right. I think it's been dead for a while. It doesn't smell like it's moved lately."

"But . . . how can you be sure, with a firebeast?" Lusa said. "I've never seen a dead one before."

"Everything dies," Ujurak said. He looked up at the sky. "Even firebeasts. Even flat-faces."

"Stop it; you're scaring Lusa," Toklo said gruffly. He was right, but Lusa could see the fur prickling along Toklo's spine, and she knew she wasn't the only one who was scared.

"I wonder how long it's been here," Kallik said. "I wonder if it left cubs behind when it died." She looked up at the sky, too, and Lusa guessed that she was searching for comfort from the ice spirits.

"Do firebeasts have cubs?" Toklo asked Ujurak.

Ujurak tipped his head to one side. "I don't know. They're not like us," he said. "Like I said before, I don't think they're really alive."

"Well, at least they can be dead," Lusa said, stepping back from the corpse of the firebeast. It gave her an awful sick feeling.

Toklo said, "Can we eat it?" He pawed at the firebeast, but his claws went *clang-clang* against the side, and he scowled as he lowered his foot.

"Let's not even try," Kallik said. "It's so old it probably has disgusting rotfood diseases."

"Come on," Ujurak said, turning back to the trail.

Lusa glanced back at the dead firebeast, alone and rotting among the trees. Had it died of old age and sickness, or had something killed it?

Something like the spirit of an angry giant flat-face? She shivered, remembering Qopuk's words about the Smoke Mountain.

Something is lying in wait there . . . something evil.

CHAPTER NINETEEN

Lusa

At sunrise they stopped to sleep for a while before continuing on. Even with the sun in the sky, Lusa didn't feel any warmer. It seemed to be getting colder with every pawstep. She was sure the smoke was getting thicker, too. Qopuk had said that meant the giant flat-face was building his fire, getting ready to kill and eat bears. As they climbed along a stony ridge, Lusa tried to see if the smoke was coming from one place in particular— the Bear Rock that Qopuk had mentioned. But it seemed to just rise from the ground, like mist.

Toward the end of that day, they came to a part of the forest where the trees grew thickly together, blocking most of the light from the sun. Toklo slowed down as he led the way through, giving the branches overhead an uneasy look. Lusa checked the trunks as they went by, but she didn't see any grizzly claw marks. It was strange that they hadn't seen any other bears . . . although from what they *had* seen—the lack of prey, the miserable weather, the smoke and the fire-beasts and the trench—she could believe that no bear would choose to live here for long.

A rumble of thunder shook the sky, and a storm opened up above them. The rain dripped down through the leaves, soaking their fur and dumping unexpected bursts of water on their heads as they sloshed through the mud. Lusa could see the gray sky through the trees, but the forest stayed dark as night. The branches scraped and rattled in the wind.

Up ahead, Toklo paused with one paw raised. In the fading gray twilight, Lusa saw him sniff the air and back up quickly.

"Flat-faces," he whispered. Raindrops rolled off his nose and he shook his head to clear his vision. "A flat-face den."

"Out here?" Kallik said disbelievingly. "But it's so far from . . . from any flat-face things! The nearest denning place is skylengths away. And I can't smell any BlackPaths."

"Well, it's here anyway," Toklo said, jerking his snout toward a small clearing up ahead. Lusa peered past him and saw the squat shape of the den, made of wood and hemmed in closely by the trees. Smoke was rising from a hole in the top.

"Let's get away from here," she said. "There's nothing for us." Toklo nodded and started to push his way into the trees, to skirt around the clearing.

"Wait," Ujurak said.

"Why?" Lusa cried. She wanted to bury her head in a pile of leaves, or climb to the top of the tallest tree in the forest and never come down. There was something wrong with this place; she just knew it. She wanted to get away from the den with every tuft of fur on her body.

Ujurak padded ahead through the trees.

"What's he doing now?" Toklo sighed.

"Well, we can't leave him to explore on his own," said Kallik. "Let's go." She set off behind the little brown bear.

"Come on, Lusa, it's all right," Toklo said, nudging her with his snout.

Lusa tried to ignore the voice in her head that was shrieking, *Run! Run as fast as you can!*

They caught up to Ujurak right outside the den. He was standing on his hind legs, peeking in through the window. Bright light spilled out of the den, and for a moment Lusa couldn't see anything inside but the blinding light.

Then she realized that there were four male flat-faces inside, sitting around a fire. They were laughing and talking in loud, boisterous voices. Two of them were holding the kind of bottles that Lusa had found in flat-face trash several times. They smelled awful and usually had a sticky liquid inside that made her head buzz when she licked it.

These flat-faces were not like the ones the bears had stolen from, in the blue and red dens. These flat-faces were bigger and noisier, and Lusa could see firesticks even from where she was standing. Several were propped around the den, leaning against the wall or hung above the fire. She let her gaze travel across the wooden floor, to the far side.

There was a head sticking out of the wall.

A *bear's* head.

For a moment she couldn't believe it was dead. She actually thought, *Why is that brown bear just standing there? Is the rest of it on the other side of the wall?*

And then she knew that it was dead. Its glazed eyes stared sightlessly into space. She knew that flat-faces had killed it—maybe even these flat-faces—and chopped off its head and then *hung that head on the wall.*

"Oh, bear spirits," Lusa whimpered.

"How . . . Why . . . " Kallik's voice trailed off. She pressed her nose to the window as if she were hoping the sight inside would change.

Toklo didn't say anything, but Lusa could see his claws flexing and his eyes narrowing.

Ujurak dropped to all paws and began to slink toward the front of the den.

"Ujurak!" she hissed. "Where are you going? Let's get out of here!"

He disappeared around the corner as if he hadn't heard her. Perhaps he hadn't. The wind and the rain were coming down hard, sweeping away their voices.

Toklo and Kallik were still peering in the window. Lusa hurried after Ujurak. Why would he want to know more about this place?

As she rounded the corner behind him, she saw him standing in front of the den with his teeth bared. She followed his gaze to the roofed area that jutted out from the front of the den.

Her heart seemed to freeze in her chest.

Hanging from the roof, blowing in the fierce stormy wind, were three empty, bloodstained bearskins.

CHAPTER TWENTY

Toklo

Even through the storm, Toklo heard Lusa's terrified shriek. He dashed toward the front of the den with Kallik right behind him.

Lusa was already racing away through the trees. He could see her tiny black paws pumping madly as she ran.

"What . . . ?" He gasped, turning to Ujurak.

His friend was staring at the den. Now Toklo saw the bearskins. Their heads were hanging loose, jaws open, eyes staring blankly straight at Toklo. Dead eyes. Their teeth snarled hopelessly at the sky. The wind caught one of the skins and flapped it so the paws seemed to reach toward Toklo. All three of them were brown bears.

Thumping noises came from inside the den, and suddenly the door flew open. The flat-faces pointed and yelled. Three of them were already holding firesticks. Toklo saw one of them raise his stick and point it at the bears.

Toklo started running, his paws thudding across the ground, slipping on the wet leaves. Bangs and shouts echoed behind him. He searched for Lusa's scent and followed it, tearing through the trees. He could hear crashing in the undergrowth that he hoped was Kallik and Ujurak.

His paws jerked and he shuddered as he imagined claws slicing into his fur, peeling away his skin. He skidded through a puddle and slammed hard into a tree, but he bounced off and kept running. One of his scratches was bleeding again, but he ignored it. He had to catch up to Lusa. That old white bear was right about this place: It was dangerous for bears.

Rain dripped in his eyes and turned the world blurry and dark. The trees seemed to shake their branches at him as he ran past. Suddenly the ground dropped out from under him and he lost his footing, tumbling head over paw down a slick, muddy bank. He braced himself for a bone-jarring impact at the end, but instead he landed in a river with an enormous splash.

He floundered to his paws and shook out his fur, which did very little good, considering that as much water was falling out of the sky as there was in the river below him.

Then he saw Lusa. She was crouching upstream from him, shivering with terror.

"Lusa!" he cried. He waded over to her and wrapped his front paws around her.

"Toklo," she whimpered. "Did you see them?" The river rushed by their noses, smelling faintly of smoke and death.

"Yes. But we knew flat-faces did terrible things," Toklo said. "It's just a shock to see it, that's all."

"But . . . they hunt bears!" Lusa cried. "They're looking for bears to kill, Toklo! And then they're stealing their skins! Why would they do that? We kill to eat, but we wouldn't keep our prey's heads around to look at!"

"That must be what Qopuk's stories are really about," Ujurak said, coming out of the woods with Kallik beside him. They slid down the bank and waded over to Lusa and Toklo.

"So there's no giant flat-face," Kallik said, wiping the rain off her snout. "No cooking fire. The smoke from the rocks must have started the legend. When bears went into the mountains and didn't come back, all their families would have seen was the smoke, and they knew how no-claws burn their food."

"So it's just real flat-faces," Lusa murmured. "With real firesticks, hunting bears." She buried her nose in Toklo's fur.

He nuzzled her, his heart still pounding. The truth frightened him far more than stories of spirits. His paws itched. They had to get away from here.

"Come on," he said, nudging Lusa up to the other side of the river. "Let's eat something and then keep going."

"I want to keep going now," Lusa insisted.

"You need to rest," Ujurak pointed out. "You're bleeding again."

"And so are you, Toklo," Kallik prompted.

He realized that it wasn't just rainwater trickling through his pelt; blood was seeping from a long scratch on his shoulder. He must have cut it while he was running from the flat-faces. "I'm fine," he said gruffly. "Lusa, over here."

She followed him to the other side of the river, which swirled around their bellies. Toklo splashed through the pebbly shallows to a tall bush, the leaves glittering with silver raindrops, and curled up in the damp shelter underneath. Lusa and the other bears squashed in beside him.

"Where's the trail?" Kallik asked Ujurak.

The rain dripped around them as they huddled together, staring gloomily back at the forest they'd run through. Toklo didn't want to go back to find the trail. He didn't think any of the others did, either.

"We'll just keep going," Ujurak said. He crawled farther under the bush and rubbed his back against the branches. "I'll figure it out."

Toklo ducked his head. "I'll hunt," he growled.

He bounded back into the river and splashed away upstream, ignoring Kallik when she called, "But shouldn't you rest, too?"

The rain rolling off his snout made it hard to concentrate on any scents, but Toklo focused his sharp eyes on the banks, knowing that his own smell would be hidden from any prey as well. Concentrating his mind on hunting relaxed him, distracting his thoughts from flat-faces with firesticks that killed bears.

Something moved in the mud on the bank to his right. He slowed down and crouched so his nose was just sticking out of the water. He hoped he looked like a log floating along . . . and that the prey would be too dumb to realize he was floating upriver. He slid quietly through the water, closer and closer.

And then, with a lightning-fast movement, he lunged out

of the water and sank his claws into the animal on the bank.

It flailed wildly with a furious hiss, and Toklo realized it was a snake. He slammed his paw into the back of the snake's head, pinning it to the ground, and then sunk his teeth into it, killing it instantly. The long, thick body lay in the mud. Toklo's belly rumbled, and part of him wanted to eat the whole thing right there by himself. But he knew he had to feed the others. He picked up the snake and trotted back down the river.

Snakes killed to eat, too—that was just life. If you were hungry, prey was prey. It made sense to kill something if you needed to eat it to survive. Did flat-faces eat bears? The thought had never occurred to him.

The other bears were still huddled together, trying to stay dry. He squeezed in next to them and they shared the snake in silence. No stars were visible through the thick covering of clouds, and the river thundered by below them. Toklo could see the water rising as it swelled with the rain.

Ujurak left the last scraps of the snake to the others and padded out to search for signs. Toklo watched the dim shape of his friend pace slowly up and down the river. The trees around them were not as dark or thick as those near the flat-face den. There was less cover, which meant more rain dripped through the leaves onto his cold nose. But there was also more room to run if they needed to.

It was pitch-dark as they set off. Slippery leaves squished and slid around under Toklo's paws. Ujurak was leading them uphill again. Toklo missed nice flat plains that didn't make his muscles ache so much.

After a while, Ujurak found a trail through the trees that looked like a large animal had wandered through several days earlier. The rain had washed away the scents, but Toklo guessed that it might have been a moose or a caribou. It wasn't as wide as the real caribou trail, but it made walking a little easier, since their paws didn't have to fight the undergrowth at every step. At one point, when he glanced up, Toklo thought he caught a glimpse of the Pathway Star glittering in the sky through a gap in the rain clouds.

He should have felt better. They were moving on. It couldn't be much farther to the other side of Smoke Mountain.

But as he traipsed through the woods, a wind rose up, tossing the leaves on the trees and tugging at his fur. He remembered the wind lifting the bearskins, their dead eyes, and the way their claws seemed to be reaching for him. He shivered and looked over his shoulder. Did the wind carry the faint scent of flat-faces?

No, he was imagining things.

There was nothing there.

He shook his head to clear the smoke from his mind.

CHAPTER TWENTY-ONE

Kallik

Kallik felt as if she were carrying a lump of ice in her stomach. Even several days after the night of the flat-face den, she could still see the bearskins splayed out in her mind. Her nose seemed clogged with the stench of death, making it hard to hunt. Whenever it wasn't raining, trails of smoke filled the air.

Her fur pricked and her sleep was full of nightmares. Now when her mother was dragged under the water, it wasn't by orcas; instead it was flat-faces with firesticks shooting her mother full of bloody holes.

Lusa was jumpier than usual, sometimes leaping right into trees when a twig snapped behind them. She was also quieter. Kallik tried to get her to tell more stories about the Bear Bowl, hoping that would cheer her up, but halfway through a story, Lusa would trail off and stare into the trees, her nose twitching.

Then there was Ujurak, who seemed less and less certain about the signs he found. Once, as they crossed a grassy meadow, he stopped and gazed at a boulder high above them.

The enormous rock, the size of a full-grown bear, was resting right at the edge of a cliff over their heads.

Toklo growled, "What is it?"

Ujurak whispered, "I'm not sure. But something is hanging over us. I feel that we're in danger."

"Well, let's stand around in the open until it lands on us, then," Toklo barked. He stomped away and the others followed.

Only Toklo acted as if he were unaffected by the horrifying sight of the bearskins, but Kallik noticed how quickly he was walking. It was as if he was trying to hurry them on as fast as he could without drawing attention to what he was doing.

She didn't mind traveling faster, though. She wanted to get away from Smoke Mountain. If she were on her own, she'd spend every day running as far as her paws could carry her. She might even have crossed all the way over by now. But she would never leave the others, and she knew Lusa couldn't go any faster on her wounded leg.

Then, as they left the trees and climbed higher into the mountains, their spirits started to lift. Toklo led them onto a craggy slope, treading carefully along narrow ledges and slippery outcroppings. A valley full of scrubby trees spread out below them. For the first time, they could see how far they had traveled from the BlackPath, and from the thick, dark forest with the flat-face den.

Kallik lifted her nose into the air. The scent of something cool and crisp and clear was drifting down from the peak above them.

"Snow!" she yelped.

Lusa stood on her hind legs and sniffed. "Wow! I think you're right." Up ahead, Ujurak and Toklo paused near a crack in the rocks and looked back at them.

"It smells like home," Kallik said, breathing in deeply. "Toklo! Can we go a little higher?" She imagined burying her paws in thick white drifts of snow. She wanted to roll and roll in it until her fur was clean and cold again. She wished she'd had one more chance to play in the snow with Taqqiq, like they used to. That was where they both belonged.

But Toklo was shaking his head. "I'm sorry, Kallik," he said. "Snow means no prey up here in these mountains. We need to stay where we can find food."

"Oh," Kallik said. She scraped a bit of moss out from between two rocks. She knew he was right, but it was strange to think of snow as a sign of hunger, when she saw it as bringing the world back to life. "All right."

The brown bears turned and kept walking. Lusa poked Kallik's side with her nose. "I wish we could go play in the snow," Lusa said. "It sounds like fun when you talk about it."

"It's not just that," Kallik said. "I feel safer when my fur blends into the landscape."

"I didn't think of that," Lusa said. "But if it makes you feel any better, you're so muddy that you blend in just fine here."

Kallik snorted. "Thanks. I feel much better."

They hurried to catch up to the others, who had stopped at an outcropping of craggy gray rocks.

"I'm going to scout ahead," Ujurak said. Feathers sprouted

through his fur, and his snout folded under, becoming hard and hooked. His furry ears melted back into his head, and talons appeared in place of his paws. In moments he was a falcon, and he flung himself into the air with a few swift wingbeats.

"Well, thanks for warning us this time," Toklo muttered. He sat down on a rock in the sun, and Lusa lay down beside him, closing her eyes. Kallik stayed in the shade under the rock, wishing she had a snowbank to roll in. She lifted her head to watch Ujurak circling far overhead. She couldn't believe he could see anything from that far away. She watched the Ujurak-falcon soaring over the territory in front of them, swooping in a long arc. Then he disappeared over the ridge.

Kallik wriggled around and peered down the mountain to the forest below, where they had just been. The trees were so small from here that it looked like she could squash them all under her paw.

Something moved in the shadows.

Kallik tensed. Had she imagined it? The woods were so far below . . . it could have been anything.

Then it moved again, and she realized that something was creeping out of the woods onto the rocky slope. It moved cautiously, stopping every few pawsteps. It was hard to tell what it was, as if it were deliberately hiding in the shadows of the rocks. Was it an animal? A flat-face? Something else?

Kallik looked up at the rock above her and realized that Lusa and Toklo were leaning over the edge, watching it, too.

The three bear cubs stared down as the moving shape crept along the bottom of the mountain. It reached the point where the cubs had left the trail to climb higher. There it stopped for a long moment.

And then . . . *it started to climb toward them.*

Toklo and Lusa slid down the rock and pressed in close to Kallik.

"What is it?" Lusa whispered.

Kallik wished she knew. The wind was blowing in the wrong direction, so there wasn't even a scent to offer a clue.

Toklo took a step backward, farther into the shadows. "I don't know," he said in a voice more full of fear than Kallik had ever heard from him.

Toklo glanced up at the sky, as if he wished Ujurak were back already.

"What's it doing?" Lusa whispered in an even smaller voice.

Kallik and Toklo exchanged glances. They didn't need to know what it was to recognize how it was acting.

Toklo answered her.

"It's hunting us."

CHAPTER TWENTY-TWO

Lusa

A *flutter of feathers behind them* nearly scared Lusa out of her fur. Ujurak was turning back into a bear. Lusa normally loved to watch him transform; she loved watching feathers turn to fur, limbs changing, a new animal appearing in his place. But now the ripples across his fur conjured up thoughts of bearskins blowing in the wind, and she had to look away.

"We have to go," Toklo said to Ujurak. "Right now."

Ujurak started trying to walk before his paws were all in place and stumbled, sending a few pebbles skittering down the slope. Lusa flinched, sure that the sound would guide the hunter straight to them.

"I know. I saw them," said Ujurak, his voice still high-pitched like the cry of a bird. "Four flat-faces with firesticks."

Four? For a moment, Lusa's legs gave way and she started to sink onto the stones.

"Let's go," Toklo said, bounding to his paws. "Come on, Lusa." He gave her a shove, and she lurched to her feet again.

"Up," Kallik insisted. "We should go up."

"But—" Toklo started.

"Listen, if it's cold for us, it'll be far worse for them without any fur. And we can climb faster than they can."

Toklo didn't argue. They hurried straight up the rocky slope, all of them wrapped in their own fearful thoughts. Lusa's legs weren't wobbling now. They were strong with terror, tingling as she pushed herself as hard as she could to keep up with Toklo. Surely if the cubs got far enough ahead, the flat-faces would give up and turn back?

Her paws scraped painfully as she hauled herself over boulders. Stones rattled down the slope behind them.

"Oh, no," she fretted. "That'll bring them right to us!"

"They already know where we are," Toklo pointed out. "We just have to outrun them."

The slope slanted up into a towering cliff wall, and Ujurak turned to lead them along a narrow ledge that ran around the peak. As Lusa edged along behind Kallik, trying not to look down, she heard a roaring sound up ahead. It was different from the roaring of the BlackPaths. For a moment she thought of the giant flat-face, but she shook those thoughts away. There were *real* dangers right behind them.

The cubs came around a corner of the ledge and saw a huge waterfall pouring down the mountain, sparkling and thundering. Their path ended abruptly in a blaze of white water. There was no way forward. They were trapped!

Don't panic, Lusa told herself. *No one else is panicking. There must be a way around it. We don't have to go back toward the flat-faces . . . no, there must be another way.*

Toklo led them closer until the spray from the falling water beaded their fur. He sniffed around the ledge and the slope above and below them. Lusa studied the waterfall. It wasn't a torrent shooting straight down from above; it ran down the cliffs on more of a slope, charging around boulders and splitting into smaller waterfalls here and there as it bounced over different rocky outcroppings.

"There's a kind of path down there," Toklo said, nodding over the side of the ledge. "If we scramble over the edge at this point, we can slide down to that trail and follow it to the bottom of the valley. Then we can cross the river down below, where the current is calmer."

"Or we could go straight up," Kallik argued. She pointed with her nose to the top of the waterfall, several bearlengths above them. "See those bushes and trees sticking out of the slope? If we could get ahold of them, we could push ourselves up until we reached the top, and then cross the river up there."

"That's if we don't get swept over the waterfall," said Ujurak.

"Climbing up might be easier," Toklo admitted.

"But going down might be faster," Kallik said. "I don't know. I want to do whatever those flat-faces can't do."

"Me, too," Toklo said.

"So maybe—" Ujurak started to say, but Lusa interrupted him.

"Let's go straight across," she said.

The other three bears stared at her. Lusa squeezed past

Toklo and stood on her hind legs, blinking in the spray from the waterfall.

"Look," she said. "If we climb up just one bearlength, using that bush above me, there's a spot up there where we could scramble across the boulders—they're sticking out of the water enough that we could get from one to the next without being swept away."

Toklo narrowed his eyes, nodding slowly. "I see what you're saying."

"I want to go first," Ujurak said. "It's my fault we're going this way; I should be the one to lead us across."

"No," Toklo said, blocking Ujurak's way with his large, shaggy shoulder. "That's stupid. We can't afford to lose you, especially now. You should change shape and fly across."

Ujurak pawed the rocks angrily. "I don't want to! It isn't fair to you. My shape-changing shouldn't be just an easy way to keep me safe while the rest of you risk your lives all the time. I'm a bear, just like you!"

"We know," Kallik said gently. "But if you get killed by a waterfall, what will the rest of us do? We'll never find the Place of Endless Ice without you."

"Please, Ujurak," Lusa begged. "We'd all turn into falcons and fly across if we could."

Toklo let out a tiny snort, as if he would never do such a thing, but he nodded when Ujurak looked at him. "Don't be salmon-brained," he said. "We're being hunted, remember? Just get out of here."

"And it was my idea," Lusa said quickly, "so *I'm* going across first." She was pleased when Toklo didn't argue with her.

"I'll give you a boost," he said.

"Okay." She stood near the slope of the mountain while Toklo crouched beside her. He braced his shoulders under her hindquarters and shoved her up toward the bush. She pushed off with her back paws and leaped, snagging her front paws in the branches. To her relief, the bush held firm. The thicket of interlocking branches gave her perfect clawholds to snag onto. She wriggled until she was safely perched on top of it, then looked back down at the others.

Ujurak's face was just disappearing into a falcon's feathers. He flapped up into the air, flew across the waterfall, turned in a circle, and then soared higher, leaving them behind.

"How does it look from up there, Lusa?" Toklo called.

"Easy," she said, studying the rocks sticking out of the waterfall. At this spot there were enough things to grip to climb all the way across—assuming her paws didn't slip and send her crashing down to her death. "Watch how I do it." She crawled as far along the bush as she could, testing each pawstep to make sure the branches would hold. From there it was only a few pawlengths to the first boulder, which stuck out of the waterfall like a bear snout. Lusa braced herself, wriggled her hindquarters, and launched herself out of the branches.

For a heart-stopping moment she was afraid she was going to miss and plunge into the torrent of water, but then her paws landed squarely on the flat top of the boulder. She gripped it fiercely, determined not to slip even a hairbreadth.

"Nice jump!" Kallik called. "Go, Lusa! That was terrific!"

Toklo didn't say anything; he just watched Lusa with a worried face.

From the boulder it was a close jump to a tree that rose straight out of the waterfall. Lusa wasn't nervous about this part. The tree must be strong to have withstood the force of the waterfall for so long. It could hold one little bear. The only thing she had to be careful about was leaping off the boulder she was on. The surface of the rock was slick and wet, and if she lost her footing as she pushed off, she might miss the tree and hurtle all the way to the rocks at the bottom.

Don't think about that, she told herself. *Don't think about those big rocks way down below. Don't think about how jagged they are. Definitely don't look down at them.*

She leaped through the air and landed in the tree, feeling the wet leaves trail across her fur in a way she found comforting. It was as if the tree spirits were saying, *It's all right; we've got you.* She wondered if there was a bear spirit living in this tree. If so, she hoped it didn't mind being soaked all the time.

The next part was a little trickier. There were two more boulders sticking out of the waterfall, but the first one was too small to fit on. She needed to balance on it while she made it across to the second one, which meant landing on both of them at the same time. She wasn't sure she could do that without falling.

But she would. She had to.

She wrapped her front paws around the tree branch closest to the far side and slowly lowered her back paws down until she was hanging from the tree. The branch dipped a little with her weight, and she felt the powerful current of the waterfall catch at her paws. Lusa swung herself back and forth to get closer to the first boulder. She let out a gasp when her claws scraped painfully against it. Now just a little closer—she stretched her back paws as far as she could—and when she felt the stone under her pads, she let go of the tree.

For a dizzying moment the water spun away below her and she thought she was falling the wrong way, but then her front paws hit the next boulder and she stopped with a bone-jarring thud, splayed across the two boulders with her front paws on one and her back paws on the other. She caught her breath for a moment, sucking in the water-soaked air, and then she shoved herself quickly onto the bigger boulder.

The slick rock rubbed against her claws, making her feel unsteady. But now there was only one jump to go, over to the dry ledge on the far side. Lusa closed her eyes and sent up a prayer to the bear spirits in the trees.

"Please help me," she whispered.

Then she crouched and leaped. Her back paws skidded on the wet stone and she flailed in the air, trying to make herself fly farther. If only she had wings like Ujurak! Her heart raced with terror.

Her front paws hit the ledge and then her chest whomped into the rocks, knocking the air out of her. She scrabbled with her back paws and dug in her claws and slowly shoved herself all the way onto the ledge. Then she pushed herself to her paws and turned back to Toklo and Kallik.

"See?" she called hoarsely. "Easy!" She doubled over in a fit of coughing.

Toklo came next. He was heavier, so the tree swayed more ominously and his paws were soaked through, but he was bigger, too, so he could reach from boulder to boulder more easily. Then Kallik followed them across. Her paws were made for walking on slippery ice, so she had no trouble with the wet boulders, although her large size also made it hard for her to navigate the smallest boulder.

But at last all three of them were standing on the far side of the waterfall, wet and exhausted, but triumphant.

"You did so well!" Lusa cheered as Kallik shook her fur dry. "I'd like to see a flat-face try that!"

"I wouldn't," Toklo growled. "Let's get going. Where's Ujurak?"

They all looked up at the sky and saw the Ujurak-falcon swooping down. He landed beside them and changed back into a bear, grumpily shaking off his feathers.

"I could have crossed with you," he insisted. "I saw the flat-faces—they're still well behind us."

"Well, we're all safe now," Toklo said. "Come on."

They followed the ledge away from the waterfall. After a few pawsteps, Lusa glanced back at the thundering spray. She couldn't see any flat-faces behind them, but it was hard to see anything through the cloud of water and mist. Would the good spirits in the mountains help them escape? Or would the bad spirits let them be hunted down like prey?

She wanted to believe that the flat-faces would give up. She hoped that the cubs' brave crossing of the waterfall would put them too far ahead for the flat-faces to ever catch up. But she remembered how the hunters had followed the bears' trail up the side of the mountain. She had a feeling they wouldn't give up so easily.

As the bears started to climb, the skies opened up, and it began to rain again.

CHAPTER TWENTY-THREE

Kallik

Rain poured down from the clouds all the rest of that day. The bears trudged through mud and sudden torrents of water that appeared like rivers rising out of nowhere. Their paws slipped on the wet rocks and their fur clung to their hungry bodies. Kallik could barely remember what it felt like *not* to be wet and scared. She worried about Lusa, who looked even smaller and more fragile with her fur drenched flat.

The cubs stopped to eat a hurried meal when Toklo caught a smelly muskrat, but even though she was so hungry, Kallik found it hard to swallow because her paws just wanted to run and run and keep running. She choked her portion down without tasting it, and they pressed on quickly.

She thought it was near sunset, although it was hard to tell through the rain, when they reached the highest peak. To her disappointment, there was no snow here, although she could see it on some of the peaks that surrounded them. It looked clean and white and crisp, and something inside her yearned for it, tugging her paws toward the icy freshness.... But unless she grew wings like Ujurak and flew, it was too far to reach. She was stuck here on this snowless, rocky mountain, with aching paws and flat-faces hunting her.

Lusa let out a whimper as she stared at the ridges and valleys that spread out in front of them. "I thought we were nearly through the mountains," she said. "It still looks so far."

"It's hard to tell from here," Ujurak said, but his voice was flat and toneless.

"Let's sleep for a while," Toklo suggested, his shoulders drooping wearily. "We won't be able to keep running unless we rest."

They had barely stopped moving since spotting the no-claw hunters that morning. Kallik collapsed onto her side and fell asleep right away.

She dreamed of no-claws with firesticks creeping closer and closer, their faces hidden by smoke and fog. Their paws crunched on the forest floor. Their smell scratched her nose, too strong and acrid and horrible, like a hundred firebeasts crawling over her tongue.

That smell—the smell of firebeasts. It was stronger than it should be, all the way out here in the mountains.

Kallik woke up with her nose twitching. A pale moon hung low in the sky, nearly hidden by thick clouds. Her friends slept soundly beside her, their fur rising and falling like ocean waves. Not even Toklo had been able to stay awake to keep watch.

Her fur prickled anxiously. She tried to figure out how much time had passed. There was a gray, cold feeling to the air, as if it were nearly morning.

And she could still smell the scent of firebeast.

Kallik twisted to look behind them.

Something was crawling along the slope of the mountain, far below them.

"Toklo," she said. The urgency in her voice brought him instantly awake. He scrambled to his paws, rubbing his face. Lusa and Ujurak shifted, slowly waking up.

"Look," Kallik said, nodding down at the small, creeping thing. She felt as if the ground were disappearing under her paws, like the ice suddenly melting underneath her. Terror flooded through her. "It's them. They're still following us." A low growl rumbled deep in Toklo's throat as he stared down the mountain.

"That's a firebeast!" Lusa gasped, jumping up. They were all wide awake now. "It's like the one we saw in the forest—the kind that can leave the BlackPath!"

"That must be how they caught up to us," Toklo muttered.

The firebeast looked tiny from their vantage point, no bigger than a fly. Kallik wished it were really that small; she'd squash it in a heartbeat. She thought she could see the flat-faces leaning out, pointing up at the peak where the bears stood.

"We ought to go," Ujurak said unnecessarily.

The sky was shifting from black to gray as they came down from the peak into a grassy valley surrounded by pine forest and snowy mountain peaks. The faint light of a silver moon still glimmered from behind the clouds, and the rain had finally ebbed away.

Kallik nearly crashed into Lusa when the little black bear stopped and stood up suddenly. Lusa twisted her head in each direction, pointing her big ears at the landscape on either side.

"I hear a firebeast!" she cried.

"That's impossible," Toklo said, spinning around. "It can't have scaled the peak so quickly."

"Could it have gone around the mountain?" Kallik asked. She tried to stand protectively in front of Lusa, but the little black bear was running in a tight circle, staring into the darkness.

"I hear it," Lusa repeated frantically, standing and clawing the air. "It's coming this way. It's angry. It's coming for us!" She twisted around again.

"I'm sure there's no—" Toklo began, but a distant roar interrupted him.

Then Kallik saw the firebeast rear above the shoulder of the mountain and plunge down into the valley. Smoke and clouds of dust rose from its paws as it ran, and its eyes glowed horribly. She felt a sudden chill over her whole body, like diving into the freezing sea. She had never seen a firebeast stray from the narrow BlackPaths before, and this one was alive and growling and *hunting her*.

"Run," Toklo said grimly.

Kallik sprang forward and began galloping through the grass. Toklo's paws thudded close beside her.

"If we lose one another," he said, panting, "meet at that tallest tree at the end of the valley."

In the distance, Kallik could see the tip of a pine tree waving above a low clump of trees at the head of the valley.

Behind her, she could hear the firebeast roaring closer and closer. Its growl rose and fell as it bounced over the rocks and tussocks of grass. How could they be so much faster than bears? She never saw them use their haunches or legs to shove themselves off. All their movement came from their strange rolling black paws.

She glanced back and saw two of the no-claws standing up with their heads sticking out of the top of the firebeast. They lifted long black sticks and pointed them at her.

Bang! Bang!

Something whizzed past Kallik's ear with a high-pitched humming sound.

Death pellets!

She thought fast. Lusa was dark and small; if she could hide in the shadows of the rocks, the no-claws might not see her. Especially if Kallik could draw them away on her longer, faster legs.

"Lusa!" Kallik yowled, looking around and finding her friend behind her. "Head for those rocks on the left—if you run behind them, they'll hide you until you can make it to the trees. Run for your life—go, *now!*" She gave Lusa a ferocious shove and the bear cub pelted away.

Kallik dodged in the other direction. In the dim, growing light, her white coat stood out like a splash of seal blood on the ice.

Bang!

Ahead of her she saw Toklo slam into Ujurak and knock him down as another death pellet whizzed over their heads.

"Change, Ujurak!" Toklo yelled. "Change! You have to!"

"No! I'm staying with you!" Ujurak shouted back. "I'm a bear! I want to be a bear!"

Bang! Bang!

"I will die protecting you if you don't change *right now*," Toklo growled, his voice low but so fierce that Kallik could hear it over her pawsteps as she sped away from them. Her own paws seemed unwilling to obey her. Part of her wanted to stay with Toklo, but she needed to lead the no-claws away from Lusa. So instead she ran and kept running, feeling sure that death was going to thud into her side at any moment, ripping her open and tearing her full of holes.

Something flapped over her head and she ducked, but when she looked up she realized it was Ujurak as a snowy owl, taking to the skies. She could still see dark patches of fur disappearing into his wings as he soared away. Toklo had won the argument.

Suddenly the firebeast fell silent, and that was even more terrifying. Now Kallik didn't know where it might be, or how close. She skidded behind a boulder and peered out.

Where were the no-claws?

She took a deep breath, trying to calm herself, and then, suddenly, she realized . . . *she could smell them.*

There was less smoke at this end of the valley, and scents were sharper than they had been before. Not only that, but the no-claws smelled very strongly of the liquid in the bottles that Lusa had pointed out to her when they raided the rot-food. Lusa had warned her that it tasted foul and musty, and it smelled that way, too. All four of the no-claws reeked of it.

She could tell that two of them had run off in opposite directions, but two of them were very close by. Could she make it to the trees before they spotted her? Crouching low to the ground, she crept out from behind the boulder.

In the gloomy shadows behind her, she heard a hissing whisper.

Turning slowly, she saw the two hunters only a few bear-lengths away. They were looking straight at her. Behind them, the firebeast waited, still and silent.

The hunters raised their firesticks.

All right, chase me! I'm the fastest bear. I'm a white bear. You'll never catch me!

Kallik drove her paws into the ground and focused on running, on the strength flowing through her limbs. She remembered racing across the ice with her mother and Taqqiq, escaping from full-grown male white bears. She remembered running away from the walruses. She knew she was good at running.

She also remembered the looks on the faces of the no-claws that she had scared back by the Big River. Maybe she was scarier than she knew. She had claws and teeth and power in her arms that these no-claws couldn't dream of. If she turned to fight them, might *they* run away from *her*?

But these no-claws had unfair advantages, like firebeasts to give them speed and sticks that could kill from far away, so that they didn't need claws and teeth.

Her sharp nose told her the hunters had split up and stopped. They were crouching, doing something. . . .

Pointing their firesticks at me, she guessed, hearing the click of metal. And she was a large white target, easy to hit even in the trees.

Kallik noticed that the ground slanted away to her left. She dove and rolled down the slope. Wet soil coated her fur as she tumbled over and over, bouncing off rocks and tree trunks. She landed with a splash in a muddy stream. Kallik rolled and rolled, coating her pelt in thick brown mud.

She stopped and sniffed the air. The no-claws had lost sight of her, though they were running toward her again. She could hear every movement and crackle of twigs as they ran. They were so loud and clumsy! She slunk up the opposite slope, checking her fur to make sure she was completely covered. Sliding forward on muddy paws, she listened for any sign that they'd spotted her. There were no shouts, no pounding footsteps.

She began to run. She could tell that the no-claws hadn't seen her, because they kept going in the wrong direction, creeping around on the far side of the stream.

What about Lusa and Toklo? Would they make it to the trees? She stretched out her neck and ran.

Spirits, protect them, please. . . .

CHAPTER TWENTY-FOUR

Lusa

Lusa's paws skidded on loose pebbles as she scrambled behind the rocks, her heart rattling in her chest. She didn't know where Kallik had gone. One moment the white bear had been shoving her along, and the next moment she was tearing off in a different direction.

The windswept boulders and mountain peaks formed a path of shadows at the edge of the valley, concealing Lusa as she sprinted forward. Up ahead she could see the clump of trees Toklo had pointed out—but before she could get there, she had to cross back through an open space.

Lusa didn't stop to think. She shot out of the rocks and ran, wild with fear, desperate to reach the trees. If she could just feel their branches surrounding her, the leaves brushing her fur, she knew she'd be safe. The bear spirits didn't want her to die. They'd save her from the flat-faces and firesticks. She'd nearly died already, and they wouldn't let her. She had to save the wild!

She heard a shout behind her. A flat-face had seen her!

Bang! Bang! Bang!

She felt whizzing death pellets fly past her fur.

Lusa squeaked with terror. She was nearly there! The trees were only a bearlength away!

Bang!

An explosion of pain blossomed at the top of her shoulder and she stumbled, but she didn't stop running. She didn't even let out a howl; she bit back her yelp, forcing her paws to keep pushing forward, carrying her toward the trees. She didn't want the flat-faces to know they'd hit her. If they knew she was wounded, they'd think she was weak. And right now, Lusa had to be strong.

With a massive leap, she launched herself at the first tree. Her instincts took over as her back claws dug into the bark. She bounded up the tree the way her father, King, had taught her, fast and nimble and determined. *I'm a black bear! No one can climb like us!*

She knew that just being in a tree wouldn't keep her safe. Firesticks could kill her as easily from the ground while she sat up in the branches like a dazed squirrel. She had to keep going. Lusa thought of Miki and the other bear cubs she'd met at the Longest Day Gathering. She could jump from tree to tree the way they did, and that might make it harder for the flat-faces to follow her.

She didn't waste time worrying about whether she could do it. As she reached the topmost branch, she scouted ahead for a strong-looking branch on the next tree only a short distance away. Her fear gave her extra strength as she jumped, and she barely felt the pain rippling through her shoulder.

Bang! went the firesticks again. *Bang!* This time they sounded farther away, but it didn't make her feel any better. Lusa's pelt trembled with terror and fury. Those flat-faces were shooting at *her friends*!

Her paws wobbled a little as she leaped to the next tree, and she had to wrap her forelegs tightly around the branch to make sure she didn't fall. Leaves tickled her nose as she scrambled up several branches. She fell into a rhythm: Check branch, launch, close eyes, land, balance. Even in the shadows of the forest, she could sense the shapes of the trees in front of her. She felt as if the bear spirits were calling to her, reaching out and catching her as she jumped.

She stopped halfway up a pine tree and perched for a moment, listening. Everything was silent. There were no more firesticks going off, no flat-faces shouting, no cries for help from her friends. She didn't know whether that was a good or a bad sign. What had happened to them? *They could have been caught while you ran away,* she thought, her fur prickling with shame. *But we all ran away. Wasn't that the idea?* She started to climb, getting as high as she could. *At least I didn't hold anyone back. That's something.*

At the top of the tree she wrapped her paws around the trunk and peered out at the valley. Nothing was moving out there. Only the last fading rays of the moon slipped through the clouds to flicker across the grass. There were no bears— not even slumped on the ground, bleeding and dying from the firesticks. Toklo and Kallik must have made it to the trees.

Maybe they were already waiting for her at the pine tree, worrying about her.

As she scrambled back down the tree, she heard the firebeast roar in the distance, out of sight beyond the trees. She froze, straining her ears. The hunters sounded like they were whooping. A few more shots rang out. Had they found the others?

Lusa's paws were quaking, but she forced herself to climb up again. The whoops and rumbling were getting fainter. From the top she spotted the firebeast bumping away up the valley, moonlight gleaming on its flanks.

Have they gone?

Are we safe?

Lusa persuaded her paws to let go of the tree and clambered down to the ground. She raced through the trees, searching for her friends.

"Please be safe," she whispered. "Please be alive."

What if she was the only one who made it? Would she have to find the Last Great Wilderness by herself?

Don't think about that, she ordered herself. *You're not alone. They will be here.*

Lusa paused to catch her breath. The trees were silent all around her. Pain shot along her shoulder as she flexed her front leg. Her fur felt hot and sticky; she hoped the pellet wasn't inside her.

Something moved in the bushes.

Lusa froze. "Toklo?" she whispered. "Kallik? Ujurak?" She braced herself to escape up the nearest tree.

A white furry head, streaked with mud, poked out of the bushes.

"Lusa!" Kallik cried. "You made it!" She leaped out of the undergrowth and raced up to Lusa, huffing in relief.

"You're all muddy!" Lusa said. "Did you fall and hurt yourself? Are you all right?"

"I was hiding my fur," Kallik explained, craning her neck to look at the thick mud caking her white fur. "I guess it worked. I lost the no-claws back there."

"Have you seen Toklo or Ujurak?" Lusa asked.

Kallik looked up. Lusa followed her gaze up to the sky and saw an owl plummeting out of the clouds. It dove toward them, and for a moment Lusa thought it might crash headlong into the ground, but at the last moment it veered up again and landed neatly on its claws. Fur and whiskers and a wet black nose sprouted from the feathers, and soon Ujurak was standing in a cloud of feather fluff, shaking his pelt.

"Oh, Ujurak, I'm so glad you're all right," Lusa said, pressing against his comfortingly warm side.

He stared at his paws. "Changing into a bird to escape is a cowardly thing to do," he said.

"That's stupid," Kallik said, sounding like Toklo for a moment. "If the rest of us could do it, don't you think we would?"

"In a heartbeat!" Lusa agreed. "Without even thinking about it! I'd have wings and be gone before the flat-faces could even find the noses on their flat faces!"

"Toklo wouldn't," Ujurak said glumly. "He'll fight anything

as a bear, and be proud of it."

Lusa and Kallik exchanged uneasy glances. "You don't think he tried to fight them, do you?" Lusa asked. "To protect us?"

They all glanced around at the quiet forest.

Where was Toklo?

CHAPTER TWENTY-FIVE

Toklo

Toklo watched Ujurak take off into the sky on snowy white feathers, then turned to race after Lusa. He saw Kallik pelting away across the grass; there was nothing he could do to help her. She was already the fastest bear of all of them. But Lusa might need protecting.

He spotted her running toward the boulders that lined the valley and chased after her. The hot, burning smell of the firebeast was in his nose, and he stumbled on rocks that he thought were shadows. His muscles screamed with agony as he drove his paws into the ground.

Suddenly the firebeast roared across his path. The blazing light in its eyes blinded him, and Toklo skidded to a halt. One of the hunters gave a yell, and Toklo heard the bang of a firestick.

He couldn't get to Lusa. The best he could do was lead the flat-faces away. Toklo turned and fled across the valley in the opposite direction. The light had dazzled his eyes and he shook his head as he ran, trying to see clearly again. Blinking, he spotted long, marshy grass ahead of him and ran for it.

Toklo's paws crashed through tussocks as he plowed through the long, brittle grass, shouldering tall reeds out of his way. He growled with frustration as prickly weeds caught on his fur. With a violent wrench, he tore himself free and dove into a clump of thick grass. Hidden by the tall reeds, he lay still with his belly fur in the mud, listening. Was he being followed?

He sniffed deeply and a powerful, pungent smell filled his nostrils. To his dismay, he realized he was lying in a patch of wild garlic. He'd crushed the plants under his paws, and now the smell was all over him. He couldn't pick up any other scents; the odor of garlic was too strong.

He couldn't smell the flat-faces coming. They could be right behind him and he wouldn't know.

Something went *crack!* behind him and he jumped, peering into the shadows. Should he stay here, or should he run for it?

He crawled backward, deeper into the grass, letting the long stems close around him. Maybe he could sneak away without being noticed. He wasn't sure how well the flat-faces could smell, but if they used their noses for hunting, it wouldn't do them much good now that he smelled so strongly of garlic, disguising his bear scent.

Toklo crept through the grass, wincing at the splash of marshy puddles under his paws. He stayed close to the ground, hoping to blend into the knobbly, shapeless shadows around him. Across the open valley plain ahead of him, he could see the grove of pine trees. There was no sign of Lusa or Ujurak, but he spotted Kallik racing toward the trees with a pair of hunters right behind her.

Toklo leaned forward, trying desperately to smell anything over the stench of garlic. Suddenly a strong whiff of something hit his nose: a sour, stale smell. . . .

Flat-faces!

Toklo whirled, ready to run.

A giant shiny cobweb flew toward him and knocked him to the ground. His paws became tangled in barbed vines that scraped his face as well as he thrashed and fought.

He was caught in a flat-face trap!

CHAPTER TWENTY-SIX

Kallik

Dim gray morning light slowly spread across the valley as Kallik and the others waited. Lusa climbed up the tree to see if she could see Toklo coming. Ujurak paced around the trunk, looking more and more agitated as he clawed the earth and bared his teeth.

Kallik didn't know what to do. Her stomach churned with worry. Should they go on without Toklo? If he was dead . . . it wouldn't be safe to go look for him, because they'd be putting their lives at risk.

But if he wasn't dead, then they *had* to go find him. They couldn't abandon Toklo, who had been so brave and struggled so hard to take care of them all.

"I'm going back," Ujurak said, stopping in front of her. He looked her right in the eyes, as if challenging her to argue with him.

"Yes. I'll go with you," Kallik said. Ujurak dipped his head in agreement.

Branches swayed and rustled above them as Lusa scrambled

down the trunk. "I'm coming, too!"

"No, Lusa, you should stay here," Kallik told her, sniffing her worriedly. She could smell the blood on the black cub, and a smell of burned fur. Had she been shot by a firestick?

"What?" Lusa protested. "No way! I want to look for Toklo, too!"

"But you're still injured," Kallik said. "One of your wounds must have opened up—I can smell the blood on you, Lusa. Did a firestick get you? I know you're hurting right now, even if you won't admit it."

Lusa was quiet for a moment. "A death pellet hit my shoulder," she admitted. "But that doesn't matter. It doesn't hurt that much. And I'm the best at being quiet. I can hide and I can sneak through the woods better than any of you. You might need me!"

Kallik wondered if she should point out that Ujurak could be any animal in the forest—he could definitely change into something quiet and sneaky if he needed to. But then Lusa went on.

"Don't leave me alone here," she said, touching Kallik's paw. "I'd rather die helping to save Toklo than sit in a tree by myself and lose you forever and never know what happened. It'd be like you and Taqqiq, when you were separated and you didn't know if he was even alive. Remember? Remember how awful that was? Please don't leave me like that."

Kallik sighed. She looked at Ujurak.

"I say we let her come," Ujurak said. "If a bear wants to be brave, I don't think it's anyone's place to stop her."

Lusa blinked gratefully at him.

"All right," Kallik said. "Let's go. But be careful. And, Lusa, if you start bleeding any more, you'll have to stop."

They stayed at the edge of the trees as long as they could before venturing back into the valley. The pine needles above them scraped against each other in the wind, and Kallik felt like she could hear voices whispering in them. Maybe Lusa's bear spirits were watching over them. Kallik peeked up at the sky, which was mostly covered by clouds. The sun was a line of golden fur on the edge of the mountains. But she could still see the twinkle of a few ice spots . . . so maybe her spirits were with her, too.

What about the spirits who watch over Toklo? Where are they?

"Ujurak," Lusa said, "do you know why the flat-faces hunt us?"

Ujurak looked uncomfortable, shifting his shoulders so his fur rippled and settled. "I . . . I think they do it for fun," he said finally. "I don't know."

"Fun!" Lusa cried. "That's horrible!"

"Well, I guess I think hunting is fun," Kallik said, trying to understand. "When there's something good to hunt, I mean, like a seal. But I do it to feed myself. And we still don't know if flat-faces eat bears." They had to cross into the open now, and she lowered her head to sniff for any sign of Toklo.

"I wish *I* had a firestick!" Lusa growled. "Is there a special forest where they grow? If I had a firestick, you can bet I'd make them leave us alone!"

"Lusa, we wouldn't know what to do with a firestick if we

found one," Kallik said. "Firesticks aren't for bears. We'd probably just end up hurting ourselves with them." They found the stream where Kallik had rolled in the mud and splashed across to the other side.

"Well, I wish I had one anyway," Lusa said.

"No, you don't," Ujurak said quietly.

Lusa opened her mouth to speak, but just then Kallik caught a scent in the churned-up mud. "I smell the no-claws!" she whispered. She bounded ahead, keeping her nose close to the ground.

The cubs tracked the scent across the grass. Mud was caked into Kallik's fur, which gave her a sort of heavy, sticky feeling. Bits of it flaked off as she walked, but she was still more brown than white, which made her feel safer as they slunk through the open space. Even though they'd heard the firebeast leave, she couldn't shake the fear that a hunter might still be lying in wait for them.

At a huddle of rocks near the middle of the valley, they picked up the scent of more hunters. All four of them had been here. And there was something else as well. . . .

"Is that garlic?" Lusa asked, wrinkling her nose.

"It smells like Toklo, too," Kallik realized. "I think he was here."

"Maybe he's still here," Lusa said hopefully. "Maybe he's just hiding until he's sure they're gone."

They all stood still for a moment. It was eerily quiet, as if they were the only living creatures in the mountains. There was no sound from a brown bear hiding close by.

Without saying anything, Ujurak padded forward into the long, marshy grass. Tussocks of earth squished under Kallik's paws as she paced behind him, trying to puzzle out all the smells. They came to a dip in the marsh where all the grass for a bearlength was trampled down and there were broken reeds all around it. It looked—and smelled—like there had been a struggle here. Kallik could pick out the scents of no-claws, Toklo . . . and blood. Her heart sank.

"Oh, no," Lusa whispered. Ujurak pressed against her silently, his head drooping.

Kallik found a trail of smashed grass leading away from the spot, heavy with the same tangled smells. "They must have dragged him away." She followed it cautiously, wincing at the tufts of brown fur and spots of blood along the trail. Lusa and Ujurak stayed close behind her, trusting her nose to lead them.

The trail led back to where the firebeast had waited. Its paws had left deep gouges in the grass as it surged back onto a muddy dirt path. Kallik stepped onto the bare dirt and sniffed; it smelled like a BlackPath. And it looked like it ran around the mountain they'd just climbed. Kallik could see the firebeast's prints heading up the path, back the way they'd come.

"Oh, no," Lusa squeaked again, her voice rising in panic. "Oh, no, oh, no, oh, no. Did . . . did the firebeast eat Toklo? Kallik, did the flat-faces feed Toklo to the firebeast?"

"I don't know," Kallik said.

She stared at the muddy tracks and the faint traces of blood on the grass nearby. The acrid smell of metal and fear made her nose hurt and her eyes water. She could also smell rain in the air. Another storm was coming.

Kallik planted her paws firmly in the churned-up dirt. She remembered feeling like this when she first lost Taqqiq, when she realized that the most important thing in the world was finding him again. "If there's even a chance he's still alive," she said, "then we're going after him."

CHAPTER TWENTY-SEVEN

Toklo

Wham! Toklo slammed into the hard side of the firebeast as it skidded around a corner. His claws scraped painfully on the slippery floor. He tried to push himself upright, but the flat-faces had tied his paws together. They'd wrapped their prickly vines around his muzzle as well, so he couldn't fight back with his teeth. They tied him so tightly that the barbs dug into his skin until he bled, leaving red smears on the grass as they dragged him to the firebeast.

The more Toklo saw of firebeasts, the less he understood them. This one had a large, flat, hollow back with two flaps, one above and one below, that opened like a mouth to swallow him up. The flat-faces dragged him over to the firebeast; it took all four of them to lift him in, especially since he thrashed and kicked and fought as hard as he could.

You wouldn't dare to fight me one-on-one! he thought furiously. *Cowards—I'd rip your skin off!*

The flat-faces slammed the door flaps shut, bellowing at one another, and climbed into the front part of the firebeast.

The firebeast roared to life and charged off down the muddy track.

Toklo couldn't tell how far they'd gone. The firebeast moved very fast, raging loudly. The ground was rough and muddy, and the firebeast kept slipping around and bouncing. Under Toklo's paws the floor bucked and rolled every time they hit a bump. He could feel the firebeast's power thrumming up through his legs. He gave up trying to stand and wedged himself in a corner, facing backward. He didn't know if they were still in the valley. He didn't know if he'd ever see his friends again. He didn't know how much longer he would be alive.

A rumble of thunder shook the sky, and the clouds opened up. Rain poured down, splattering against the transparent squares on the sides and back of the firebeast. Toklo huddled miserably in the corner, trying to brace himself so he wouldn't hit the sides so hard every time the firebeast swerved.

The firebeast pulled onto a winding trail that sloped down and around the mountain at the head of the valley. Toklo scooted himself over to peer out the back and saw the cliff yawning below him. The firebeast's paws churned frighteningly close to the edge of the steep drop. Far below, Toklo could see a brown river foaming with rapids and whirlpools.

The flat-faces whistled and hollered every time the firebeast skidded on the mud. Toklo closed his eyes tightly. He had never felt so terrified or so sure that he was about to die . . . or so alone. How would the flat-faces kill him? With a firestick or with claws? Would they kill him before they took his skin, or peel it off while he was still alive? How long would it take him to die? His body shook with horror.

For the first time, Toklo could understand the way Lusa saw the stars. The other animals up there weren't taunting the lonely bear in the sky—they were his friends. They kept him company. They kept him safe and gave him something to live for.

Toklo missed Lusa, Kallik, and Ujurak. His heart ached; he wished he could see his friends one more time before he died. He hoped Ujurak wasn't still angry at him—at least changing into an owl meant that Ujurak had escaped and was safe now. He hoped they all found one another and made it to the Last Great Wilderness without him. Kallik was getting better at hunting all the time. . . . Maybe she could protect the others now that he was gone. . . . Maybe she could keep Lusa safe.

Something shrieked inside the firebeast and Toklo's head banged against the floor as the firebeast slammed sideways into the mountain wall. Its paws churned frantically in the mud, but the force of the impact was too strong. The firebeast skidded out to the edge of the cliff—and tipped over.

The flat-faces screamed as the firebeast went careering down the muddy slope. Toklo howled with fear as it crashed into a tree, bounced off, crashed into another tree, shot out into empty space, and finally landed with a bone-jarring splash in the river.

The front of the firebeast hit the mud at the bottom of the river and the entire creature flipped over, then crashed heavily onto its side. Toklo's head whammed into the roof as it tipped and fell, and for a dizzying moment he lost consciousness.

He was jolted awake by icy water covering his nose. The river was surging into the back of the submerged firebeast through the top back flap, which was wedged partly open. The water was rising quickly around his paws. A jagged piece of metal had peeled up from the side of the firebeast and sliced through the vine around Toklo's legs. As Toklo watched, the water tugged the vine loose.

Toklo! He thought he heard voices in the river. Was it Oka and Tobi? Were they here to help him?

Toklo, get up! Hurry!

His whole body wailed with agony as he shoved himself upright, shaking off the last of the vines. He carefully scraped his muzzle against the sharp piece of metal, cutting through the vine holding his mouth closed. He winced as it scratched against the side of his face. He blinked through the rain, searching for a sign of his family's spirits in the surging river.

Get out! You have to get free! Toklo, hurry, fight!

Toklo waded across to the back, fighting the current of the river pouring in. The gap was too small for him to squeeze through. He pounded on the back flap of the firebeast, but it was rammed against a giant rock. The firebeast was filling with water fast. He couldn't see the flat-faces, but he could hear them yelling on the other side of the wall. Were they stuck, too?

The water sucked at his chest fur and he looked down. It wouldn't be long before the river reached the top of the space . . . and then Toklo would drown.

Of all the ways he'd thought he might die today, this one hadn't occurred to him. Drowning—his worst nightmare.

"Help!" he shouted, battering the side of the firebeast with his paws. "Somebody help me! *Help!*"

CHAPTER TWENTY-EIGHT

Lusa

Rain splattered in Lusa's eyes, and the wind howled down the mountain as if it were trying to push her off the path. Her heart was racing as fast as her paws. Ahead of her, she could barely see Kallik's haunches pounding along the firebeast's trail. The dirt path here was narrow and bumpy, barely a path at all, and it curved around the mountain with a steep drop-off beside them. Lusa tried not to look down at the sharp rocks and roaring river below. Everything was gray and blurry under the dark covering of clouds, and her paws kept slipping on the muddy tracks of the firebeast.

They skidded around a corner, and for a terrifying moment Lusa's paws flew out from under her. She crashed onto her backside and slid down the next stretch of slope, scrabbling for a pawhold. The edge of the cliff loomed in front of her.

Ujurak leaped in her way and Lusa smashed into him, but he dug his claws in and stood like a rock to stop her headlong tumble. Lusa breathed a sigh of relief as she scrambled upright again. And then they were off once more, tearing through the firebeast's muddy pawprints.

Toklo, hang on! Lusa thought. *We're coming for you!* A wild fury drove her paws faster. *They'll see how fast bears can run! Not even the firebeast can escape us!*

Lightning ripped the clouds open like a jagged claw. Only a breath later, thunder boomed, so loud it sounded as though the sky were caving in. As the thunder faded, Lusa realized she could hear Kallik around the next bend, shouting something. She threw herself forward and nearly slid right into the muddy white bear.

Kallik was standing at the edge of the path, looking down the slope to the river below. All around her the dirt had deep slashes in it, and mud was spattered higher than a full-grown bear up on the mountainside. Where Kallik was standing, the firebeast tracks veered off the path and plunged down the cliff.

"Toklo!" Lusa shouted, bounding to Kallik's side and peering into the darkness. "Kallik, are they down there? Why did the firebeast leave the path?"

"Maybe it didn't mean to." Ujurak puffed as he caught up to them. "Look how the mud is churned up, like the firebeast was trying to stay up here. Come on; let's follow it."

Diving off the cliff sounded like madness, but Lusa was not going to be the one too scared to do it. She held her breath and leaped off the path. As soon as she hit the mud below, she lost control of her paws and went skidding madly down the hill. She covered her head with her front paws and huddled in a ball, praying that none of the things she was crashing into would kill her before she reached Toklo. A tree branch whipped across her face, and her shoulder howled with pain as she bounced off a broken tree stump.

Splash! Lusa landed headfirst in the river and struggled to the surface, gasping and spluttering for air. She flailed her paws and felt the sharp stones of the river bottom under her.

When she stood up and shook the water from her eyes, she spotted a large shape lying in the water not far away. It was the firebeast!

"Toklo!" she yelled, floundering over to it.

"Lusa!" It was Toklo's voice! He was alive! "Lusa!" he shouted. "Lusa, help! I'm trapped!"

The water was deeper around the wrecked firebeast, and Lusa had to swim the last bearlength over to it. She couldn't see the flat-faces anywhere. She was sure the firebeast was dead—it was lying on its side with its head buried in the water, its eyes were dim, and it wasn't even struggling to escape. Carefully she hooked her claws into a gash along its side and hung on, peering into the dark water around it.

A flap at the back of the firebeast was wedged open a few pawlengths. Lusa spotted Toklo's nose poking through the small gap.

"Toklo!" she cried, splashing over and pressing her nose to his.

"Lusa! Help!" he called again.

The river surged around Lusa's paws, and she realized the back of the firebeast was filling with water.

Splash! Splash!

Lusa heard Kallik and Ujurak tumble into the river behind her. She twisted around and saw them flounder to their paws, dripping with mud.

"Kallik!" she yelled. "Hurry! We have to open the fire-beast!"

"What?" Kallik gasped, splashing over to Lusa.

"Toklo's trapped inside."

Kallik blinked at the firebeast. "Let me try." The white bear braced her paws on the rocks and hooked her claws in the gap. She tugged and heaved, but the flap didn't move. Ujurak tried to add his strength, but his paws slipped on the wet surface and the flap held fast.

"We're coming, Toklo!" Lusa called.

"It's stuck! I'm going under the water to look." Kallik took a deep breath and dove under the firebeast. Lusa let go of her perch and dropped into the river, following Kallik down to the spooky dark mud at the bottom of the river. The current dragged at her fur, and she had to catch onto parts of the firebeast to pull herself forward. It was eerie touching a dead firebeast, but it was even stranger than she expected because it didn't *feel* like a dead animal. Its flesh was hard and slippery under her paws.

Kallik moved like a fish in the water, smooth and graceful. She looked around at Lusa and pointed with her snout to a giant rock that was wedged up against the flap. The white bear waved her paws, and Lusa realized that she was saying they needed to roll it free.

Mud swirled around the two bears as they sank their paws

into the river bottom. In the murky greenish brown water, Lusa could barely see the bulky shape of the big rock. Her claws scraped painfully against it as she scrabbled to brace herself. Something brushed against her snout, and she nearly sucked in a mouthful of water, but she managed to hold back her yelp. It was only Ujurak, paddling down to wedge himself between them.

Lusa's lungs were starting to ache. She leaned into the rock with all her strength and felt her friends heaving and shoving as well. The rock shifted slightly, stirring up a spiral of muddy silt. Her head was dizzy. She needed air. But so did Toklo. They had to move the rock. The river mud sucked at the boulder while the current tugged on their fur.

River spirits, please help us! This is for Toklo!

Suddenly the rock seemed to pop free from the mud. Lusa fell backward as it rolled sideways, knocked into the flap, and landed in a cloud of mud. Paddling madly, she surged back up to the air. Her snout broke the surface and she gasped, blinking in the rain. Kallik and Ujurak popped up beside her.

"It didn't open!" Kallik cried.

In a flash of panic, Lusa realized the rock had banged into the flap as it fell. The open gap had disappeared, and the back flap of the firebeast had slammed shut again. Now there was nothing holding it closed, but no way to pull it open, either. She pressed her nose to the small window in the back, trying to see through the muddy water inside. Kallik and Ujurak started clawing at the sides, trying to find another way in.

"Lusa," Toklo called weakly, pounding on the walls of

the firebeast. Water swamped over his snout, drowning out his words. The back of the firebeast was flooded, and Toklo didn't seem to have the strength left to keep his nose in the tiny air space left at the top. Lusa scrabbled at the back of the firebeast. What made it open?

A bit of metal stuck out of the bottom flap, and suddenly Lusa remembered the cage she had escaped from, way back at the beginning of her adventure. She'd pretended to be sick, so the flat-face guides took her out of the Bear Bowl in a cage and left her in a room full of silvery things. Escaping from that cage and climbing out a window had been the first steps of the path she was on now—the first pawsteps toward these friends and the majestic place they were looking for.

And saving the wild, she thought.

Now she just had to remember how she'd opened that first cage door. It hadn't been too complicated. She pawed at the metal bit and it moved a little. Encouraged, she grabbed it in her teeth and tugged. Ignoring the horrible sharp taste of it, she waggled and pulled on it with ferocious intensity. *Open, you horrid thing,* she thought furiously. *Open and let my friend out!*

There was a muffled clang and the door suddenly swung toward Lusa. She let go and shoved it aside with her back paws. In a cloud of swirling mud, she poked her head inside the firebeast.

Toklo had sunk under the water, a limp pile of brown fur.

"Kallik!" Lusa yelled. "Ujurak!" She swam through the door and thrust her head under the water to grab Toklo's scruff in her teeth. She yanked on him as hard as she could.

Bubbles floated up from Toklo's mouth as his head slowly lifted toward Lusa. His eyes opened and met hers.

Lusa let go of his scruff and head-butted him in the chest, trying to get him to move. His paws seemed to shift with agonizing slowness as he pushed himself up. She desperately paddled backward, dragging him through the door. She felt Ujurak and Kallik swim up behind her and reach past with their front legs, helping Lusa heave Toklo out of the firebeast. In a rush, his heavy body shot through the gap and bobbed up to the surface of the river.

Toklo gasped as air hit his lungs. He came suddenly to life, flailing his paws to stay afloat. Kallik supported him to the side of the firebeast, and he clung to it with his front paws, coughing up water.

"I knew it!" Ujurak said, paddling in place beside him. "I knew you weren't dead! You wouldn't do that to us!"

Toklo spluttered, still catching his breath.

"Let's get to shore," Kallik said, shoving her shoulder under Toklo to support him. Lusa took his other paw and they helped drag him onto the muddy riverbank, where all four cubs collapsed, exhausted and trembling.

Suddenly Lusa sat bolt upright. "Where are the flat-faces?" she asked. "Did they die with the firebeast?"

"No," Toklo mumbled. "Not all of them, anyway. I heard them shouting and swimming away."

"Then let's get out of here," Kallik said. She climbed to her paws and shook out her fur, although it did very little good, since the rain was still pelting down through the thin trees around them.

Lusa glanced back at the river. Where did the flat-faces go? She peered into the blinding rain, feeling a shiver of fear that they might be peering back at her.

Then her ears picked up a sound over the drumming rain-drops. She leaned forward, listening, and realized that it was a flat-face noise—one of them shouting loudly.

"I think I hear them," she said. "They sound like they're in trouble."

Lusa edged closer to the river and peered out at the fire-beast. Suddenly she spotted a floundering shape in the water, just downstream from the firebeast. It was one of the flat-faces; it looked like the current had caught him and dragged him away from the firebeast as he tried to swim to safety. Now he was clinging to a fallen tree trunk. Why didn't he swim free? Couldn't flat-faces swim?

She boosted herself onto a rock and peered up and down the riverbank. Her heart thumped as she spotted two of the other flat-faces. They were lying faceup in the mud only a few bearlengths away from the cubs. Their eyes were closed. But she could see their chests rising and falling. They were still alive. But they weren't getting up to help their friend. Maybe they couldn't.

Lusa looked back at the flat-face still in the river. His paws were turning white as he clutched the tree's branches. In moments he would lose his grip and be washed away. She could see the fur covering his chin, and his pale forehead. He reminded her of one of the feeders from the Bear Bowl—a flat-face who brought her berries and scratched her back.

Part of her still hated this flat-face who had hunted them and captured Toklo and nearly *killed* him, but part of her . . . a big part of her . . . couldn't let him die. Bears weren't supposed to kill flat-faces, and if Lusa watched him drown without trying to help him, she would be responsible for his death.

"Lusa, where are you going?" Kallik cried as Lusa waded into the river.

"I'm going to help," Lusa said. She jumped into the deep water with a splash and started paddling fast so the others couldn't stop her.

"Don't be stupid!" Toklo shouted. "Lusa, come back!"

Lusa swam around the firebeast, hanging on to it with her claws when the current felt too strong. Water swamped over her snout and she sneezed.

The flat-face spotted her when she was only pawlengths away. He let out a high-pitched yell of surprise and nearly lost his grip on the tree. She dove under the water and saw that his back paw was caught between two of the tree's submerged branches. He must have gotten stuck when the current dragged him downstream. That was why he couldn't swim free.

She seized one of the branches with her paws and pulled herself closer. It was a funny feeling, like climbing a tree underwater. She reached to free the flat-face's paw and he started jerking and splashing around like he thought she was going to eat him. *I* should *eat you!* she thought. *That would serve you right!*

Since she didn't think she could touch his paw without getting kicked in the head, she focused her attention on the branches that trapped him. Lusa poked the thinner of the two branches with her front paw, then grabbed it in her teeth and yanked. It snapped off and she nearly spun backward into the rushing current. But the tree's other branches caught her, holding her so she could regain her grip.

When she finally made it to the surface again, she saw the flat-face swimming away with huge splashing movements. Up on the bank, she saw one of the other flat-faces stand up and start looking around him. He pointed at Lusa and shouted something at his friends. From the way he was searching the mud, Lusa guessed that he was looking for his firestick. Were flat-faces really so dumb that they didn't realize she'd just saved his friend's life?

It was time to get out of there.

CHAPTER TWENTY-NINE

Kallik

Despite their aching paws and bleeding wounds, the bear cubs didn't stop to rest until they were back in the valley. Kallik licked the long scratch on Lusa's shoulder as they flopped down in the grove of pine trees. The death pellet had only grazed her, but there was a lot of blood. Kallik opened her mouth to the pelting rain to wash away the hot, sticky taste of it. Lusa leaned against her side, drowsing. She was limping from the scratch, but at least the pellet hadn't lodged in her skin. Kallik still couldn't believe Lusa had done everything she did to rescue Toklo with an injury like that.

"They won't catch up to us without the firebeast," Ujurak said to Toklo, who was standing at the edge of the trees, looking back.

"I hope you're right," Toklo said. He paced over to lie down on the other side of Lusa. "But let's keep going if we can." He nudged Lusa with his nose.

"Mmmmph," she mumbled, covering her snout with her paws.

"I'll see what's on the other side of the trees," Ujurak said. Kallik tilted her head, watching for feathers to come sprouting out of his fur. He met her gaze. "As a *bear*." He trotted away through the trees, which were slick with rain.

A branch above Kallik dripped raindrops right on her nose, but she was too tired to move away. She closed her eyes and listened to the humming whoosh of Lusa breathing. Even Toklo started to snore.

Kallik jolted awake at the sound of snapping twigs. Ujurak was galloping back through the trees toward them. His eyes were bright.

"You have to see this," he said. He nudged Toklo's side and the brown bear grunted, shaking his head. "Come on, all of you."

Wearily, Kallik climbed to her paws and helped Lusa up. Wet pine needles clung to her fur as they trudged behind Ujurak. The rain had washed away some of the mud, but Kallik didn't think she'd ever feel clean again.

The ground sloped up through the trees and she could see a glimmer of sunlight ahead. They emerged onto an open, pebbly stretch of earth with a mountain wall rising up on either side. Kallik blinked. Straight ahead of them, the ground ran smooth and flat between the mountains for almost a skylength. And beyond the mountain walls, in the distance ahead—just sky and rolling plains.

"Where are the rest of the mountains?" Lusa asked.

"This is it," Ujurak said. "We just have to get through this gap, and we'll be in the foothills. On the other side of Smoke Mountain."

"Really?" Kallik gasped.

Toklo's eyes widened. "Let's go!"

Kallik's paws thrummed with new energy as they sprang forward. It was amazing to run on flat ground again, instead of climbing, always climbing, on bare, sharp rocks. The wind ruffled her fur, and she felt the rain start to taper off. They ran and ran as the day wore on.

The clouds parted and a beam of sunlight, low in the sky, cut across their path as they burst into the open air. The mountain walls were behind them, and ahead lay a rolling, grassy meadow that sloped down to a faraway forest. The setting sun lit up tiny spots of color in the grass—bright yellow and blue wildflowers amid the green.

Kallik turned to look back at the tall ridge of mountains spread out against the sky behind them. They seemed blurry and unreal now, as if she were seeing them through a cloud of smoke. She inhaled deeply, realizing that for the first time in what felt like moons, the air smelled fresh and clean.

"Did we make it?" Lusa said wonderingly. "I think . . . I think we did. We survived Smoke Mountain!" She buried her nose in the grass, then lay down and rolled with her paws in the air.

"Good-bye forever, you horrible place," Kallik said.

"We did survive the mountain," Ujurak said with a nod. "But we still have a long way to go."

"Oh, fabulous," Toklo grumbled.

"Cheer up, you old walruses," Kallik said. The crisp smell of the air was almost like snow-sky, and she felt like running and leaping through the long brown grasses ahead of them. "We're alive! We survived the flat-face hunters!" She lifted her snout and saw the Pathway Star glimmering in the dark blue sky ahead of them. "All thanks to the ice spirits watching over us," she added.

"And the bear spirits in the trees who helped us through that waterfall and saved me in the river," Lusa said.

"Those were the river bear spirits!" Toklo insisted. "They're the ones who helped us the most!" He and Lusa had been having this argument most of the past day, as they ran through the mountain gap.

Ujurak let out a snort of laughter. "At least we can agree to be thankful, whoever it's to."

Kallik nodded and yawned. Exhaustion was finally catching up with her. They all lay down right there in the grass and slept, fur brushing fur.

Bright light woke her, and she realized the sun was high in the sky. They had slept through the night and well into the next day. Lusa was still asleep, but the two brown bears were gone. Kallik squinted through the grass and saw Toklo trotting toward them.

He dropped a rabbit at her paws and shook himself. "I'd forgotten what it was like to be dry!"

Lusa's nose twitched. "I smell rabbit," she mumbled with her eyes still shut.

"That's because I brought you rabbits," Toklo said, poking her. "Squirrel-brain."

Lusa's eyes popped open. "Food!" she cried, scrambling to her paws.

They each ripped off a chunk of flesh, saving some for Ujurak, who was bounding through the meadow not far away. Kallik wasn't sure what he was doing, but it looked as though he were chasing a butterfly. He joined them after a few moments and they all lay in a circle, chewing contentedly.

"Let's keep walking while it's daylight," Kallik suggested when the newkill was all gone.

They walked through the foothills all the rest of that day and most of the night. The Pathway Star shone brightly ahead of them, guiding their path. Kallik's paws stopped aching, and her body tingled with anticipation. Despite Ujurak's gloomy prediction that they still had a long way to go, she felt sure that it couldn't be much farther. The Place of Endless Ice was calling to her. She could practically smell it in the air.

When they stopped to sleep beside a shallow stream, Kallik dreamed of catching a plump seal, her teeth sinking into its rich flesh. The nights were truly getting longer now, giving them more darkness to sleep in.

The next day she trotted even faster, wishing she could race across the grassland at full speed. They could see wooded mountains ahead of them, green and tipped with white snow. Was that it? Was that the Last Great Wilderness?

The air was turning colder as well. Kallik knew she was the only one who was happy about this; the others anxiously glanced at the sky, and Toklo muttered about catching enough prey for the cold season. But her paws trembled at the thought of touching ice again.

As they began to climb into these smaller mountains, a flurry of snow whirled through the air. Kallik could barely hold in her excitement. It was the first snowfall she'd seen in moons and moons. Even though it didn't stick to the ground, she felt it drift across her fur and tickle her nose. She felt like the Great Bear Silaluk coming back to life.

Lusa, Ujurak, and Toklo were fascinated by it. They watched transfixed as their fur turned white. Kallik wondered if they'd be so enthusiastic if the snow settled up to their bellies and higher. These bears weren't made for the cold like she was. Would it be her turn to feed them and look after them now?

And then finally, as they came over the ridge of the mountains, they saw a great plain spread out before them, stretching for skylengths in all directions. They all stopped on a shelf of stone and stared down. From their high perch, Kallik could see animals everywhere—a herd of caribou grazing, long-legged moose strolling slowly through the grass, wild ducks and geese flying overhead. She even thought she spotted some furry shapes that might be other bears.

"It's beautiful!" Lusa cried.

Kallik's gaze drifted to the horizon, where a vast sea of green-blue water sparkled and glittered in the sun.

"Look at all that water," Ujurak said, blinking in astonishment.

"That's the biggest lake I've ever seen," Toklo agreed. "Even bigger than Great Bear Lake."

Kallik snorted. "That's because it's not a lake, seal-brains. That's the sea!" She stood up on her hind legs and stared at it. Suddenly she gasped.

Ice!

In the distance, sparkling pure and white against the blue ocean, she could see the sea-ice clearly. It was there, solid and real, even in the time of burn-sky. It didn't reach all the way to the shore, but as the weather got colder, it would. And then she would be back where she belonged, among seals and fish and other white bears.

"We've made it!" she cried. "This is it! Look, Lusa, that's the ice—that's what I've been telling you about for so long."

"The Last Great Wilderness," Lusa whispered. "We found it! Ujurak, you did it—you brought us here!"

Ujurak stared down the slope and didn't say anything.

Toklo shook his head. "I must admit, I wasn't sure it was real," he said. "I thought we might be on a wild-goose chase. But here it is. You were right after all, Ujurak."

"Of course he was!" Lusa said.

"And Mother was right, too," Kallik said. "She told me about the Place of Endless Ice. I wish she could be here to see it." *And Taqqiq,* she thought with a pang of sadness. *I wish he could have believed enough in the ice spirits to make the journey with us.*

Lusa pressed close to Kallik's fur. "Your mother is here," she said. "She's watching you now; I know it."

"You don't look as thrilled as I thought you'd be," Toklo said to Ujurak.

The smaller brown bear turned his gaze slowly to him. "This doesn't feel right," he said.

"What?" Kallik said. "Why not?"

"I don't know," Ujurak said, shuffling his paws.

"But it's perfect!" Lusa cried. "It's the most amazing place I've ever seen! Ujurak, why don't you love it?"

"I do," Ujurak said, trying to sound bright. "I think I do, anyway. But . . . "

Toklo poked Ujurak in the side with his snout. "What?"

"If this is *really* the end of the trail," he said, "then why don't I feel it?"

"You're a worry-face, that's why. We're here, and now we're going to enjoy it." Toklo looked around at the others. "Who's starving?"

"Me!" Lusa yelped, bouncing on her paws. "*I'm* starving!"

Toklo nodded down the slope. "Come on; let's hunt!"

Without waiting for an answer, he bounded through the grass toward the herd of unsuspecting caribou below. Lusa shot after him, her ears perked forward. Kallik took a step down the hill, then glanced back at Ujurak.

"Come on, Ujurak," she said. "Race you!"

He nodded and got to his paws.

Kallik bounded off after Toklo and Lusa, her paws feeling light as snowflakes. She could hear Ujurak pounding behind her.

Everything was just as Qopuk had described it. Was there anything that wasn't perfect about this place? There were herds of prey to eat, places to shelter, and *ice*.

Kallik opened her jaws and breathed in the sharp, empty air. She could hardly believe it. After all this time, they had come to the end of their journey.

They had reached the Last Great Wilderness.

But as she ran, Ujurak's words echoed in her mind.

If this is really the end of the trail . . . then why don't I feel it?

SEEKERS

BOOK FOUR
THE LAST WILDERNESS

Ujurak

Wind buffeted Ujurak's fur as he plunged down the mountain slope toward the rolling foothills below, where the caribou were grazing.

It was late burn-sky, and after the recent rains the air was filled with delicious scents. Ujurak drew them all in with every breath: scents of prey, of green growing plants, and underlying it all the salt tang of the sea.

As he bounded down the slope he glanced around at his friends, and his paws felt light as a summer breeze. The white bear Kallik raced beside him, her stride as smooth as flowing water, her twitching nose sniffing the air. After so many moons of traveling through dark forests and over sun-baked rocks, he wondered if she could smell the sea-ice at last.

He heard a *whoomf* and glanced to his other side as the black bear Lusa tripped over her own paws in her haste to keep up. She rolled several bearlengths before scrambling up and continuing to pelt downward.

And charging ahead, his ears pinned back by the wind, was the brown bear Toklo—always out in front, always the first. After facing many dangers together, they had reached their journey's end. They'd found the last wilderness.

Down on the grassy hills, the caribou raised their heads as the bears hurtled toward them.

"Watch out!" Ujurak snarled. "Here we come!"

Toklo glanced back over his shoulder. "They're too big to hunt, feather-brain!" he called.

Ujurak *wuffed* with amusement—he hadn't meant what Toklo had thought he'd meant. He was simply enjoying the feeling of running.

On the bears rushed. They began crossing the foothills, rushing through the herd of grazing caribou. Close-up, the horned beasts were huge, and they swung their heavy heads to give the bears lazy glances, unafraid of Ujurak and his companions. There were so many of them, and their pelts gave off a powerful musky scent.

Ujurak took happy breaths as the bears charged up a green slope then down the other side. On the plain beyond he could see patches of white where flocks of geese had alighted to feed in the damp grassland.

This is the wilderness Qopuk promised us. And it's everything he said it was, and more!

As he ran, Ujurak became aware of a sharp pain in his belly. The journey through Smoke Mountain had been a hard one, with little prey, and the sight of the geese awakened his hunger. He swallowed as his mouth filled with saliva. *Goose flesh*, he thought. Then as he bounded down off the foothills, Ujurak felt his legs tingling and saw his forelegs begin to lengthen and grow thinner; his pelt prickled as his brown fur transformed into a rough, gray pelt. *Wolf!* he thought.

His snout grew longer and he could feel his vision narrowing, the edges darkening as he focused on a single flock of geese on the plain. *One flock.* The sounds around him faded to insignificance and all he could hear was the flock's honking and yakking, growing louder and louder.

His stride lengthened. He felt swift; as he raced passed Toklo he thought he heard the brown bear growl. But the sound seemed to come from far away. It meant nothing to Ujurak. The hot reek of the geese engulfed his senses. His tongue lolled as he pinpointed his prey: a fat white bird feeding at the edge of the flock. *One goose.* He could almost feel his teeth sinking through its feathers, crunching its bones. He smelled its blood and heard its heartbeat.

Kill . . . one bite into warm prey . . . then feed.

The plain whirled past him in a blur. He reached the edge of the flock; the birds flew up in a storm of flapping wings and terrified squawking. Snarling, Ujurak leaped on his chosen prey. His fangs closed on its neck. He shook it; it battered him with its wings, then went limp.

Ujurak stood erect, his prey dangling from his mouth. *Feed now . . . taste blood . . .* But something was gnawing at his mind. He couldn't eat yet. Reluctantly he turned and began trotting back the way he had come.

Ujurak felt his rangy wolf body begin to grow compact;

brown fur replaced the shaggy gray pelt. His heartbeat slowed as the wolf's rage for blood died away.

Gradually he began to notice the plain around him. The flock of geese was settling again a little way off. The geese's raucous cries faded. Ujurak could hear the rattle of wind in the reeds and the splashing paws of an arctic fox as it darted from one clump of bushes to another.

He blinked in confusion as he saw three other bears approaching him, just coming off the foothills onto the plain. Black, brown, white . . . he felt that they ought to be familiar.

"Ujurak!" The small black bear bounded forward to meet him. "That was a great catch!"

"Uh . . . thanks . . . Lusa." Ujurak's confusion vanished as he hurried back toward them and dropped the prey at Lusa's paws. Of course he knew who she was, and the other two bears padding up to him were his friends Toklo and Kallik. The long legs he had as a wolf had rapidly outdistanced them. "Come and share," he invited them.

Toklo growled his thanks as he tore off a part of the goose and retired a couple of paces to flop down and eat the newkill. Ujurak waited for the two she-bears to take their share before he settled down to eat, too. The goose was a fat one, and there was plenty of meat for all of them. It tasted delicious, warm in Ujurak's belly.

"Thish ish—mmmm—won-erful!" Kallik said, chewing a mouthful then swallowing. She raised her head from her food and sniffed at the air. "Can you smell the ice? Soon the sea will freeze closer to shore, and I'll be able to get back to the white bears' feeding grounds."

"But . . . there's no . . . shelter . . . on the ice," Lusa objected, her mouth full of juicy meat. "The wind will blow you into the sea."

"No, we dig dens there," Kallik explained. "Then we curl up together, and it's so warm!" Ujurak saw a shadow of sadness creep into her eyes as though she was remembering her old life with her brother and mother. Then she blinked, and the shadow vanished. "And we hunt for seals through holes in the ice. You've never tasted anything as delicious as seal!"

"I'll settle for the brown earth under my paws, and the prey I can catch on it." Toklo jerked his head toward a distant ridge that was thickly covered with trees. Ujurak could see birds wheeling over it, and sense the throbbing life of small animals under the branches. "That's the best sort of place for brown bears—right, Ujurak?"

"Right," Ujurak replied.

"Look at all those trees," Lusa said, pawing a feather from her muzzle. Her dark eyes sparkled with anticipation as she looked across at the tree-clad ridge. "I love sleeping in the branches, with the sound of the wind and the bear spirits close by."

Toklo tore off another mouthful of goose flesh. "What—mm—I like about . . . this . . . place," he said, gulping the food down and swiping his tongue around his jaws, "is no flat-faces. No BlackPaths. No firebeasts. No flat-face dens."

"Just open land and sea, wherever you look," Kallik said.

"And all the prey we can eat," Toklo added.

Lusa sprang to her paws. "What shall we do next?" she asked. "I want to find a tree to spend the night in."

"Let's rest for a bit." Toklo batted a paw at the enthusiastic little bear. "There's plenty of time."

Ujurak finished eating his share contentedly. He liked listening to his friends as they chattered excitedly about their new home. He was licking his paws, feeling his belly full of warm meat, when a soft voice inside his head whispered: *Not the end.*

Ujurak lifted his head, his pelt prickling like it was crawling with ants. He quietly rose to his paws and stepped away from his friends, pretending to drink from a pool of water. Then he listened in case the voice came again.

He had heard this voice before.

Many moons ago it had spoken to him one cold night under a blaze of stars. *Follow the Pathway Star,* it had said and when he had looked up, that cold night, he had seen one star twinkling more brightly than the rest. He had chosen to ignore the voice at first. But it had whispered to him in the quiet moments as he curled up to sleep and before he rose in the morning. *There are those that will travel with you,* it had told him.

"Like who?" Ujurak had asked, and for some reason he had addressed his question to the stars in the night sky. Then he met the brown bear Toklo, and his question was answered. He'd started to listen to the voice after that. If ever he had doubted the journey they were making, the voice inside his head urged him on, soft and insistent. Over time, he'd thought he'd come to know who it was.

Ujurak lapped the ice-cold water from the pool, his eyes gazing upward. A single star glimmered faintly in the dusky gray-blue sky. *Not the end,* the voice whispered again.

I don't understand, Ujurak silently answered, gazing up at the Pathway Star.

The voice was silent.

Then, over the mountains, he saw a tiny black dot moving in the sky—no, there were three black dots. They moved closer, following the line of the ridge, and he could hear a distant buzzing. The dots grew bigger and he saw the flash of evening sunlight on metal. *Metal birds,* he thought with alarm. He glanced back at his companions. They hadn't noticed them. They were too busy arguing about which was better, trees or caves.

He watched the metal birds fly away into the distance, shivers running up and down his spine. Metal birds, he knew, were flat-face things—firebeasts of the air. So what were they doing here? Like Toklo had said about this place, *No firebeasts. No flat-faces.*

Ujurak looked back to his companions. He saw Lusa cuffing Toklo, pretending to be angry with him. *They look so happy,* he thought. He felt his heart pounding in his chest.

But I have brought them here—to this place, he told the voice inside his head. *There is nowhere left to go.*

Not the end, said the voice.

But what am I supposed to do, Silaluk? Ujurak asked.

He listened for an answer. But the great star bear was silent and Ujurak felt more afraid than he'd felt in his whole life.

DON'T MISS

WARRIORS

SUPER EDITION
BLUESTAR'S PROPHECY

Waking, Bluekit could feel the weight of her sister Snowkit lying on top of her. Moonflower's belly rose and fell rhythmically beside them. Swiftbreeze was snoring and Poppydawn wheezed a little as she breathed.

Bluekit could hear Leopardkit and Patchkit chattering outside.

"You be the mouse and I'll be the warrior!" Patchkit was ordering.

"I was the mouse last time!" Leopardkit retorted.

"Was not!"

"Was!"

A scuffle broke out, punctuated by squeaks of defiance.

"Watch where you're rolling!" The angry meow of a tom silenced them, but only for a moment.

"Okay, you be the warrior," Patchkit agreed. "But I bet you can't catch me."

Warrior!

Bluekit wriggled out from under her sister. A newleaf

breeze stirred the bramble walls; it drifted through the gaps—the same fresh forest smell her father had carried in on his pelt when he'd visited. It chased away the stuffy smell of moss and milk and warm sleeping fur.

Excitement made Bluekit's claws twitch. *I'm going to be a warrior!*

For the first time, she stretched open her eyes, blinking against the shafts of light that pierced the bramble roof. The nursery was huge! In darkness, the den had felt small and cozy, but now she could see the brambles arching high overhead, with tiny patches of blue beyond.

Poppydawn, a dark brown tabby with a long bushy tail, lay on her side near one wall. Bluekit recognized her because she smelled different from Swiftbreeze and Moonflower. There was no milk scent on her because she didn't have any kits yet. Swiftbreeze, in a nest beside her, was hardly visible; curled in a tight ball with her nose tucked under her tail, her tabby and white pelt blotchy against the bracken underneath her.

The most familiar scent of all lay behind her. Wriggling around, Bluekit gazed at her mother. Sunshine dappled Moonflower's silver-gray pelt, rippling over the dark stripes that ran along her flank. Her striped face was narrow, and her ears tapered to gentle points. *Do I look like her?* Bluekit looked over her shoulder at her own pelt. It was fluffy, not sleek like Moonflower, and dark gray all over, with no stripes. *Not yet.*

Snowkit, lying stretched on her back, was all white except for her gray ear tips.

"Snowkit!" Bluekit breathed.

"What is it?" Snowkit blinked open her eyes. They were blue.

Are mine blue? Bluekit wondered.

"You've opened your eyes!" Snowkit leaped to her paws, wide awake. "Now we can go out of the nursery!"

Bluekit spotted a hole in the bramble wall, just big enough for two kits to squeeze through. "Patchkit and Leopardkit are already outside. Let's surprise them!"

Poppydawn raised her head. "Don't go far," she murmured sleepily before tucking her nose back under her tail.

"Where are Poppydawn's kits?" Bluekit whispered.

"They won't arrive for another two moons," Snowkit answered.

Arrive? Bluekit tipped her head to one side. *Where from?*

Snowkit was already heading for the hole, scrambling clumsily over Moonflower. Bluekit tumbled after, her short legs uncertain as she slid down her mother's back and landed in the soft moss behind.

The nest rustled and Bluekit felt a soft paw clamp her tail-tip to the ground. "Where do you think you are going?"

Moonflower was awake.

Bluekit turned and blinked at her mother. "Outside."

Moonflower's eyes glowed and a loud purr rolled in her throat. "You've opened your eyes." She sounded relieved.

"I decided it was time," Bluekit replied.

"There, Swiftbreeze." Moonflower turned, waking the tabby and white queen with her satisfied mew. "I told you she'd do it when she was ready."

Swiftbreeze sat up and gave her paw a lick. "Of course she would. But my kits opened their eyes sooner." She swiped her paw across her muzzle, smoothing the fur on her nose.

Moonflower turned back to her kits. "So now you're going out to see the world?"

"Why not?" Bluekit mewed. "Leopardkit and Patchkit are already out there."

"Leopardkit and Patchkit are five moons old," Moonflower told her. "They're much bigger than you, so they're allowed to play outside."

Bluekit opened her eyes very wide. "Is it dangerous?"

Moonflower shook her head. "Not in the camp."

"Then we can go!"

Moonflower sighed, then leaned down to smooth Bluekit's fur with her tongue. "I suppose you can't stay in the nursery forever." She studied Snowkit. "Straighten your whiskers." Pride lit the queen's amber gaze. "I want you to look perfect when you meet the Clan."

Snowkit ran a licked paw over each spray of whiskers.

Bluekit looked up at her mother. "Are you coming with us?"

"Do you want me to?"

Bluekit shook her head. "We're going to surprise Patchkit and Leopardkit."

"Your first prey." Moonflower's whiskers twitched. "Off you go then."

Bluekit bounced around and sprinted for the gap.

"Don't get under any cat's paws!" Moonflower called after them as Bluekit barged ahead of her sister and headed through the hole. "And stay together!"

The brambles scraped Bluekit's pelt as she wriggled out of the nursery. When she tumbled onto the ground beyond, sunshine stung her eyes. She blinked away the glare and the camp opened out in front of her like a dream. A vast sandy clearing stretched away to a rock that cast a shadow so long it almost touched her paw-tips. Two warriors sat beneath it, sharing prey beside a clump of nettles. Beyond them lay a fallen tree, its tangled branches folded on the ground like a heap of skinny hairless legs. Several tail-lengths away from the nursery, a wide low bush spread its branches over the ground. Ferns crowded a corner at the other side of the nursery and behind them rose a barrier of gorse so tall that Bluekit had to crane her neck to see the top.

Excitement thrilled through her. This was her territory! Her paws prickled. Would she ever know her way around?

There was no sign of Patchkit or Leopardkit.

"Where've they gone?" she called to Snowkit.

Snowkit was staring around the camp. "I don't know," she meowed absently. "Look at that prey!" She was staring at a heap of birds and mice at the side of the clearing. It was topped by a fat fluffy squirrel.

"The fresh-kill pile!" Bluekit bounced toward it, her nose twitching. She'd heard the queens in the nursery talking about prey, and she'd smelled squirrel on her mother's fur. What would it taste like? Thrusting her nose into the pile, she tried to sink her claws into a small creature with short brown fur and a long thin tail.

"Watch out!"

Snowkit's warning came too late. Bluekit's paws buckled as the plump squirrel rolled off the top of the pile and flattened her. *Ooof!*

Purrs of amusement erupted from the two warriors beside the nettle patch. "I've never seen fresh-kill attack a cat before!" meowed one of them.

"Careful!" warned the other warrior. "All that fluff might choke you!"

Hot with embarrassment, Bluekit wriggled out from under the squirrel and stared fiercely at the warriors. "It just fell on me!" She didn't want to be remembered as the kit who was jumped on by a dead squirrel.

"Hey, you two!" Bluekit recognized Patchkit from his nursery-scent as he padded out from behind the nursery. "Does your mother know you're outside?"

"Of course!" Bluekit spun around to see her denmate for the first time.

Oh.

She hadn't expected Patchkit to be so big. His black-and-white fur was smooth like a warrior's, and she had to tip her head back to look up at him. She stretched her legs, trying to appear taller.

Leopardkit scampered after her brother, swiping playfully at his tail. Her black coat shone in the sunshine. She stopped and stared in delight when she saw Bluekit and Snowkit. "You've opened your eyes!"

Bluekit licked her chest, trying to smooth down her fluffy

fur and wishing her pelt was as sleek as theirs.

"We can show you around," Leopardkit mewed excitedly.

Snowkit bounced around the older kit. "Yes, please!"

Bluekit flicked her tail crossly. She didn't want to be shown her territory. She wanted to explore it for herself! But Leopardkit was already trotting toward the wide patch of ferns near the gorse barrier. "This is the apprentice den," she called over her shoulder. "*We'll* be sleeping there in a moon."

Snowkit raced after her.

"Are you coming?" Patchkit nudged Bluekit.

Bluekit was gazing back at the nursery. "Won't you miss your old nest?" She felt a sudden flicker of anxiety. She liked sleeping next to Moonflower.

"I can't wait to move into my new den!" Patchkit yowled as he darted toward the apprentices' den. "It'll be great to be able to talk without Swiftbreeze telling us to be quiet and go to sleep."

As Bluekit hurried after him, the ferns trembled and a tortoiseshell face poked out between the green fronds.

"Once you start your training," yawned the sleepy-looking apprentice, "you'll be glad to get some sleep."

"Hello, Dapplepaw!" Patchkit skittered to a halt outside the den as the tortoiseshell she-cat stretched, half in, half out of the bush.

Bluekit stared at her pelt, thick and shiny, the muscles on her shoulders rippling as she sprang from the ferns and landed beside Patchkit. Suddenly her denmate didn't seem so big after all.

"We're showing Bluekit and Snowkit around the camp," Leopardkit announced. "It's their first time out."

"Don't forget to show them the dirtplace," Dapplepaw joked. "Whitepaw was complaining about cleaning out the nursery only this morning. The place has been filled with kits for moons, and there are more on the way."

Bluekit lifted her chin. "Snowkit and I can keep our nest clean now," she declared.

Dapplepaw's whiskers quivered. "I'll tell Whitepaw when she gets back from hunting, I'm sure she'll be delighted to hear it."

Was she teasing? Bluekit narrowed her eyes.

"I can't wait to go hunting!" Patchkit dropped into a crouch, his tail weaving like a snake.

Quick as the wind, Dapplepaw pinned it down with her paw. "Don't forget to keep your tail still or the prey will hear you swishing up the leaves."

Patchkit pulled his tail free and straightened it out, flattening it to the ground.

Snowkit stifled a purr. "It sticks out like a twig," she whispered in Bluekit's ear.

Bluekit was watching too intently to reply. She studied how Patchkit had pressed his chest to the ground, how he'd unsheathed his claws and tucked his hind paws right under his body. *I'm going to be the best hunter ThunderClan has ever seen,* she vowed.